Does the approach of a full moon make animals restless? I think I hear them at night," Skylar said.

ow she was pushing things. She was an idiot.

avin came closer than she should have allowed nd faced her squarely. He smiled, but with an xpression of sadness. Heartbreaking sadness.

Vhy?

Vhatever she had expected, it hadn't been that.

As he slowly moved toward her, she felt every inch he traveled as if the air between them had been compressed. When he stopped, they were nearly chest to chest, and she had to look up to see his face.

Liquid lava coursed through her veins. She was hot enough to be combustible and was breathing hard…all these reactions serving to confirm that she hadn't been wrong about one thing. Something was going on between them on a crazy personal level. Their chemistry had been instantaneous and impossible to ignore.

Animal magnetism taken to extremes.

Lust at first sight.

Dreams trespassing into the realm of reality.

SEDUCED BY THE MOON

LINDA THOMAS-SUNDSTROM

MILLS BOON

Published in Great Britain 2015
by Mills & Boon, an imprint of Harlequin (UK) Limited,
Eton House, 18-24 Paradise Road, Richmond, Surrey, TW9 1SR

© 2015 Linda Thomas-Sundstrom

ISBN: 978-0-263-91563-1

89-0815

Printed and bound in Spain
by CPI, Barcelona

Linda Thomas-Sundstrom writes contemporary and paranormal romance novels for Mills & Boon® Desire™ and Mills & Boon® Nocturne™. A teacher by day and a writer by night, Linda lives in the West, juggling teaching, writing, family and caring for a big stretch of land. She swears she has a resident Muse who sings so loudly, she often wears earplugs in order to get anything else done. But she has big plans to eventually get to all those ideas. Visit Linda at lindathomas-sundstrom.com or on Facebook.

To my family, those here and those gone,
who always believed I had a story to tell.

Chapter 1

Skylar Donovan was being haunted by the same dream.

Four nights in a row.

An erotic, half awake, half asleep nightmare from which she awoke in tangled sheets, body slick with sweat, with her hand between her thighs.

Looked like nothing had changed tonight, either.

The minute Skylar closed her eyes, the dream returned. Moonlight lit the mountains. Shadows edged that light. And through the dark came the echo of a man's voice: a mesmerizing wordless whisper that was the equivalent of a highly charged sexual invitation.

Her dream guy was there again. Hell, it was impossible to tune him out. The remote Colorado cabin she bunked in had no TV for white noise, and she'd left her headphones behind.

He called to her, and she responded to the raw sensuality in his voice. Though his words weren't clear, his provocative tone left her ready to do something about the effect he had on her, whether he was real or not.

These damn dreams would have topped the charts as the best wet dreams ever...if it were an actual man she lusted for instead of a hallucination. Something her mind had created as a distraction from recent painful events. Everyone knew that fantasy was a notoriously viable way of coping with loss.

Problem was, this nighttime lustfest wouldn't stop. Neither would the questions she didn't dare acknowledge out loud.

Who was he?

What was he?

What would this creature's skin feel like against her? How about his mouth? With a voice so totally seductive, surely the rest of him would be sublime.

Although Skylar knew the difference between dreams and reality, there were no clear-cut definitions here. With her eyes closed, she fell under his spell. His image stuck to her with supernatural glue.

Wide shoulders above a broad muscular chest. Thick torso. Narrow waist and hips. Dark hair worn long. His stance was determined, his face sometimes raised to the star-filled sky. And over everything was an aura of wildness that catapulted things into nightmare territory. Because there wasn't the slightest chance of mistaking her nocturnal seducer for a normal human being. He was, in fact, anything but normal.

He was a magnetic combination of man and beast with a ridiculous twist on the DNA sequencing of two species that couldn't share the same physical space in reality. A unique being with its own name.

Werewolf.

Hell. Yes. Werewolf.

With a presence powerful enough to sift through REM.

Of course these were just dreams. She got that. She wasn't an idiot.

Well, maybe she was. Because…

She was so very hot for the creature that stood on that hilltop and looked like a man at times, though that outline was deceptive. She felt vulnerable when he was around, and slightly out of control. But maybe she was only an cavesdropper, and he waited for someone else. Some*thing* else.

Was the moon his mistress? Wasn't that how things worked for werewolves?

Why, then, was he yanking her chain?

A sudden spike in her heart rate, far beyond the usual range, jolted Skylar's eyes open. Anxious, she rolled over on the mattress and sat up, sweat trickling between her breasts, heart pounding too damn fast.

Tonight was different somehow. This time the voice had seemed closer and very, very real. It left an echo in the room.

Not dreaming now?

To prove that, Skylar slipped from the bed and padded to the window. She moved the curtain, expecting to catch sight of her velvety tormentor, wondering again why she allowed a figment of her imagination to continue to interrupt what should have been a good night's sleep.

She saw nothing out there, but God, had she actually expected to?

Resisting the urge to laugh at herself, Skylar rested her forehead on the cool window glass. Probably she had allowed her mind to supercharge some poor nocturnal creature's cry into something it wasn't. That's all those sounds were.

Not a voice.

She wasn't nuts, just tired, worn out and sleep deprived.

She also supposed that these nighttime escapades could be tied to the power of suggestion, caused by the discovery of her dad's cache of items in the attic. That old trunk and the things she found inside it.

Her dad, it seemed, kept dirty little secrets to himself here in Colorado, so far away from his family. And it had taken coming to this remote cabin to go through his things for Skylar to realize she hadn't really known David Donovan at all.

One more glance outside, at the night, and she turned back to the bed. Curling up on the mattress with her knees to her chest, she used her usual abundance of common sense to reason things out.

Maybe dreaming about a supernatural lover merely showcased a healthy need to get past the termination of her relationship with Danny, her ex-fiancé. She had left him a couple of months ago, before actually getting to the altar, and everybody needed time to adapt.

It wouldn't take a professional opinion to point out that the sexy dreams she seemed committed to having could be her mind's way of filling the void made by that kind of change, especially since it was followed fairly closely by her father's untimely death…

The father who, as a famous psychiatrist dealing in other peoples' problems, had, it turned out, sometimes dabbled in his own world of make-believe.

Werewolves were his idea, after all.

Not only had her dad believed those creatures existed, he must have thought they roamed the mountains of Colorado, right outside this cabin's door—which was likely the reason he often retreated here under the premise of needing alone time.

Beasts, for God's sake.

Like the one in my dreams.

So maybe fantasies were contagious and could be inherited, and stumbling on her father's secrets had spawned her own nocturnal reveries.

Skylar pulled the blanket up to her neck. Seconds later, she flipped onto her back, staring at the ceiling of the small rustic bedroom.

"Screw the pity party," she murmured. Because truthfully one thing, at least, was clear. She felt liberated by the empty spot on her ring finger.

Seeking comfort in the lavender-scented feather pillow, Skylar vowed to stick to her plan: finish going through and packing up her father's things and then return to her apartment in Miami, where her wedding dress still hung on a hanger. The dress would have to be returned eventually. If she ran into Danny, she'd just have to deal.

She could do that.

In truth, her life sucked sometimes. No mother, no father and no fiancé…but what the heck? She had three loving sisters and the deed to this cabin.

"Bring it on, sexy nightmare!"

Plumping up the pillow, Skylar blew out a breath and dared to close her eyes. Refusing to behave, her heart spiked again.

Swear to God, she was sure the man in her dreams was out there now, waiting for her. Whispering to her. Compelling her to listen.

And why the hell shouldn't she?

Gavin Harris turned his face to the night wind, catching a whiff of a fragrance completely foreign to the rest of the forest smells surrounding him. It was a sudden sensory bombardment that didn't belong here and was, even as he breathed it in, a detour from his agenda.

Eyes shut, he wrapped his senses around the uniqueness

of the rich, sweet scent, separating each component with his fine-tuned wolf senses.

Female, he concluded. *Young, supple flesh. Musky pheromones. Traces of soap and denim.* Tantalizing feminine scents that weren't in any way related to the more monstrous odors he sought tonight, but were oh so compelling.

He shook his head hard to ward off the distraction, and muttered, "Forget it." Investigating the source of these new smells would mean detouring from his objective, which had to remain his greatest priority. He was on watch, hunting his own version of big game.

That objective was an important one. Vital.

But damn...

The rosy feminine perfume floating to him from the cabin in the clearing below him caused a visceral physical reaction similar to being shocked by a cattle prod. All the little hairs on his arms stood up. Tingling nerves made his muscles twitch.

He smelled the woman in that cabin as easily as if she stood in front of him, in person.

And she was alone.

Stepping forward brought the cabin into view through a gap in the trees. Gavin leveled his gaze on the dark windows and inhaled deeply, concluding that the woman down there was the only human in the area at the moment. She occupied a cabin that had been originally been built by old Tom Jeevers, making it smell a whole hell of a lot better than its line of former occupants had.

Something else?

The agitated, tinnier scent of anxiousness wafted to him, adding a second, spicier layer to the woman's floral bouquet. Either she was anticipating something, or was in some kind of trouble. A fight with a companion, lover or husband, maybe, that caused a ruffle in the atmosphere? The long-anticipated arrival of a lover who was late?

"Lucky bastard," Gavin muttered. If she had a husband, that guy would get to smell her every damn day.

With a quick glance up at the sky, Gavin widened his stance, knowing he shouldn't linger too long in the moonlight. Though the moon wasn't completely full tonight, that bugger was close enough to that phase to affect him in adverse ways. All the enhanced senses were just a start.

A quick glance down the length of his body found it not actually foreign, but increasingly unfamiliar as each lunar phase progressed. The extra muscle that he hadn't worked out in a gym to maintain helped to add bulk. His height had stretched a good inch or two above his normal six-one.

His jeans were tighter. Shirts now strained at the seams. The only measurements remaining the same were his feet, slammed into his boots.

Then there was his hair. The tangle of chin-length waves were darker and much longer than he was used to, tickling his ears, making him wonder how long he'd been patrolling this section of the mountain ignoring most of the perks of civilization.

Could it have been two years?

Damn if everything hadn't changed in the span of those years. Out of necessity, he'd pretty much become a loner. And though he patrolled this area of the Rockies regularly, during those past two years four people had died. One of them was the last man to occupy the cabin now emitting a woman's enticing pheromones.

Oh, yes. And within those two years he, Gavin Harris, Colorado Forest Ranger, had regrettably, unforgettably, become a beast tethered by a silver chain to the devilish disk in the sky. *Moon.* As absurd as that seemed.

He closed his eyes again, shook his head. Having a

woman down there, so very close, and smelling like heaven, served to highlight his shitload of personal issues.

People who abused the clichéd phrase *no crying over spilt milk* had never experienced their skin turning inside out or their muscles expanding to nearly twice their size in the span of sixty seconds. They'd never felt the pain of fingers splitting open to spring a full set of razor-sharp claws, and a jaw disconnecting bone by bone.

After taking another deep breath, Gavin dropped to a crouch. The sultry smells floating upward from the cabin were disturbing to him for so many reasons. One major problem was that they could easily mask the other, more feral odor he'd been out here searching for.

The woman's presence was trouble, any way he looked at it, and also a reminder he didn't need about the better times in his past. And the woman in that cabin might be in danger out here from bigger, badder things than him.

Who are you? he wondered. *Hasn't anyone warned you about this place? Told you that four deaths in and around the area are four too many, and that a woman by herself might be asking for trouble?*

Determined to let this go, Gavin straightened and half turned. That woman wasn't his problem. He had more serious things to worry about. There was a damn good possibility he wasn't the only monster nearby, and if that theory proved true, odds were less than good that he'd ever see another sunrise.

"Leave her alone. Get out of here. Let her be," Gavin warned himself.

Not so fast...

An additional beam of light drew his gaze.

He turned back.

The cabin's door opened, throwing a narrow strip of yellow across the boards of the covered porch. A figure emerged to stand in that beam, and although the features were shadowy from this distance, Gavin's heart exploded in a flurry of racing beats.

The woman stood in the open doorway as if his thoughts had drawn her out. As if she knew he was there, watching her, and felt his presence.

Seeing her jolted the beast inside him.

He'd been right about this woman. Anxiousness rode the breeze. She was tense, uptight and high-strung, like an animal about to spring.

But she was also small, blonde, and only half-dressed.

Gavin stared at the half-dressed part, and the long, lean, very bare legs that melted into delicate ankles and shoe-less feet.

His inner wolf gave a soft, muted whine that scattered when he cleared his throat.

Christ, temptation was a bitch.

So was being a goddamn werewolf.

As for you, woman...

His attention snapped to identify another smell.

Metal.

The woman on the porch had a gun?

Gavin realized with a sudden flash of intuition that the icy chill now ripping through him wasn't due only to the alluring sight of the woman, or the scent of her weapon, but to the thing closing in on them from the mountain.

He must have gauged the strange lure of this area correctly if the prodigal beast he sought returned two days early. Forty-eight hours shy of that next full moon.

"Ah, hell..."

With renewed wariness, he glanced again at the cabin and the beauty on the porch whose white T-shirt high-lighted her slender torso, and whose face was hidden by a cloud of fair hair. He already felt protective of her. Felt as though he knew her somehow.

She might have courage enough to try to protect herself, but no gun he knew of would save her if the thing he chased turned its attention her way. He whirled, his boots digging up clumps of dirt. *No time to waste.* If the visitor heading this way was what he hoped it might be, he needed to lead that abomination away from the cabin.

With a final look over his shoulder, Gavin took off at a jog because his gut told him he needed to stop this killer before it claimed another poor soul.

Chapter 2

Although no one showed up to confront her as she stood on the porch, Skylar knew she was no longer alone, and that she wasn't dreaming this time. Not a chance in hell.

Her father's gun felt heavy and cold in her hands. It was loaded, and she knew how to fire, just as all the Donovan girls did. Their father had been diligent about his daughters' self-defense.

That didn't stop the shaking, though. She had to hold the gun with both hands as she faced the unknown. Someone was out there. This was real. And at this time of night, that felt like bad news.

Of course, it could be a lost hiker. Maybe it was her father's crusty caretaker coming by to check on the property, or out for a late-night stroll. But the persistent flush of internal heat told her that those possibilities were false and that someone else was here.

Instead of retreating inside and locking the door behind

Seduced by the Moon

her, Skylar stood her ground, scanning the night beyond the meager pool of porch light where evidence of a visitor lay in the sudden silence of insects.

Biting her lip hard enough to taste blood, she ventured a call. "Where are you? Who are you?"

The silence was unnerving. She worked at drawing a breath.

"Not going to show yourself? I'm here, waiting." She pointed the revolver at the trees on the hillside, upped her volume. "And I'm not happy about it."

The taunt produced no results, but she couldn't give up. Someone was there, somewhere. What if it wasn't some innocent hiker? Suppose her father's killer had returned?

She had to consider that possibility. She refused to believe that her diligent, first-rate climber dad might have fallen to his death. The conclusion she'd come to, independent of her sisters' opinions, was that if David Donovan had fallen, someone must have pushed him.

"So who are you? Have you come for me?" she said to the quiet night, getting nothing back. No response at all.

"No time for hide and seek," she called out in a last-ditch effort to make contact as she backed up slowly, crossing the threshold in a shuffle of bare feet.

A change in the air made her pause. Moving the gun, she refocused her aim on a point just south of the path up the hillside.

"Best to stay inside," a man's voice advised from somewhere near the closest trees. "And lock the door. It might also be a good idea to leave here tomorrow."

Skylar's heart skidded over one too many beats, leaving her breathless. "Who are you?" she called out.

"Ranger, patrolling the area. There's been some trouble around here."

She waved the gun. "I know that, and I know how to use this."

"Better to move on before you have to use it," he said. "A woman alone is far too tempting as a target."

"How do you know I'm alone?"

"It's my business to know who's in the area."

"You've been watching the cabin?"

"As much as I can, but right now I'm needed elsewhere."

"Where's your car, or whatever rangers use to get around in?"

"Over the hill behind me."

"You run around on foot in the dark?"

"There aren't too many paths worthy of a vehicle around here, beyond the main road."

"I don't need you to stand guard," Skylar said. "Thanks, but you can get on with your business."

"Fine. Just offering a friendly warning. Can't be too careful this far out of town."

Skylar waved the gun again. "I'm well aware of that."

"Well, good night, then," the invisible ranger, if that's what he really was, said.

"Good night," Skylar echoed.

The night air changed again, rearranging itself as though something heavy had been removed and the darkness filled in the vacuum left behind. The result was a powerful charge that left Skylar swaying on her feet.

This could have been her imagination, she supposed as she shrugged off a new round of chills. But one thing was clear. She had no doubt whatsoever that this ranger's voice was the voice from her dreams.

The same damn one.

She'd bet her life on that.

* * *

"You're too far out there," Trish said over the phone the next day in the authoritative tone reserved for bossy older sisters.

"It's temporary, so I don't mind." Skylar rubbed her bloodshot eyes. Ten minutes of sleep while sitting by the window all night, gun in hand, wasn't nearly enough for a clear head.

"I need to get this cabin boxed," she added, like she did every time she spoke with Trish, which was every day. Sometimes twice.

"I'll come and help," Trish said.

"No, you won't."

"Then Lark can visit. She can ask for time off."

"I'd rather choke."

Trish's voice deepened. "Do you know any of the neighbors?"

Like most lawyers, Trish didn't like being crossed or argued with for any reason. As the oldest Donovan sister, Trish would lay out her argument logically and plan on wearing her down with repetition.

Skylar didn't want to go home and didn't want company while she explored the circumstances surrounding her father's death. Unless hell froze over, she wasn't going to share that objective with her sisters and get them all riled up.

Besides, the good Lord only knew what would happen if she were to utter the word *werewolf*, or mention being harassed by someone who hadn't really shown themselves last night. If Trish knew any of that, half of Colorado would be on their way over before the phone disconnected.

Which might not have been such a bad idea, actually, if Skylar's stubborn streak would have allowed it.

"The caretaker for this place lives a couple of miles down the road, Trish. I have his phone number right here."

Trish snorted her disapproval. "Miles? Like that's comforting?"

"I have a gun."

Skylar's announcement preceded a beat of silence over the line.

"You what?" Trish eventually said.

"It was Dad's. I took it from the trunk."

"What trunk would that be?" Trish asked. *Demanded*, really, in her best cross-examination style.

"The one I found in the attic here. It's loaded and I know how to use it. We all do."

Trish sighed unhappily. Trisha Lilith Donovan saw far too many weapons in her job as a prosecuting attorney to be comfortable with any of them. And Trish, as the eldest sibling and the only Donovan kid not named after a bird, felt responsible for the rest of the motherless girls.

"I suppose being engaged to the cop for twelve months also had its perks in the weapons department?" Trish suggested.

Skylar lowered the phone to take a deep breath so that Trish wouldn't hear it. Trish had said "the cop," avoiding the use of Danny's name.

Skylar raised the receiver when she heard Trish calling her name.

"Skye? Skylar?"

"Sorry. I have something cooking on the stove. Can we talk later?"

"You're putting me off. We haven't discussed—"

"Good. Thanks," Skylar interrupted. "I'll call you tomorrow morning."

"Skye, wait. I'm sorry I brought up the cop. Really sorry."

"No sweat. I've moved on, that's all."

"I know, but…"

"It's all right. I haven't been a baby for twenty-three years now. Nor have I ever needed help in making up my mind about something."

"I know that, too. But you will always be my baby sister. You can confide in me."

"I'm all right, I swear. My fiancé was a bastard, and it took me too long to figure that out. I'm off the hook now. That's how I look at the breakup. Possibly it was an act of divine intervention in my favor. I feel relief, if you want the truth. We'll talk again tomorrow. Okay?"

"Oh, all right."

"Bye, Trish."

Skylar signed off before the arguments could start up again, and with them the apologies about things not working out with Detective Danny Parker, who had gotten her close enough to matrimony to actually buy the dress.

But it had never been a match made in heaven, and she'd known that, deep down inside. She'd merely been going through the motions.

Worse, in terms of regrets, was realizing she'd gone along with Danny's little mental abuses, and had been swept up in them, rather than openly exerting her true rebellious personality. That hadn't been like her at all, really. And she hadn't been lying to Trish about the relief.

Palming her cell phone, Skylar checked the screen for calls, half expecting Trish to call back. Then she set the phone on the table. Service was spotty in the mountains, and only seemed to like this small area in the front room of the cabin—a fact that wasn't exactly comforting, she supposed, though Trish didn't need to know that, either.

"And if you knew what else I found in that trunk of Dad's, Trish, you'd send in the tanks," she muttered.

Not only had she found the gun in that trunk, well-oiled and ready to go, it was loaded with unusual ammunition that had to have helped shape her dreams. She was sure that silver bullets weren't the norm for anyone, outside of people chasing their own form of madness.

Glancing up at the ceiling as if she could see through the rough wooden beams, she said, "Neither are they standard in a psychiatrist's medicine bag."

In the past, she would have called Danny to talk about this, but she was on her own now—which left her imagination wide-open. Because shiny silver ammunition, unless merely something a collector might covet, was de rigueur for hunting…

"Werewolves."

Skylar turned toward the window, attuned to the drop in temperature that signaled another day's end. Nightfall wasn't far off.

"Damn it, Trish. I need to find out what our father was up to, and why it might have killed him."

Solving the mystery of her father's frequent disappearances was paramount, as was finding out why he needed so much time away from everyone he supposedly loved.

But hell, Dad. Silver bullets?

In all truth, she had to admit, being in this cabin for a few days by herself, with her dad's things, had caused her more discomfort than seeing Danny's face when she told him the engagement was off.

The men in her life were gone, and she was far too intelligent to imagine that velvet-voiced rangers could have stepped out of her dreams.

As for monsters…

The moon would be completely full in another twenty-four hours, a big deal in werewolf lore, at least in the movies. If the approaching moon was some kind of supernatural stimulant, all werewolves would be affected. If there were such things as man-wolf creatures, her dream lover would be affected, too. And with her dad's gun under her pillow, she'd be ready for anything that dream had to offer.

Chapter 3

Gavin hadn't found the trail of the creature he sought. Although he'd gotten close enough to taste its feral presence, one too many detours had brought him back, time and time again, to stare at the cabin, wishing to see *her*.

He hadn't meant to circle back. He had, in fact, been heading in the opposite direction. Yet here he was again, staring down at the blasted cabin, telling himself, "Don't be an idiot. No one needs a woman that bad."

Obviously, he didn't believe that on some level.

The beast he hunted, which had a fondness for blood and sacrifices, disappeared just after midnight. After following its malevolent stench south, the damn thing vanished into thin air. He'd spent a fruitless night backtracking all over the mountain, and more time searching throughout the day to make sure he hadn't missed anything crucial. Now, once again, darkness wasn't far off, putting him a hell of a lot closer to the phase of the moon that counted.

He eyed the cabin warily, figuring that if his interest in the woman down there kept up, he'd have to chain himself to the Jeep to avoid showing up on her doorstep, in person. The next time he confronted that woman, she might do more than point the weapon in his direction. She might actually pull the trigger.

He thought about that gun, and what it might do to him.

It was possible that he could he survive a bullet at close range, but it would certainly slow him down. When the beast inside him took over, several bullets might be required to make a permanent dent.

In theory, anyway.

He'd only tested his survival skills once, when he was accidentally hit by an arrow fired at him by mistake. That hunter now spent time in a cell.

And by the way...that arrow had been a bitch.

Gavin searched the clearing.

The cabin looked quiet in the evening light, though he knew the woman hadn't taken his advice and hit the road. A ribbon of gray smoke rose from the chimney.

Stubborn streak?

Who in their right mind remained resistant to a ranger's warning, or stepped outside in the middle of the night to face anyone or anything that might be out there?

Not courageous, necessarily. More like impulsive.

Maybe she gets off on danger.

And just maybe he'd make it his business to find out.

Besides, he was ravenous for company, and the smoke coming from the cabin carried the smell of food. If he knocked on the door, was there was a remote possibly she'd invite him in for a bite?

Gavin shook his head, rubbed his eyes.

She shouldn't be alone. The last death out here had been gruesome. Some poor doctor found in a gulley, sliced to shreds. Gavin had an idea about how that might have happened, and that idea didn't include a slippery trail. But he couldn't speak of it to anyone. Who'd believe him?

The doctor who had occupied the cabin died just ten days ago, which made the new occupant's tenancy a quick turnaround. Possibly the woman was part of that man's family.

She'd probably have her pants on today.

Smiling felt strange. So did the compulsion to go down there. He didn't know why this woman's presence was so intriguing to him that his vow of celibacy strained at its leash.

He was way too hungry for everything that cabin had to offer, for anyone's good.

As for women? He hadn't dared to sleep with one since he'd been mauled by a hell demon and his life, as he'd always known it, had ceased to exist. He had no idea how the beast, now an integral part of him, would deal with emotion. He wasn't sure if this nightmare could be passed to others by way of something as insignificant as a scratch or a kiss.

There seemed to be no rule book for werewolves. No manual. Hell, it was possible there were no others like him, and he'd have to continue to play it by ear.

"Sorry," Gavin whispered to the female below, though his insides quaked with a longing for what she could offer that bordered on visceral greed.

He craved warmth and closeness and the freedom to fill his lungs with the perfume surrounding this woman like an aura. He wanted to run his hands over every inch of her, and see where that led. Test himself. Push himself.

But he had a job to do and a vow to fulfill. He'd find the beast that had ruined his life, and take that beast down.

"Not her," he said to quiet his inner wolf. "Definitely can't bother this woman."

Want her, his wolfish side protested with a sharp stomach twist.

"Yes. Okay. I suppose I do," Gavin admitted as he started down the hill toward the cabin as if pulled there by an invisible chain.

"Stop right there."

Obliging, the man by the fence stopped at the gate.

Even if she hadn't guessed that her nighttime visitor would return, Skylar's first thought actually would have been *ranger* due to the light green pants and the shirt with a badge on the pocket.

She wasn't sure how she noticed the clothing details though, given her initial surprise over how incredibly attractive the rest of him was and how well he fit her dream guy's stats.

Tall and rangy, his outfit did little to hide masses of lean, well-honed muscle. Other dreamed attributes were there, too: the broad shoulders and narrow waist, the dark brown hair with its loose waves curtaining a chiseled face. From where she stood, it appeared that every body part seemed perfectly balanced and in accord with his beautifully united whole.

Just as she'd imagined.

This was downright uncanny, and maybe even a little scary. Still, while the hunky outdoorsman looked strong, he didn't look primeval. His fingers didn't end in razor-sharp claws, though she seemed to recognize him on whatever level of consciousness telegraphed heat.

Skylar felt her temperature begin to rise. Sensitive spots at the base of her spine tingled—a sign that though he hadn't spoken yet, this guy truly was last night's visitor, in the flesh.

"You've lost your gun," he finally observed.

Velvet. Yes. His voice was like a velvet blanket, the vocalization of his appearance.

Skylar's heart fluttered in her chest.

"Do I need it?" She regarded this guy almost rudely, unable to stop the flood of internal warnings about the impossibility of dreams coming to life.

But she couldn't have made this guy up. He was standing in her yard in the last light of a long day, and was close enough for her to see his face.

She wasn't dreaming now. That face and its perfectly symmetrical features struck her as being way too familiar.

"The apron suits you," he said in a teasing manner that might have been inappropriate since they were strangers outside of her fantastically naughty dreams. Nevertheless, she smiled and ran one hand down the front of the dish towel she'd tied around her waist, glad she had on jeans for this reunion.

Her other hand clutched the gun hidden behind her back.

"I guess you're determined to stay, ignoring the advice of the locals," he went on.

"I have business to conclude here."

"Can I ask what that business is?"

"Cleaning up my father's things. He lived here on and off until recently."

The ranger kicked dirt off his boots and looked down, suggesting that he knew what had happened to her dad.

"I'm sorry for your loss." He glanced up again to meet her scrutinizing gaze.

Nervously, Skylar glanced away. The flutter inside her chest spread to her arms. She gripped the gun tighter so she wouldn't drop the damn thing.

"Were you watching my father, too? He had an accident, they said."

Skylar let the word *accident* hang in the air before continuing. "Was anyone patrolling around here when he died?"

Unable to resist the urge to look at him again, almost as if he requested it, she dragged her focus upward until their gazes connected across the small front yard.

Shudders rocked her with the immediacy of the connection, and she shifted from foot to foot to cover the quakes. He stared back at her with a seriousness that set off more alarm bells. His penetrating eyes were very light against his bronzed skin. Though she was unfamiliar with the dream man's eyes, she was sure these were his.

You're a handsome sucker, I'll give you that.

But how do I know you?

Why have I modeled a dream after you?

If she'd met this guy before, she would have remembered, and yet her treacherous body was responding to him as though he'd stepped right out of her dream and was presenting himself to her now in order to culminate all those pent-up feelings.

While reading body language was a trick both her father and her own classes in medical school had taught her, this situation was different. Meeting his gaze was like sharing secrets without having to speak. It felt weird, and also incredibly sexy in a messed-up way.

"Two of us were on duty that night, but not near here," he said in answer to the question she'd almost forgotten.

"Night?" she echoed. "Dad was hiking at night?"

"I don't know that for a fact," he replied. "Sorry again."

Even in stillness, the ranger seemed to be moving, evidence of the wild streak he harbored. Chances were good he was a loner, preferring to live on the fringes of the city, communing with trees. Weren't all forest rangers born with some kind of special calling for the great outdoors?

How about werewolves?

Glad she hadn't said that out loud, Skylar fisted her free hand in the dish cloth, trying on the word *figment* for size. This ranger, so like the man in her dreams, was quite possibly a figment of her overwrought imagination.

"You don't need the gun," he said in a lowered tone. "Not with me."

Although his blue-eyed gaze held steady, Skylar also noted a hint of weariness in his features. He might have been up all night. He could have been near here the whole time, either guarding this cabin's sole resident, or drawn to her for reasons that went beyond being neighborly. Reasons like sharing unusual dreams or offering genuine condolences in person for her loss.

Fingers tight on the gun behind her back, Skylar smiled. "Do all rangers have X-ray vision, or just you?"

He shrugged. "Merely an educated guess since you showed me the gun last night."

"It's a precaution. After all, how do I know you're what you say you are?"

"You're right to mistrust strangers. That's a good sign."

"A good sign of what?"

"Wariness, where it's necessary. Caution. A healthy respect for self-preservation."

He pulled a small radio from his belt and held it up. "This is how I check in." He spoke to the radio. "Harris here, on the eastern slope."

An answer crackled back from the radio, and Skylar heard enough to make her feel better about believing him. His voice, as he spoke, also made her familiarity with it more unsettling. Disconnecting from the dream was proving to be tough.

Puzzled, she said, "I recognize your voice."

Ranger Harris nodded. "We spoke last night."

It's so much more than that. What though?

"Why did you come back today?" she asked.

"I thought I'd check on you. Make sure everything is okay."

"Do your rounds take in all of the cabins out here?"

"Usually. But very few people are in residence right now."

"I passed four cabins on my way to this one."

"Most folks don't live in them year-round. And those who do have taken off for a while."

Breaking the disconcerting eye contact, Skylar looked to the east. "Because of what happened to my father?"

"Your father had an accident."

"So they say."

Other than offering a brief nod, he didn't react to her remark.

"You're alone out here. I just thought you might like to know we're around," he said.

"Rangers, you mean?"

"Yes."

Skylar crossed her arms over her chest, bringing the gun front and center. If nothing else, she needed the weapon to protect her from herself. This guy's gaze made her feel naked, though he didn't appear to be staring at anything other than her face. Outwardly, he acted like a gentleman, the warden of this place, but the sparks tickling her insides weren't appeased by his surface calm, his coolness or his distance.

Hearing him had set off a chain reaction. Too many of her fantasies were built on that voice. In the flesh, this guy, whoever he was, stranger that he might be, was like catnip to a serial dreamer.

Skylar reached for the flush creeping up her neck, hoping to stop it from reaching her face.

"How did they find him?" she finally asked.

Ranger Harris tilted his head to ponder the question.

"Who found my father's body?"

"Hikers, I believe," he replied.

"Near here?"

"On the other side of this hill."

"At night?"

"He was found sometime after sundown, I heard."

Skylar lowered the gun. "He was barely recognizable."

"Then I hope you didn't have to see that, Miss..."

"Donovan. Skylar Donovan."

He nodded.

"No one in my family saw him. His partner at the hospital identified his body, and she believed it best we didn't see him...under the circumstances."

"I'm sorry."

Sorry for what? she thought. *For my father's death? For making me want to forget we're strangers?*

Pressing back a strand of hair that had slipped from her ponytail, Skylar remembered how Danny preferred her hair shorter than she wore it. He hadn't liked her in jeans like the ones she wore now. Her cop had been critical about so many things she liked to do and certainly never would have approved of her being out here alone. *Control freak* would have been a good description of his personality.

She had gone along with Danny's preferences for the sake of trying to appear normal, feel normal, be part of a couple...when she had always known it wouldn't work out in the end.

Her next shiver was in the bastard ex-fiancé's honor.

"Are you okay?" the man across from her asked.

"Yes," she lied. "Anyway, I suppose accidents happen."

"Too often," he agreed.

"Especially in this kind of terrain?"

"The trails are tricky," he concurred. "Moreso when wet."

He hadn't budged from his position near the gate. Skylar wondered if he wanted to but was afraid he'd frighten her. Realizing how nuts it might be to trust him at all, she said, "Would you like something to drink? I've got lemonade."

"Lemonade would be nice. Thanks. It's been a fairly warm day, despite the end of summer, and I didn't take time for lunch."

"Come in, then. We can sit on the porch."

"I'd like that. Mind if I wash my hands?"

"There's a hose by the corner of the cabin, and a bar of soap in a pail."

The ranger opened the tiny gate and closed it behind him. Having him on her side of the fence gave her an unanticipated thrill, despite the fence being no more than hip high and easy enough to knock over with one good shove.

The closer he got, the more her body reacted to him. She wanted to get close to this guy, feel him, smell him. She wanted him down and dirty, filthy hands and all.

That damn dream...

Ranger Harris was a delectable mixture of all the things that made a man a man. Equally rugged and elegant, he moved with the casual, effortless grace of an animal, sinew and muscle seeming to work without the impediment of an underlying bone structure. Predatory animals moved like that. Tigers, lions, cheetahs.

Wolves.

Skylar nearly dropped the gun and fumbled to secure it in her grip. Hell, did she have to distort everything?

This guy, with his badge and radio, was not the creature of her dreams. He wasn't a *creature* at all. Her idea that he could be one virtually screamed of her desire to get over what had happened with Danny. Her imagination was twisting situations to match wishes that were nothing more than a bunch of dangling loose ends.

"There's a towel on the rack," she called out.

"Thanks." He crouched down to lift the hose, his green shirt stretching across his shoulders and threatening to tear at the seams. His dark hair, thick with a slight curl, brushed against the back of his collar when his head tilted forward.

She had always loved hair like that. Hair made for running fingers through. Hair that would tickle bare skin in moments of intimacy, and provide something to hang on to.

Skylar cringed, and gave herself a stern silent reprimand.

I will not take this guy to bed.

No way was she going to indulge in her first one-night stand in the middle of a forest, even if he were willing to take her up on what she was thinking.

That's what her mind said.

Her body told her otherwise. There had been far too many erotic thoughts about rugged men lately to ignore what was right in front of her. And he was interested in her. He couldn't hide that fact any more than she could hide her interest in him. He kept looking her way.

Something came to life within her as she watched him. The sensation wasn't familiar, and was centered so deep down inside her body it mimicked the feel of a rising sexual climax.

Working hard to keep from sliding a hand between her thighs to ease the pressure building there, Skylar withheld a sigh that might have given away her fanciful state of neediness. Everything about this cabin and what happened around it was strange. She felt strange…and very much like the predator here.

How's that for a switch?

"I'll get the pitcher," she said as the internal flares going off reached unbearable levels, threatening to burn her up if left untended. She wanted to rush into this guy's arms. Would he be shocked if she did?

"I'll be right back," she said. Yet she didn't turn away, fascinated by the way the ranger's pants adhered to every line and curve of his masculine, muscular backside. Fully aware of how forceful his thrusts into a woman would be with powerful musculature like that.

The oncoming twinge of greed made Skylar cross her legs. Danny had been in good shape, but this guy was exceptional. Almost too perfect. If she looked harder, would she find proof of a hidden wildness that made perfection an art form? One little slip on his part, and he'd growl? There'd be fur in unusual places and spring-loaded claws on those wet hands?

He was looking at her intently.

She'd forgotten to go for the lemonade.

Cheeks flushed with heat, Skylar tried to smile. "I was wondering if you're working tomorrow night, too."

He turned off the water and got to his feet. "I'm here all week."

"Should be easier to see tomorrow, with the moon full."

"You're right." He dried his hands on his pants, forgoing the towel.

There were no claws on those hands.

"Does the approach of a full moon make animals restless? I think I hear them at night," Skylar said.

Now she was pushing things. She was an idiot.

He came closer than she should have allowed, and faced her squarely. He smiled, but with an expression of sadness. Heartbreaking sadness.

Why?

Whatever she had expected, it hadn't been that.

As he slowly moved toward her, she felt every inch he traveled as if the air between them compressed. When he stopped, they were nearly chest to chest, and she had to look up to see his face.

Liquid lava coursed through her veins, pumping, scorching, flowing fast. Her forehead dampened. Her heart raced. She was hot enough to be combustible and breathing hard. All these reactions confirmed that she hadn't been wrong about one thing. Something was going on between them on a crazy personal level. Their chemistry had been instantaneous and wasn't to be ignored.

Animal magnetism taken to extremes.

Lust at first sight.

Dreams trespassing into the realm of reality.

In that moment, she wanted no backstory or history with a man who spoke of relationships and marriage. No rules governing behavior and no regrets of any kind. This was the man she desperately wanted with an all-encompassing physical desire. His hands on her, for real. His mouth torturing her mouth, right now. His body inside hers, his every move making her writhe with pleasure.

Hell...she wanted to bite and scratch and become the beast. She wanted to dig her nails into him and wrap her legs sinuously around his waist. She wanted desperately to let go and be who she really was inside, without anyone else riding shotgun on her behavior.

Screw the dreams. These fiery cravings were real and pulsing and painfully acute. If she acted on them, she wouldn't wake with her own hand between her legs because this guy would be there to do that for her.

"I've changed my mind about the porch." Her voice was throaty and pitched low.

His eyes kept her riveted, casting a familiar spell. Skylar

heard thunder, though the skies were clear. She felt lightning strike her, stapling her to the ground, and yet she was able to move.

Brazenly, she reached for his hand. She brought it to her breast and spread his long fingers over the thin fabric of the blue linen shirt covering her. His heat blended with hers, forcing her heart into a frantic tempo.

Miraculously, his face showed no surprise at this kind of sexual aggression. Maybe, like her, he'd known what was going to happen. With his free arm, he gathered her tightly to him. Warm lips brushed her forehead with the softness of a sigh.

Why in God's name was she doing this?

Because she felt an unearthly attraction to this man, that's why. No, not just attracted to, *possessed by*, and therefore willing to ditch caution for him, and for what they were about to do.

She looked into light blue eyes that sparkled with curiosity and contained no visible wolfish variation. *Just a man, then. A really sexy man.* One she didn't have to have a future with, only a passing moment of eroticism that would be a culmination of her one-sided bed play.

She brushed off the little alarms going off in the back of her skull in favor of the quakes and the heat of the ranger's seductive nearness. It was hardly surprising that she'd go for this. She needed to take the risk.

This guy wasn't Danny. Danny lacked in some departments and was intimidated by her lust for sex. She had tamped down those lusts the entire time they were together in favor of hiding her wilder side. After being corralled so long, some of those needs were pushing back.

The man holding her stroked her face, sending waves of little shivers through her body. Did he understand what was happening to her or was this blatant offer of female physicality merely every ranger's wish come true?

He moved first, backing up, his breathing as labored as hers. Calmly, he took the gun from her and tucked it into his belt. Then he reached for her hand.

She said nothing, couldn't have managed one word. His touch was electric and uncommonly sensuous.

In silence, he led her up the steps toward the front door of the cabin of secrets, where some of those secrets, scary as they might be, strange as they had become, were about to be shared.

Only then did Skylar whisper a curse and a prayer.

Chapter 4

Secrets.

Desire unleashed.

Gavin had touched this sexy woman and was still standing there in human form. His hand had been on her breast, and that hand had remained his own without altering its shape or hurting her.

So maybe he could do this, he thought. Perhaps in the grand scheme of things that made monsters of men, he'd prevail in something he wanted so badly.

The cabin was small, a one-bedroom affair, so the bedroom wasn't hard to find. Once they reached it, Gavin lifted the woman beside him into his arms. In silence he held her, fearing to speak, afraid to ruin what was going on between them. He was sure she felt as strongly about it as he did.

Her eyes told him so. Big green eyes in a pretty oval face, with a small tapered nose, high cheekbones and beautifully arched brows—all of those features expressive and showing her impatience.

She looked young and felt light, almost buoyant, in his arms, but she buzzed with energy as she laced a slender arm around his neck and snaked her fingers into his hair, just above the nape of his neck. Heat flared white-hot in the spot she touched, and he held back a groan.

He could not afford to come unglued.

Pulse soaring, body hardening, Gavin checked a growl when her lush pink mouth parted and she ran her tongue over her lips, unconsciously wetting them in a seductive sweep without taking her eyes from his.

Siren.

Seductress.

Put here to tempt him. Push him. Test his limits.

Her exhaled breath smelled like the lemons she'd used to make the drink offered to him, but her lips offered so much more, if he dared to cross a line he'd set for himself so achingly long ago.

Gavin wanted nothing more than to devour that pouty mouth and draw from her a moan. He was close enough to her to do that, yet he didn't kiss her, could not kiss her now, because that level of intimacy was too dangerous and might be too much for either man or wolf to bear.

Already her closeness was tricky. His skin rippled with tension. Nerves were firing, exaggerating his pulse, sending it skyrocketing. These reactions might have been normal when facing a situation like this—a beautiful woman offering herself to him on a warm evening, and out of the blue. But of course nothing about this meeting was normal. He sensed this, and so did the creature he carried inside him.

The wolf was stirring, wanting in on the deal. How far would he get? How much did he dare?

He'd have to put this woman on the bed in order to find out, and couldn't make himself release her. Tight against him, she was safe—a prisoner, his captive. *Christ!* He felt her need melt into him. Her anxiousness called him out, and the wolf inside him twisted into knots, wanting to accept her challenge.

Did this woman feel how fast his heart was beating?

"Kiss me," she said, meeting his eyes, tugging him forward with both of her hands fisted in his hair. "Make it real."

Real? Was that just her way of telling him to get on with it?

Take your time, Gavin.

Don't listen.

The excitement he felt had to be measured. Nothing was to be taken for granted or rushed.

He didn't kiss her. Not yet. One step forward and his knees bumped the mattress. Gavin loosened his grip on the sleek body he wanted to tear into. She was covered in faded jeans and a fitted shirt—a lot of layers to peel back while testing himself.

She felt so damn good, and smelled even better. Her body was slim, taut, pliant. Through the shirt, her ribs were ridges beneath his fingers. In place of curves, she was composed of lovely muted angles.

Gavin liked all of this.

He knew exactly what to do and how to do it, if he dared to press this further and face the consequences of accepting the woman's gracious invitation so close to the full moon.

Not long now and he would become the beast, at least in part. Thank God his mind remained his own and in the driver's seat when that happened. The same couldn't be said for the monster that had savaged him not far from here.

Not far from this cabin.

The woman's hands moved, and Gavin sucked in a breath. Warm fingers slid beneath his collar in a meeting of overheated flesh.

God. Help. Him.

He had to be cautious, careful, diligent. He had to keep sharp and pay attention when all he wanted to do was lose himself in the woman's succulent body and bury himself inside her, where he'd forget the rest of the world for a brief time.

He wanted that very much.

He set her on the bed. Her arms came away from him, limbs falling, muscles wired. She continued to look at him as if she knew him already, as though this wasn't the first time they faced each other in this way. That should have bothered him, Gavin supposed, but it wasn't the time for reasoning. His hunger was growing, and so far he was okay.

All right.

He sat down beside her on a lavender-scented bed not intended for two. The woman watched him with her eyes wide-open and her lips quivering ever so slightly.

I can do this.

This is what I need.

When she blinked slowly, he felt the loss of her gaze, as if part of him had been torn away. In her eyes he was a man, not a freak.

"Look," he whispered to her. "Look at me."

She did, letting out a breath.

With careful hands, in quick movements, he pulled the shirt over her head and tossed it to the floor. The sight of her creamy ivory bareness made him pause to take stock. She was splendid, flawless, made for him. The back of Gavin's neck prickled with appreciation.

Small, rounded breasts rose from a smooth chest beneath a graceful slope of shoulders. The delicate lace of skimpy blue lingerie covered those breasts, held in place by thin ribbons that ran up and over her shoulders to disappear beneath a tangle of tawny golden hair.

Pressure rose in Gavin's chest and groin as he waited out a moment of incomparable agony. Then he eased those ribbons down, leaving them to cross her fair skin like slender slashes of watercolor shadow.

He closed his eyes, aware of the irony.

He was that shadow.

When she touched him, he jumped. She'd tucked a hand inside his shirt, between the buttons, so that once again their fiery skin met. Gavin fought back a sound he was sure would have fallen somewhere between a groan and a growl.

Her touch spurred him on.

Captivating scents, rich and floral, saturated her skin, the see-through lace covering her and the pillows behind her. He had smelled this fragrance before, from afar, and it was what had brought him here, to her.

Her skin was dewy, soft. A flat stomach stretched to the button on her low-slung jeans. Sharp-edged hip bones raised the denim, highlighting the concavity between them that, wolf willing, he'd get to settle himself into. But that was wishful thinking, and he was getting way ahead of himself.

Lowering his mouth to her breasts, Gavin placed a kiss between them, feeling relatively safe if he stayed away from her mouth. With a spike in his pulse, he absorbed the ungodly pleasurable sensation of the delicate lace against his lips.

He placed a second kiss on the exposed edge of one rounded breast, knowing this might be pushing things and that he was about to become undone.

Taking his time wasn't going to work. Climbing into bed with her wasn't, either. He was starting to sweat, burning up from the inside out, and his hands were quaking. Maybe she was the wrong woman to try his luck with. He'd never ached for a woman this badly, and he didn't want to lose the connection.

Damn it, how would he explain stopping this now?

She was too exquisite to be a test run for his current predicament. He was rock hard, his body begging to be inside her. That kind of inner turmoil tended to spark the wolf to life.

He felt the wolf rising now in direct proportion to the stiffening of his cock. His throat was no longer his own. He didn't dare make a sound with this pressure building.

In hindsight, he should have known better than to come here, this close to a full moon, for any reason. Being drawn to this woman only made matters worse.

Wildness coated the underside of his skin. Although fur wouldn't burst from his pores tonight, the wolf's drive was what Gavin feared. He couldn't be entirely sure which needs were ruling his desires, his or the wolf's. Surely the wolf's hunger had become his own.

Gavin brushed a stray tendril of gold from the woman's forehead, fighting to remain sane when the wolf desired powerful thrusts and the slapping sounds of bodies fiercely merging. The wolf wanted to bite and bruise and voted for ruined beds, broken furniture and swollen mouths.

Fast. Hard. Take it now. That was the way of the wolf. And maybe also the thoughts of a man who had long gone without.

Be careful.

Keep control.

Gavin's teeth slammed shut when she whispered in his ear.

"Now," she said. "You and me, here, now."

To get a grip on a restraint that was rapidly slipping away, Gavin shut his eyes.

If I do as you ask, I'll never be able to see you again.

I'll never look into your eyes again or feel the softness of your skin. You'd know me for what I am, what I've become. My secret would be out.

Those were words he could never say out loud. But the truth was that she didn't want him to stop this. She was trembling and ready to take him on. The look in her eyes explained it all.

She reached for his shoulders, dug her fingernails into his shirt as if to tear away barriers and accept everything he had to give.

Forgive me...

He could try to be a man, and only a man, one more time.

For you.

Pulling her from the pillows, Gavin released the clasp keeping her lacy bra between them. As she fell back, he covered one of her breasts with his hot, breathless mouth.

The wolf swam in his bloodstream, causing his heart to thunder as Gavin drew her in, circling the pink raised tip with his tongue. A lick and a draw and then he bit down lightly, teasingly, sweating with the effort of holding passion back. None of this was enough by far, yet it was clear that he wouldn't get much further if he hoped to maintain some control.

More thunder hammered his skull and beat at him from behind his ribs. Beneath his belt, his body was demanding this union, though shadows lengthened in the room, darkening the floor. Night was near, and inside of that darkness roamed a monster this woman needed protection from.

Two monsters, actually.

When he looked down, it was to find his shirt hanging open from mid-chest down, with a few buttons missing. The woman beside him was running her hands over his stomach with a touch like hot coals—over his abdomen and halfway around to his lower back. He arched with each incendiary caress, maintaining eye contact, holding his breath.

Her nails grated against his ribs to leave long red grooves. She let out a sultry, sexy-as-hell sigh that shook Gavin to his core. This was her own growl of need and longing, an expectation of the otherworldly boundaries she planned on obliterating with him, and a promise to see this through, whatever he had in mind.

"Who the hell are you?" he whispered as his chest met hers.

Her lips separated, luring him into a kiss, daring him to devour her. And what the hell, he would have done it any-way, damn the beast, damn the curse that mocked his life.

Or so his thoughts went until he heard a distant sound that froze him inches from her, and kept him from taking that beautiful mouth for all it was worth.

The roar echoed in the clearing around the cabin and instantly chilled Gavin to the bone. He hesitated for several agonizing seconds, horrified. "No. Not now. Not yet," he whispered.

The woman in the bed also heard the noise. White-faced and wide-eyed, she sat forward, her heart beating as furiously as his.

"What was that?" she asked.

"Nothing you'd want to meet." Even that much of an explanation seemed to expose too much, Gavin thought.

Damn the timing. He should have known better than to put his mind and energy elsewhere when he was sure the monster had returned.

On his feet in a flash, Gavin reached for the radio still tucked into his belt before deciding against using it. Who would believe him or want to face whatever made that awful roar?

With a graceful swing of one arm, he retrieved the gun from the floor and set it on the bed.

"I'm sorry." After taking one last look at the woman who'd distracted him into nearly forgetting a vow, and with his heart filled with regret for having to pass up what she offered here tonight, he added, "Really sorry."

Then he turned for the door.

She scrambled after him. He heard the sounds of her bare feet on the old wooden boards. "What was that?" she repeated. "Tell me."

"Wolf," he said. "Big one. Badass. Doesn't belong here."

"You have to go after it?"

Her voice kept him hard and hating the separation.

"I have to find that beast before it finds other things to harm," he explained.

"Aren't wolves usual out here?"

Gavin stopped at the front door thinking that people were so damn naive. But though this woman looked bewildered, she didn't appear to be the slightest bit hurt by his hasty withdrawal, and only truly curious about the sound they'd heard. She didn't ask him to explain his abrupt behavior. She was looking at him with hunger dilating her beautiful green eyes.

Grabbing her by the shoulders, Gavin tilted her head back with a small shake. She didn't object, just bit her lower lip hard enough to bring up a droplet of blood with her tiny white teeth.

"Christ!" He wanted her so blessed badly, and to prove it, he kissed her mouth so savagely, she uttered a cry of surprise.

He kept on kissing her, deepening the union of their mouths, devouring all he found, breathing her in, tasting her sweetness. And she met him with the fervor of a storm.

God, yes, she was a storm encased in fragile human

skin. But it was okay. He could get away now that he had an excuse. She wouldn't have to see what might happen to him if he stayed.

Unsure of how long the kiss lasted, Gavin finally drew back. He'd done it, kissed her, and felt a kind of weary triumph about that. But he had to go, leave her, take care of this. Although he wanted nothing more than to stay, the monster out there in the dark had torn him apart, injected a beast into his bloodstream and then left him to die. That beast was outside right now, close enough to reach out and touch.

He had no choice here.

"Close the windows and lock the door," he said with his lips inches from hers. "I shouldn't have come here like this. I should have known better than to let it get so close."

He turned to go, torn and hurting.

"What do you mean? What's getting close?" she called after him as Gavin, broken and unfulfilled, strode across the yard, vaulted the fence and headed for the hillside, leaving perhaps the sweetest night of his life behind.

Chapter 5

Skylar didn't call for the ranger to stop as she stood in the doorway staring at the darkness settling over the mountains. The noise they'd heard hadn't just interrupted her first unplanned one-night stand, it had jangled her nerves.

Harris's haste in getting away from her would have seemed like a slap in the face if it had been for any other reason than going after whatever had made that terrible sound. His disappearance gave her breathing room to contemplate what she'd been about to do—to him, with him.

This whole night had proved a fairly spectacular hiccup in her present situation, and she wasn't all that clear about what she wanted right then—a man or a creature that was more than a man. She wasn't certain that a mere man could have done it for her.

Freud would have had a field day with that information. So would her big sister.

Trish, as the most stable of the four Donovan sisters,

wouldn't appreciate that her sibling was in heat and lusting for a tryst with anyone who came along, let alone lusting for a werewolf. After a conversation like that with Trish, there'd be a reservation in a white padded cell and some little blue pills—a scene that hit too close to home.

Skylar stared outside.

Harris had warned her to lock the door. Yet as far as she knew, wolves, no matter what size, couldn't handle a doorknob. So what good would a lock have done to protect her from the animal Harris said he needed to chase?

Reason told her that Ranger Harris had lied, that he might be hiding something.

Part of her wanted to listen to his advice anyway. The other newly rebellious part that would have taken a stranger to bed urged her to follow him and see for herself what was urgent enough to end their lovemaking session before the real fun began.

The guy had been seriously distressed over the sound they'd heard. There was no way she'd imagined that. And though her body, too, was trying to warn her about this sound, and shudder after shudder rocked her stance in the doorway, Skylar couldn't let lies and secrets become an integral part of her new reality.

She was different here. She was letting go of her own secrets, one by one, and open to taking new risks.

Should she go after the ranger? In the dark?

What if her father had fallen to his death while chasing figures from his dreams?

She wasn't familiar enough with the trails to find footing or have directional cues without proper sightlines. Her cell phone wasn't good for much because the GPS was almost nonexistent.

As for wanting to jump into the sack with this guy, maybe she just needed a night with an honorable man for a change. Harris, at least, ran out on her *before* placing a ring on her finger.

Backing up, Skylar listened hard to Harris's fading footsteps. With him went the rest of the evening's light.

Her heart refused to slow as she backed from the doorway. Confusion reigned. The room dimmed around her, but Skylar didn't reach for a lamp. Seconds flew by, then minutes.

Finally, she shut the door and leaned against it with her eyes closed, picturing Harris's tight, tanned flesh pressed to her bare skin. Feeling, even now, his breath on her face.

Gavin picked up the trail of the monster much more easily than he could have hoped, almost as if the bloodthirsty beast wanted him to.

He didn't know what to make of that, but it was too late to consider anything other than finding his prey. His blood was up. His muscles were seizing. The beast inside him recognized this other beast in an unseemly way.

I'm not like you, Gavin wanted to shout. *I'm no killer.*

But shouting would amount to a calling card and telegraph his presence…if the thing didn't know already.

As he jogged up the steep path, the old thoughts returned, though answers to his questions had never been within reach. If he wasn't like that monster, he had to suppose that the blood passed from beast to beast somehow got diluted in the transfer.

His wounds made him suffer a change, but until he knew more about what had happened to him, he had to think of his cursed condition as a disease.

Hell, the differences between him and his maker had to be studied. He couldn't exact a physical change without a full moon, yet he'd been attacked without one. Feelings inside of him shifted, internal stirrings came and went, but no full transformation happened for him without that commanding silver light. When he did morph, he became a strange mixture of both man and wolf, and not more of one thing than the other.

This damn beast was wolfish, with a lot of something extra added that had no relation to *Homo sapiens*. There was no full moon tonight, nor had there been the night before, which solidified the supposition that this monster either remained permanently furry, or could fur-up at will, with or without the moon's kiss.

So different. Yet I sense you, beast, as though what I've become isn't too far removed from what you are.

Part of that beast truly had become part of him.

Gavin's thoughts kept churning as he climbed the hillside trying to sift through facts, in search of answers.

He'd tried locking himself away to avoid the moon's treacherous call, which only made things worse. Unable to change its form, his body had betrayed him anyway. He'd nearly gone mad with the shakes, unconscious spells, roiling stomach upheavals and bouts of fever. His mind had eventually succumbed to the madness. He'd lost control of his temper, lost his mind to the pain of withholding the transformation and ended up in some godforsaken place on the mountain with no recollection of how he got there or what he might have done while his mind was in a fog.

Lesson learned. It was a freaking sharp-witted curse that developed immunity to thoughtful manipulation.

He had to give in to the physical changes in order to remain in charge mentally. Succumbing to the moon's lure was necessary. As long as he changed shape, he was okay. Keeping as far away from other people as was possible near the full moon had allowed him to weather this out.

He got that now, and guessed that without the wolfish form there'd be no survival of this monster's horrific species, hence the absolute need to shift. That furry demon's teeth and claws had created another similar freak, and so that had to be the way the moon's cult passed on. If he stayed in these mountains whenever there was a full moon, he'd be safe enough, he hoped. Others would be safe.

Gavin stopped suddenly, skin chilling, senses wide open.

The atmosphere around him had changed, creating new pressure that was like a punch to his chest. He heard rustling sounds and thought them ludicrous for a monster excelling in stealth, as though the beast were leaving him a trail of breadcrumbs.

There was no mistaking the smell. He knew this monster's scent, having been up close and personal with it. Why was it here? Did it want to finish what it had started two years ago? Finish him off?

Is that why you stuck around?

Gavin's heart rate accelerated. He'd left his weapon in the car before visiting the woman in the cabin. Damn it, he should have borrowed her gun.

The wolf inside him clawed at his insides with nails like talons, sensing trouble. An icy shiver of anticipation ran up his spine.

"Come out."

He spoke at a normal decibel, feeling the presence of Otherness as if it were a bad rash.

"You can't possibly imagine I don't know you're there, or what you are."

More rustling noises came from his right. Gavin slowly turned toward the sound, saw something. Felt something.

The creature he'd sought for so long was here, all right, and standing its ground.

Against the outline of the trees, nearly hidden in the shadow, a huge form took shape. Bigger than anything he

could have imagined, the giant specter loomed over the surrounding brush like the main character in a horror movie.

On that fateful night, the thing had moved so fast, Gavin
hadn't seen what was coming. But he saw something of its
outline now and his inner alarms went off like a string of
firecrackers.

This was no mere man-wolf combination. Nor, as he'd
guessed, was it anything remotely like him, at all.

Its massive shape left little for Gavin to appeal to, speak
to, reason with. Thoughts of getting close to it with any
kind of hand-held weapon were absurd. Killing it with a
spray of bullets seemed equally as unlikely. He hadn't really
expected this abomination to allow him another close-up
this soon—he had meant to chase it away from the cabin.
Hell, seeing it now, he wanted to run the other way.

No doubt this monster would be faster.

"So here we are," he made himself say to ease a small
portion of the fear knotting up his insides. "Should I call
you family?"

There couldn't be more than one of these beasts, he
hoped, because where'd be the justice in that?

"It had to be you who did this to me. Can you recognize
another freak?"

His nemesis didn't move, making this potentially deadly
scenario all the spookier.

"What are we to do now, since I can't let you go around
killing and maiming people?" he asked, having to talk
though this creature could strike at any moment. Talking
seemed necessary. He felt like shouting. One more night,
and he would have been stronger, at least. He would have
had claws and speed and double the muscle. Though his
humanness danced on a thin thread of control tonight, there
was no full moon to help him.

"I was supposed to protect those people who died. That's

my job. Now what? You do whatever the hell you like?" he said. Then he paused to regain the strength in his voice. "If not exactly like you, I'm no longer like them, either. Not like those people."

Like the aftershocks of an earthquake, a series of low growls shook the ground beneath him. Darkness wavered. Leaves rustled. This beast's rumble was terrible, threatening, ominous, but the monster stayed in the shadows.

When Gavin let loose a responding growl, the creature stepped forward on legs the size of a grizzly's. Transfixed, unable to get a handle on the creature's exact size and girth, and fairly sure he didn't want to, Gavin jumped back. This was a damned nightmare.

"Son of a…"

Gavin tried to ignore the tingling in his hands. Angling his head, he heard a crack of bone on bone. Licks of white-hot fire made every joint ache as a wave of lightheadedness washed over him, twisting his stomach into fits. He knew this feeling, recognized these sensations, and they came as a shock.

The beast in front of him was able to call forth Gavin's beast, and maybe even set it free early. Was that because what stood across from him had created him? Blood calling to blood?

Through a slowly revolving whirl of turmoil, Gavin heard his own growl of angry protest. "I'm not like you!"

And though it seemed impossible for anything else to get through the pain and shock of what he was experiencing, something else nipped at his attention, dragging him away from the outrageous situation at hand. Too riled up to put a name to that distraction, and feeling too ill to respond to it, Gavin kept his focus riveted to the beast less than ten feet away from him. He was close enough to hear it breathing. He heard its giant canines snapping, and the memory of teeth like that tearing into him, ripping the flesh from his bones, made his stomach turn over.

This was no werewolf. This truly was a demon. And Gavin's mind warned that he might not be able to get out of this in one piece. Not this time.

When the creature's growls suddenly ceased, the world went deathly quiet with a silence that seemed surreal. Though Gavin's muscles ached to transform and his fingers stung with the threat of popping claws, the grip this specter had on him loosened. It, too, had noticed the distraction, and turned its mind elsewhere.

The enormous werewolf, which could have squashed him like a bug, advanced no farther. After waiting out several hundred of Gavin's thunderous heartbeats, it turned away from him. Uttering a low roar of grumbling displeasure, it drifted away as completely and swiftly as if it had merely melted into the night.

Sounds from behind made Gavin spin around, afraid the creature had reappeared at his back. Lunging forward, taking the advantage, he rushed toward the sound, striking an object hard, taking it to the ground.

His breath whooshed out. His muscles screamed for the strength necessary to do some damage to the thing that had damaged him so very badly.

"This ends here, one way or the other!"

The moment he said those words, Gavin realized it wasn't the beast he'd tackled. The body beneath him was small, fragile, and it squirmed beneath his weight, smelling like soap and the soft fabrics covering it.

Closing his eyes, Gavin fought back an oath. This wasn't the monster. Not even close.

When he reopened his eyes, he found a familiar face

looking back. A small white circle of features that were pale enough in the moonlight to be almost transparent.

"What the hell?" was all he managed to say between deep, rasping breaths of mortified relief.

Chapter 6

"You can get off me now."

Breathless from the momentum of the attack, Skylar shook so hard, she stuttered.

Without being able to see Harris's expression in the dark, she felt every racing beat of his heart through the chest pressed to hers.

"What are you doing here?" he demanded.

"Following you."

"I asked you to stay inside."

"About that. I seem to be going through a rebellious streak that makes me impervious to reason. I'm sorry if I startled you."

"Hell, woman, my warning must not have been nearly strong enough to convince you of the danger."

"I was pretty sure you could handle one lone wolf."

"Lone wolf? You have no idea…"

Maddeningly, Harris didn't finish the statement as he fought for his breath.

"I thought you heard me coming," she said. "You were speaking to me, weren't you?"

"I was talking to myself."

"Is that a habit rangers often pick up?"

"Yes." He took some time to go on. "It's not safe here. Not safe anywhere near here. It was foolish of you to ignore me."

"Yes, well, right now the problem is being able to breathe."

Harris only then seemed to realize he was on top of her. Slowly, he backed onto his knees. Seconds later, he offered her his hand and a word of caution. "We have to get you out of here."

Skylar took his hand and let him pull her to her feet. The man was little more than a dim outline in the dark, but she saw him turn his head as if expecting someone else to appear.

Holding tightly to her right wrist, he said, "I can't do my job if people run all over these hills in the dark. There are always a few who think they're above the rules."

Skylar stumbled forward when he snapped his arm. "Meaning I'm one of those."

He didn't challenge her remark.

"Did you find the wolf?"

"No."

He was lying again. She could tell by the way her inner radar was going off.

"I'll go with you to look for it," she suggested.

"You'll do no such thing. You can leave this place as quickly as possible. In fact, I'll take you."

"I don't need a chaperone."

"On the contrary, I have every reason to believe you might."

He began to walk, more or less dragging her with him.

"Please listen to me, Skylar. There's a dangerous animal on the loose, and that's no joke. If you're out here, I'll worry about you. Distractions can make these situations so much worse. Surely you can understand that?"

They slid in a damp patch of dirt on the slope, but righted easily enough. Skylar resolved to pay more attention to her feet. She wasn't going to be the bimbo of horror flicks who always tripped and fell in the scary scenes. She had always been fleet.

She wasn't afraid to be out here with Harris beside her, yet she felt uneasy, and as if they were being watched.

"I think my father might have been chasing a wolf when he died," she confessed, matching Harris's lengthy strides. "If so, then I want to see it skinned."

Harris's sharp intake of air wasn't her imagination. Something out here had bothered him, and bothered him still. He was wired and on edge. He kept looking around.

"I'd like to hear about that, but this isn't the time or place for conversation. You'll have to trust me on this."

"Okay," she said.

The relief in his voice was evident. "Good."

The odd feeling of them not being alone stuck with her on their steep downhill descent until she had to speak of it.

"I think we're being followed."

His response was to utter a choice four-letter word and to walk faster. Skylar wasn't going to argue with him about getting to safety this time. The new presence she sensed was heavy enough to siphon some of the air from her lungs. The night had grown colder, and each breath she struggled to take felt icy after the day's heat.

"Maybe it's a ghost," she whispered.

Harris urged her into a jog.

Thing was, she thought, if ghosts existed, this one hovering in the woods might turn out to be what was left of her father. But if it was her father, why did the spirit feel so dark? Why was she suddenly afraid?

She let Harris lead her through the night, clinging to his hand. She'd been right. They were being followed, and the man in front of her knew this as well as she did. Clearly whatever he had been chasing out here now stalked them, and it was something Ranger Harris feared.

Halfway down the path, Skylar resisted the impulse to stop and face whatever tracked them. Only then would she confront the awful fear building inside her.

Her guide didn't seem to share her impulse to stop. His hold on her wrist remained unyielding as he led her over rough, unfamiliar terrain ignoring holes and vines as though he saw every detail in the dark.

She couldn't see a blasted thing.

He didn't produce a flashlight, either, seeming to rely on his own internal GPS system. She supposed that rangers had to be familiar with the areas they patrolled and that Harris walked these same paths over and over on a daily basis. All she saw were glimpses of his back, highlighted whenever the moon peeked out from the clouds.

Deliberately, she didn't offer the use of the flashlight she'd used to find him in the first place, now tucked inside her pocket. She was fascinated by how Harris maneuvered and afraid that if she shone that light behind her, the sanity she presently held on to might desert her. She was sure something otherworldly lurked on this hillside.

She thanked God that Harris wasn't the kind of creature she'd almost expected him to be—though the voice he shared with the man in her dreams continued to plague her. He didn't use that voice now, though there were questions that sorely needed answers. Questions having to do with wolves being bold enough to stalk two humans, or if it might be some other Colorado animal. Mountain lion. Bear. Recently escaped homicidal human.

The icy sensation of being tracked didn't ease up as they ran. Traversing the downward path, Skylar felt positive she heard sounds of the creature breathing beyond the two of them.

She kept as close to Harris as possible and his grip on her remained a comfort. But although they had gone a fair distance already, the cabin's porch light didn't appear. Were they lost?

A gravel road suddenly loomed up out of nowhere, noticeable by its ghostly gray color.

"Stop," she said, tugging at Harris's hand. "This isn't anywhere near the cabin. The road to Dad's place is dirt."

"Just a few steps more," Harris urged.

When she saw the car, Skylar remembered what he'd told her about leaving it there. "We're on the opposite side of the hill. Are we driving to the cabin?"

"I'm thinking it might be better to take you someplace else for the rest of the night."

"You heard that stalker, too?"

"What stalker?"

More lies, in the form of withheld information. The rigidity of Harris's arm gave away the fact that he knew much more than he let on.

"Answering a question with a question won't get us very far," Skylar pointed out.

"Maybe not, but my Jeep will."

They reached the car, found the doors unlocked.

"That's all you're going to tell me?" she challenged, facing him over the car's roof.

"I don't want to scare you."

"It's too late for that. Is the rush in honor of a dangerous outlaw on the loose? I have a right to know."

"Would that make you get into this car?"

"I'd just like to know what we're running from."

Harris blew out a breath. "I don't know what it is for sure, okay? I only know that something is out there, and my job is to keep you safe."

The moon was brighter here, away from the trees. Ranger Harris gestured for her to get into the car.

"I'll take you to town, where you can get a room for the night," he said.

"You, too?"

"Afraid not."

Did he sound regretful about that? Skylar wished she could see his face more clearly.

"Should I trust you?" she asked. "We're running from the unknown, but I don't know you, either. Is it wise to get into a car with you?"

"True. I am a stranger to you. But at the moment, I solemnly promise you that I'm the lesser of two evils on this mountain."

Cooperating, Skylar climbed into the vehicle. The worn leather seats smelled like the great outdoors. Like dirt and greenery and Ranger Harris.

She said, "Maybe I should have taken a closer look at that badge on your shirt."

He pulled the badge off and tossed it to her as he slid into the driver's seat. "Be my guest."

Without a doubt, this guy could be infuriating. But what he had tossed her felt like a real badge. She'd seen a few in her time, so this probably meant Harris was one of the good guys.

Skylar closed her fingers over the metal as if it were a talisman to wield against things that went bump in the night.

"Anything you need we can pick up at the store," he said. "I have an account there."

"Does this store have alcohol?"

Harris turned the key and started the engine. "I'm sure it does." After a pause, he added, "We don't have to talk about what happened tonight if you'd prefer that."

"You mean about what chased us, or what nearly took place in my bedroom?"

"Should I apologize for acting on that last one?"

"No." Skylar closed her eyes briefly, listening to the familiar nuances in his voice that fanned her inner heat. "It wasn't your fault."

The car kicked up a spray of gravel as it moved. Skylar felt Harris's attention on her.

"I needed a diversion," she explained.

"From what?"

"The rest of my life."

"Losing your father?"

"That's the most recent blow."

"Then I'm sorry we were interrupted, though it was probably for the best." Harris sounded earnest.

"Yes. For the best," Skylar agreed, leaning sideways as the car made a sharp left turn around a stand of pine trees. "It wasn't really a wolf that made you run out on me, was it?"

Harris glanced in her direction without comment.

They rode in silence after that, which made the bumpy ride more uncomfortable. Eventually it became clear that the man beside her wasn't going to offer anything resembling a decent explanation for what had happened in or around the cabin tonight. Then again, neither could she.

"You might want to pack your father's things during the day and stay in town at night," he suggested some time later.

"Being in town most of the time would be inconvenient."

Again, Skylar felt the intensity of his silent appraisal.

"As a favor to me, then," he said.

"Do I owe you one?"

"If not, you might humor me as the local law enforcement."

Skylar winced. Because of Danny, the words *law enforcement* had a sour ring to them. In essence, she'd gone from one kind of cop to another without thinking. This was far better than the werewolf dream, though.

"Well, I can't jump out of a moving car, so I guess tonight's a done deal," she said.

"Good."

As they rounded another dark curve in the road, the soft glitter of distant lights appeared. Skylar supposed her safety would be assured down there among the masses, if safety was really an issue.

It was that rebel part of her—the part that had sent her traipsing up a mountain path after dark and had given her an appreciation for sensuous dreams, gorgeous werewolves and strangers with seductive voices—that told her to ignore this ranger's plan after tonight and instead find out what the hell was going on.

Her dad had kept secrets, and that hadn't ended well. The man beside her kept things to himself. She had to know who or what was out there, and whether being followed tonight had anything to do with her father's death, less than two weeks ago. She had a hunch that it did.

With good old Donovan perseverance and a dash of stubborn determination, she vowed get to the heart of these mysteries if it was the last thing she ever did.

With or without the man next to her…in her bed.

Chapter 7

Gavin read Skylar Donovan easily and checked his concerns. She was only his business up to a point. After that, his feelings for her couldn't interfere with a task that was too weighty for distractions.

He'd seen the demon. Facing it again, he had survived. And that was one hell of a mystery.

The thing hadn't attacked. If it had scented him and identified him as a Were—one it had created in a bloody mess of poisoned flesh—surely Skylar Donovan's presence should also have piqued its interest. All that succulent ivory skin and her sweet, sweet perfume that right now made him want to look at her instead of the road.

The beast couldn't have missed that.

No beast could have missed it.

Case in point was his own inexplicable longing for her. More than anything, he wanted to stop the car and show her he could maintain some control if he was allowed to have her.

It wasn't only his vow to protect the public that made him want to see to Skylar's safety. It was sheer, unadulterated greed. He wanted to save Skylar Donovan for himself.

She was the sum total of everything he'd lost when that beast attacked him, and so much more. She was lace and perfume, defiance and mystery in a slick feminine casing that escalated his need for those things. He'd be damned if he'd allow the monster to harm one hair on her beautiful head.

Despite this newfound possessiveness, he realized that Skylar really wasn't his to keep. She was human, and he wasn't. Oil and water didn't mix. Neither should wolf and human DNA.

He'd kissed Skylar and wanted his mouth on hers now. Her plush lips were all he thought about when they weren't confronting giant rabid werewolves that by all rights shouldn't exist.

I shouldn't exist, either, as I am now. You deserve better, Skylar.

But maybe she'd been sent here from the heavens as the kind of distraction that would keep him sane and grounded?

Don't look for excuses.

He might be torn apart by the depth of his longing for her, but he had to let this woman go, keep his distance, harness his thoughts and get away from her as soon as possible because his resolve was already weakening where she was concerned, and his energy was needed elsewhere.

The beast had returned. He'd seen it. Instead of taking it down, he'd been seriously unprepared, due in part to Skylar.

"No more kissing."

Though he muttered this softly and to himself, she heard it.

"Is that a promise?" she said.

Grimacing, rubbing his forehead, Gavin felt conflicted. By being here with Skylar he was allowing the monster to get away. By allowing it to get away, he was helping Skylar Donovan avoid the ugly fate that had befallen him.

"Nothing personal," he said to her.

"If you say so."

Lights appeared around them too quickly. Gavin drove the car into the motel parking lot at the edge of town and switched off the engine. They got out of the car without speaking.

She slammed the door.

"Just give them my name." He pointed to the office.

"Ranger Harris has carte blanche here?"

"It'll do unless you run up a tab."

She tilted her head. "You actually have a tab in this place?"

Gavin nodded. "I sometimes need to crash before the long drive home."

"Then you don't live close by."

"Close enough when I haven't been up for several nights in a row. Way too far away otherwise."

Skylar Donovan walked around the car and right up to where he stood. "You're going back out there, aren't you?"

"I'm on duty for another hour or so."

He worked hard to keep his hands to himself, unsure of why he was so attracted to Skylar that he'd want to push the limits of his self-control, or delay his highly charged personal vendetta.

This leggy blonde was just so blessed tempting, the choice seemed tough. It was as if she'd gotten under his skin and nestled there alongside the wolf.

"Does that mean you have to be alone?" she asked.

"Tonight it does."

"Why? Why would you take that chance and go back out there when you know we were followed?"

"It's what I do, Skylar. It's something I have to face and take care of without risking harm to others."

Skylar. He liked her unusual name and liked saying it. Outside of her evident ornery streak, he liked everything about Skylar Donovan that he'd seen so far. Maybe he even liked that stubborn streak.

She might be small, yet she was no shy flower. She was too courageous for her own good, though. She had walked up that mountain alone tonight without being sure of finding him.

Somehow, at that moment, she seemed a lot more than just temptation in tight blue jeans. The delicious scent that had lured him to her in the first place wafted around her like a corona. Golden hair caressed her shoulders in un-combed waves highlighted by shafts of moonlight escaping the cloud cover. The same moonlight that made his forehead dampen with the strain of withholding his wild side.

"So you admit we were followed and have no idea who it might have been?" she asked.

He shrugged to hide the evidence of another unruly spike in his heart rate that pulsed upward and into his jaw. Hell, he wanted to get under *her* skin, seize the moment and take some long-overdue R&R while he could. Surely that was fair after what he'd been through?

When she'd left the cabin, after what had almost taken place in her bedroom, Skylar had tugged on her shirt—the same shirt he'd removed in a fit of passion—without properly stretching it into place. Narrow sections of bare skin showed above the waistband of her jeans—smooth, pale and terribly seductive.

No way.

Can't have you.

I've got to go back out there.

All true warnings, but Gavin's body argued adamantly

against them, and against reason. Having sampled her, tasted her, felt her beneath his hands, his body repeatedly returned to those sensations as though she'd been imprinted on him. After looking into her big green eyes and finding a shared connection, Skylar Donovan truly did feel like part of his future.

This wasn't right, of course, or normal. She was just a woman he had stumbled upon who'd ended up striking his fancy. Her open-mindedness in terms of sex and lust and freely meeting her own needs had sealed the deal. That was all. He hadn't met anyone like her in a long time.

"Will I see you tomorrow?" She ran her hands over the warm hood of the Jeep the way he imagined her running them over him, and his body responded with a ripple of lustful tension.

With his pulse erratic and a new pressure in his chest, Gavin said, "In the morning I'll be back to take you home."

"Okay. Until then."

When she turned from him, Gavin briefly shut his eyes to block the sight, attempting to keep his distance, keep himself from pulling her back and making a complete fool of himself.

He watched her walk away. Her hips swayed in the fitted jeans he hadn't been lucky enough to get off her. The taut, slender back that had arched passionately during their kiss emphasized a small waist he'd like to encircle with his hands.

Rebuking himself for staring at her like this, Gavin didn't stop looking. He'd sent her away, and she'd obliged. Her allure might be strong, but he couldn't let it rival the moon's—the moon at that same moment sending out signals that he intercepted as clearly as if the giant orb contained a telepathic intelligence.

Tomorrow night he'd change into something that would

scare Skylar to death. All thoughts of closeness and intimacy would be a thing of the past if she were to witness
his transformation.

In this new reality, however, Skylar had become as potentially dangerous to him as the moon that ruled his shape.
She'd become both a distraction and a necessity in no time
flat. He had to let her go and didn't want to.

Really didn't want to.

"Definitely no kissing," Gavin said aloud to bolster his
willpower.

Over her shoulder, Skylar Donovan smiled. "Don't be
too sure about that, Harris. I'm here for a few more days."

Gavin took two steps backward, and then two more, his
heart beating out a protest about getting into the car. His
fingers curled against his palms. His muscles rippled and
twitched. As absurd as it seemed given that he had known
this woman for only one day…leaving Skylar Donovan was
just about the hardest thing he had ever done.

Skylar heard the car drive out of the parking lot, and her
determination to remain independent faltered. In spite of
everything she'd been through, she felt forlorn and alone.

Still, she had to admit that Harris's behavior bordered
on chivalrous. He was willing to foot the bill tonight at this
motel in order to see to her safety, which meant he did believe there might be trouble out there in the dark.

"A civilized ending to a strange night?"

Resigned to her current fate, Skylar gave the motel a
wary once-over. It was a standard two-story, U-shaped
design from the fifties. The building wrapped around the
parking lot on three sides, with all the rooms and doors
front-facing, and two sets of stairs leading to the second-
floor balcony. Most of the windows were dark. A small
blue neon sign pointed to the reception area.

Skylar went inside.

A middle-aged woman with short blond hair, wearing a red fleece vest, greeted her from behind a counter and raised an eyebrow when Skylar mentioned Harris's name. Gratefully, that woman kept what she might have been thinking about a woman showing up in this place on his dime, to herself.

Handing over a key, this receptionist said, "Room twenty-one. That's his favorite," as if being in his favorite room mattered. She then produced an ice bucket and a glass, and looked past Skylar for the missing luggage.

"Will you need anything else?"

"A toothbrush would be nice."

Skylar smiled as though nothing were out of the ordinary about not having a purse or a toothbrush, omitting the explanation of not being able to stop at the cabin for some of life's conveniences because a madman might show up there.

Or a wolf that knew how to open a door.

"Emergency amenities are on the bathroom counter," the woman said, returning the smile with less enthusiasm and leaving Skylar to assume that Ranger Harris had more than one female fan in the area. "The room is on the second floor."

"Thanks."

Skylar climbed the stairs and waited for several minutes before attempting to go inside room twenty-one, which, like the rest of the rooms, overlooked the mostly empty parking lot. Summer was over, so tourists would be scarce. Since no lights were on, she guessed she might have this floor to herself, and dreaded that.

She wished the ice bucket came with a bottle of wine. Suddenly ravenous, she wanted a salad and a steak. This wasn't the kind of motel with room service, though, and since she had no wallet, dinner wasn't in the cards. Her growling stomach would just have to suck it up and deal.

Staring out at the lot, and up at the nearly full moon emerging from the clouds, she felt lost and slightly out of sorts. The cozy cabin stuffed with her father's things made her feel more at home and part of something. Here, in a strange motel without her credit cards or her cell phone, she was cut off and isolated.

"You shouldn't have brought me here, Harris. I've never really been good on my own. Too much time to think."

Her gaze rose from the card key in her hand to the parking lot. "You really shouldn't have left me."

She added wistfully, "Come back."

Her heart kicked out a thump when the Jeep reappeared. Hopping part of the curb, it halted as far away from the building as possible and sat there idling as if the engine were trying to make up its mind about something.

The man inside it sat there, too. Skylar wanted to call out to him. Over the ether, or however such things worked, had he heard her plea? Did he know she was in need of company and felt like screaming?

"Stay," she said, willing Harris to hear her when it was absurd to imagine that he could. "Stay for a while."

The Jeep's engine died. Skylar's heart thundered when the door opened and Harris got out. From across the parking lot he stared up at her over that car door.

She didn't move, just stared back and said softly, "Damn you. Don't make me beg."

The car's door closed silently and the man she knew only by his last name began to walk in her direction, each step renewing Skylar's insatiable longing for company. Harris carried something in his hand. A white paper bag. Skylar smiled, unable to pinpoint what she hungered for most—

the food that bag might contain, or the man who'd been thoughtful enough to bring it to her.

No. There really was no question about which thing she wanted most. Her body buzzed with pent-up need for everything Harris had to offer. Without being near to that hillside now, she'd have his full attention if she were lucky.

He didn't return her smile when he reached her. Hoisting the paper bag, he said, "Dinner." But he was quick to catch her expression and what that expression might mean. His hand lowered. His next remark died on his lips.

"Well, damn," he said seconds later.

In a silence filled with racing heartbeats and a rush of adrenaline coursing through her, their eyes met, held. Then he took the key from her and opened the door.

The sound of the paper bag hitting the floor echoed faintly as his body crushed hers to the wall inside the room before the door had fully closed behind them.

Chapter 8

It was a mindless, drowning kiss...deep, passionate, carnal, endless. Eyes closed, and with her fingers wrapped in Harris's thick, silky hair, Skylar breathed him in, absorbed him, became one with the sensations flooding her as his mouth transported her to a place where unadulterated greed reigned and consequences didn't matter.

They went at each other like fiends.

Through some kind of miracle, he'd heard her and returned to help fill the emptiness inside her with companionship, strength and matching ardor. Her prayers had been answered.

She kissed him fiercely in the dark, rewarding him for listening to the words he couldn't have heard. Taunting him with her tongue and teeth, she sucked his lower lip between hers, cupped the back of his neck with shaky hands, only briefly wondering if he did this often, in this room, with other women.

But what the hell. She needed an outlet for the excess energy, and tonight he was hers.

His lips slid to her cheek, her forehead, her right ear, then back to her mouth, his breath enticingly heated. Strong, warm hands wrapped around her, pulling her from the wall and into a tight embrace that Skylar wouldn't have wanted to escape, even if she could have. If this was to be a union for only one night, and spent with a stranger, her body and her mind were willing.

His hands slipped under her shirt, his sexy, masculine warmth chasing away the chills riddling her lower back. She hadn't been wrong about him being like an inferno, and she found his heat thrilling.

He kissed her with wild abandon as his hands moved up the length of her spine, working their incredible magic. This is what she wanted, what she had always wanted—to give herself over completely and accept everything in return. Strangers had a certain kind of freedom where sex was concerned. Relative anonymity worked in her favor here.

When he paused, allowing her a breath, she shook her head. Through swollen lips she whispered, "Nowhere to run this time, ranger."

Their sense of connection careened through Skylar like a shocking current of wayward electricity. Streaks of fire filled her chest, her belly, ending up as an ache between her thighs, in a place that had never been reached or addressed like this by anyone.

Unable to restrain herself, Skylar jumped into Harris's arms, caught easily by this man who seemed to possess the strength of two. Wrapping her legs and arms around him with her body pressed tightly to his, she said, "No wolf here for us to chase, unless it's you."

Harris, with his devastatingly handsome face and a body like living sin, gave a heavy sigh as he turned for the bed.

* * *

He could have been wrong, Gavin thought as he laid Skylar on the mattress and leaned over her quivering body. Wrong about catching a whiff of something buried inside this woman, far beneath the perfume and outward perfection, that caused both man and wolf to need her so greatly. But his hunger wouldn't be assuaged. Skylar Donovan had become the embodiment of an addiction.

Though he didn't know much about her or her life, he'd already figured out one thing: she was cutting herself loose from old ideas and hindrances, and using him to do it. She also, it seemed to him, had something to prove.

They met here with the impact of two clashing thunder clouds. He couldn't see enough, taste enough, get enough of her. Perhaps this test of his personal limits is what made the affair so dangerously thrilling.

His wolfishness was growing more substantial by the minute, a reminder about how close he was to being moon-whipped.

He hoped that being with Skylar, and the depth of emotion that entailed, wasn't a self-destructive act. He wanted to be here, now. In the darkened room he'd gather the will-power to hold back his inner beast. He'd do anything for this chance at being more like the kind of man he once was.

"Light." Her request was a groan of anticipation.

"Not yet. Feel me. Feel everything, my lovely Skylar, in the dark."

In the light, you might see me for what I am.

He didn't tell her how easily he saw details in that darkness—her face and her expression, if not the color of her eyes. He watched her chest rise and fall, noted the outline of her breasts beneath her shirt and the hardness of her nipples. He heard her heart pounding out a crazy rhythm that mirrored his and laid his hand on her chest to feel the beat.

Her eyes fluttered shut.

"Yes. That's it." He tugged her shirt over her head, confronting her sensuous bareness for the second time that night, and with the determination to see this encounter through.

The question was how much time he could take.

Slow wasn't going to cut it. Neither were lengthy explorations or the kind of long, lingering foreplay he'd have given an eye tooth for. He was riled up. His blood thrashed in his veins, and inside that blood a beast swam upward, in search of moonlight.

"Can't wait," he groaned, reaching for her zipper, entranced by the sound of that zipper sliding downward and the thought of what lay behind it.

"Don't." She lifted her hips to help him peel the jeans off. "Don't wait."

Her shoes hit the floor, along with her pants. Gavin's fingers hesitated on her flimsy panties. "So fragile and feminine. These things are made for a man to appreciate before he tears them off."

The lace slipped over her thighs soundlessly, and she kicked the panties aside. Seconds later, she was off the pillows and going at him with the hunger of a lioness in heat.

Pulling him down, she tore at the buttons on his shirt that were left from their last unscheduled meeting in a bedroom. Yanking the shirttails from beneath his waistband, she went for his belt buckle.

He helped her with that, wild and ready to burst. Feeling high as he floated on waves of raw sexual greed.

"I can do this." He voiced those words aloud without meaning to, knocking back a rising growl.

"Did you doubt it?" she asked through lips that were for him the highest form of pleasure. "Because I didn't."

On her knees on the bed, her hands flew over his pants, finding the zipper, easing it down. But she wasn't willing to wait for him to undress completely. His bare chest and what lay behind the zipper seemed good enough for her at the moment.

Instead of lying back down to prepare for the entry of his hardness, she again wrapped her arms around his shoulders. Unfurling her long legs, she curled those legs around him, leaving the spot he'd dreamed about entering poised above his pulsing erection.

"Don't stop. Don't wait." She whispered her command in his ear and nipped at his earlobe with her sharp little teeth.

Gavin groaned and spat out an oath. "Christ!"

He lifted her up with his hands beneath her firm, naked ass. In one smooth move, she was on her back on the bed, her thighs open for him, with nothing in the way that might remotely have stopped their joining.

He stretched out on top of her with the tip of his cock against the doorway to what he knew would turn out to be a delight beyond belief. Letting go of his control, he was inside her in a single thrust. He groaned, sighed, cursed silently as the exquisite softness surrounding him threatened to overtake him and give his darker side away.

He let the growl out, and felt better for it. She laughed. But the lightness was short-lived and only the briefest release from the growing sexual tension between them.

Desiring more friction of skin on skin, Gavin's hands grasped hers. As their fingers entwined, his lover made a soft moan of satisfaction that made his blood boil.

Any touch was going to do it for them—fingers sliding across fingers, palm resting on palm, lips meeting. But Skylar Donovan would have it all, and this was just the start.

When he moved his hips, she responded in kind, grinding against him provocatively, wrapping her molten femininity around him.

Gavin closed his eyes.

Drawing back, he waited...waited while his pulse beat like a drum in this throat and he ached all over with the buildup of the pressure of long withheld needs.

He'd gotten this far, barely. His inner animal was rising, growling, urging him to hurry this along and get to the good part. The part where all three of them would be joined.

Gathering his strength, corralling his body's urges, Gavin thrust into her again. This time she cried out as she reached for him. He remembered the feel of her nails raking his skin the last time they'd been on the verge of intimacy, and the sting of cool air meeting with warm injured flesh. The minor discomfort kept him focused.

He liked it.

His next plunge went deeper into her body. Eyes still half-shut, heart hammering, he repeated the action of pulling back, collecting himself and then burying himself in her plush heat over and over.

Moving faster, harder, he created a rhythm and kept it going, putting all of himself into every move as he stroked her fiery insides until he sensed, felt, absorbed the shudders that rocked her as her body hurled the mother of all sensations forward to meet him.

She let out a groan that became a cry. Arching her back, limbs rigid, she hung on to him, both inside and out. With sharp nails, she scored his back, digging into him as if clinging to the moment in every way possible.

Pain and pleasure merged in a rush of color behind Gavin's eyes. The scent of blood wafted in the air. His blood. But it was only a little, and it somehow fit the degree of intimacy they were sharing.

He ground himself into Skylar Donovan, pelvis to pelvis,
hips to hips, his length fully embedded in her wet, flaming
heat. And when her orgasm claimed her, he held her there…
pinned her there…with Skylar writhing beneath him in
blissful agony and the wolf inside him begging for release.

Skylar's voice rang out with a silence-shattering cry.
When he could take no more, Gavin groaned and backed
up, afraid to let himself go, not knowing where that might
lead.

Embroiled in the emotion, spurred on by the fight, the
wolf inside him soared through his veins, seeking a way
out, a way to share in this taking. But it wasn't time for
wolf play.

Skylar belonged to the man.

Chapter 9

Drowsy, Skylar woke to darkness. Still drifting hazily with the slow rhythms of a long overdue sleep, she stretched her legs, wincing at the intensity of the aches stiffening her body. She winced again after discovering the vacant warm spot in the space beside her on the bed.

She was alone.

No. Not alone, her senses told her.

Tired enough to only turn her head, she saw him. Against a thin crack of light, he stood silhouetted at the window in a way that seemed part of a familiar dream. Highlighted by the light of outside electrical bulbs, the man who had fulfilled her sexual cravings several times over stared out the window with his back to her. A guardian. Her incredible protector.

"You're still here."

"Yes." He glanced over his shoulder, his voice igniting her internal furnace in the same way it did every time she heard it.

Though her body tried to rebel against the fatigue making her limbs heavy, it was no good. Real sleep had eluded her for so long, she didn't stand a chance against it.

"Thanks," she whispered, shutting the vision of him off, letting herself, lulled by the presence of her lover watching over her, fall toward the luxury of another forty winks. No dreams interfered with her rest. No call from the mysterious distant male came, because she had found and lain with him.

When Skylar next woke, it was with a start that signified change. She shot her hand out, searching again for warmth next to her. Not finding it, she sat up. Harris wasn't beside her. He wasn't at the window. Without having to search further, she knew he had gone, and that he'd left her recently. Maybe only minutes before. His scent remained strong— in the air, ingrained in her lungs, clinging to her skin. His taste was in her mouth and on her bruised lips.

The pinkish light of dawn streamed in from the gap in the curtains.

Well, okay. He'd disappeared, and she deserved the no-excuses abandonment for both her risky behavior and for wanting more of him than he was willing to give. She had to face facts. Harris had been a heck of a one-nighter, but with the arrival of dawn, that one night was over.

She sat up slowly, her skin cool now that their heat had faded. Her throat felt dry. Her body signaled the needling pains of having been well-used. For all that, she appreciated that Harris had stayed with her until daybreak. The thought of that small consideration was comforting.

"Don't worry," she said with a glance at her chill-riddled nakedness already beginning to show faint purple marks. "I'm not stupid."

Their night of passion had been driven by lust, and nothing more. After the first round of mind-blowing sex, they'd gone at each other like animals, free to explore and be explored. Free to be wild, and hold nothing back. That would have shocked Danny. Her ex wouldn't have been able to cope with the things she and Harris had done. The big bad cop might have wondered how she'd known about half those things.

She had moved on in one hell of a way.

As for her ranger...

It was possible he'd disappear for good now and would send someone else to drive her to the cabin. Maybe that kind of avoidance was for the best. Facing him today would be awkward. What could either of them say? *Thanks for the fuck?*

At the moment, she felt satiated and worn out. Sex and sleep had worked miracles to calm her highly tuned nervous system. Nevertheless, it was too bad she hadn't thanked Harris for the meal she'd ignored in favor of blistering carnal pursuits. She could have used some added fuel now.

The upside of a night with a stranger? Chances were the erotic dreams would stay away now that she'd indulged with a real man who fulfilled the lust quotient. If those fantasies did return, it would prove her overly greedy. In fact, she felt greedy now, with a whole new set of parameters. She wished for Harris to come back and start the circuit all over again—the talented hands, lips, and all the rest.

Listening to the rumble of hunger in her stomach, Skylar sagged against the pillows with her arms crossed over her eyes.

Until the knock came.

"Skylar? Miss Donovan?" a husky female voice said. "Gavin left something for you."

Gavin?

Wrapped in the blanket, Skylar opened the door to find

the woman who'd checked her in last night holding a brown paper bag. She wore the same red vest.

Skylar looked at her inquisitively.

"Breakfast." The woman eyed Skylar right back, probably noticing the swollen mouth and nakedness beneath the blanket.

"Ranger Harris left this?" Skylar asked.

The woman shrugged. "Before he left."

Skylar took the bag.

"Don't get your hopes up, hun. It's only a couple of doughnuts. There's coffee in the lounge if you'd care to come down."

"Thanks."

"Don't mention it."

As Skylar started to close the door, the woman said, "He also left the Jeep for you. The keys are under the floor mat. Gavin said he'd get it later and to tell you it's full of gas."

Skylar pressed her back to the closed door and let out a sigh. She'd been right in assuming Harris might prefer to avoid her this morning. At least he'd been thoughtful enough to leave her some wheels so that she wouldn't have to explain about her night in the motel to anyone else on duty with him.

"Aren't we polite?" she muttered. She tossed the bag on the bed and jumped in after it. Two bites into her first meal since breakfast the day before, she silently thanked her lover for this small reward. She'd have to see him again eventually, when he came for the car, and she equally dreaded and looked forward to that.

Thoughtfully, she stopped chewing and lowered the second doughnut. What if she was being harsh, and there was a positive spin to his actions? Maybe Gavin meant the loan of his car to be read as a promise to her of a future face-to-face meeting instead of avoidance.

Don't get your hopes up. Hopes can ruin a perfectly good memory.

Moving to the window, Skylar searched the parking lot. Spying the beat-up Jeep, she slid down the wall to sit on the floor.

Somehow, *thanks for the fuck* didn't sound as fulfilling or sarcastic as it had moments ago. It sounded more to her like the excuse of two desperate souls dancing around the problem of celibacy and loneliness without knowing how to handle themselves after the night they'd had.

"Who are you, Gavin?"

She posed the question aloud, wanting an answer to that particular question even more than she wanted to finish the food he'd sent. She was determined to banish the coward hiding in the nooks of her own personality. The coward who until last night had kept her true feelings and needs hidden from everyone and who now feared she wouldn't be able to go back to the way things were before.

Uncontrolled sex with the ranger had been exquisitely satisfying. Damn if she didn't want more.

Gavin hitched a ride with the grocer's wife as far as the old logging road, and hoofed it up the dirt track leading to Skylar's cabin.

He'd taken time for a shower, a quick bite and a cup of coffee, courtesy of the motel's overseer, Marian Smith, who'd refrained from asking questions.

He was fairly sure Marian could keep some things private and would do so. If sharing a room with a newcomer got out, it would obliterate the gossip that he'd achieved monk status as far as women were concerned, and turn the tide on incoming dinner proposals.

He didn't need that kind of gossip getting around. Though he'd enjoyed every minute with Skylar, he had almost forgotten about the monster he'd faced, and its odd behavior.

He shook those thoughts off in favor of deciding what to do next.

If he'd been thinking with his head, instead of what lay in his pants, he'd have wondered earlier about the fire in Skylar's old wood stove, which they'd left overnight. The safety of leaving that stove untended should have been a concern. Then again, who could have predicted that Skylar would follow him?

Also, if he hadn't had the run-in with a wolfish demon *and* the fright of Skylar showing up and placing herself in danger, he might have taken more time to get to know her.

Instead they'd skipped past all the "getting to know each other" parts, and delved straight into the realm of really incredible sex. Incendiary stuff. Without a werewolf's one positive perk of nearly miraculous healing powers, he would have had the bite marks from her tiny human teeth to prove it.

But it was a new day, and there were other things on his agenda. Thinking about Skylar any more than he already did would get him nowhere.

He had to find out about that monster.

But first, a couple of stops were necessary. He wanted some background on the Donovans.

Tom Jeevers lived on the road Gavin walked now. The old man rarely left his house, summer or winter, and was listed in Gavin's written log as the caretaker for Skylar's father's cabin.

The old guy, once a great craftsman in and around these parts, had built that cabin with his own two hands before turning his attention to a new spot farther north and closer to the main road. Gavin wanted to question Tom about Skylar's dad. He also wanted to see if Tom might have seen anything strange in the area lately.

Of course, there didn't have to be a connection between the abomination hiding out in the mountains and this particular area, but it seemed to Gavin to be more than coincidental that the creature kept returning here, of all the places it had to choose from in and around the Rockies.

Getting wind of it on the hillside above Skylar's cabin made Gavin extremely wary. Hearing that Doctor Donovan had been found with his face half gone made him warier still. Whether this meant Skylar might also be in danger due to the isolation of the cabin was a further concern. If anything happened to Skylar, he wasn't sure what he might do. Last night seemed to have sealed some kind of unspoken deal between them.

Jeevers's house appeared around the next bend. Made of logs and mortar, with a green metal roof and a large front porch, it complemented the woods surrounding it by blending in.

A long walkway of wood chips led to the rustic house. The intricately carved wood door opened before Gavin set a boot on the steps.

"Ranger," Tom said. "To what do I owe the honor of this visit?"

Gavin smiled. "Wanted to have a chat, Tom. I need some information about the man who bought your other cabin some time back."

"Donovan."

"That's the guy."

"Sorry affair, Harris. He took a nasty fall, I heard. Come and sit. I've got the coffeepot on the stove, and you look like you could use a cup."

Gavin followed Tom into the house, and looked around.

Though the place could have used a lighter touch in terms of furniture, and carried a faint scent of dust and strong coffee, the parlor was roomy and pleasant.

Since he'd been here twice before, Gavin made himself at home on a leather sofa covered in an elaborate blanket of Hopi Indian design.

"Black, right?" Tom handed him a steaming mug filled with an aromatic brew.

"Perfect. Thanks, Tom."

Tom settled himself into the chair opposite and crossed his aging legs at the knee. Gavin noted that Tom, a bachelor for as long as anyone could remember, wore clean overalls and a plaid flannel shirt. His gray hair was neatly combed. The image he presented this morning was pretty much the opposite of what most people thought about true mountain men.

"What kind of chat are we having, Harris? An official one or a neighborly exchange?"

Gavin wrapped his hands around the mug, waiting for the coffee to cool. "Both. You know that the doctor's daughter is staying at your old cabin?"

Tom nodded. "Pretty girl. Young. Doesn't look much like her father."

"She's going through her father's things and seems at a loss over his death. I'm curious about this guy. Is there anything else about the doctor that you can tell me?"

Tom nodded. "He was a serious man, though friendly enough. When he first bought the place, he came around now and then for friendly chats."

"Did he ever mention why he bought the cabin?"

"As a matter of fact, he did mention that once. Said he needed to get away from hectic hospital work from time to time, and that Florida was too humid to spend his downtime in."

Gavin said, "They're from Florida? I didn't know that."

"Miami, if memory serves me right. Can I ask why you're asking about the doc?"

"His daughter has questions about how he died."

Tom nodded again. "Only one of them is here."

Gavin looked up from his coffee. "One of what?"

"The doctor's daughters. There are four of them, he told me, all fairly close in age. No wife, though—at least that's what I deduced from the fact that he never mentioned one."

"His daughters haven't been here before?"

"Not as far as I know."

"Donovan kept mostly to himself, then?"

"I rarely saw him in person after his first couple of years visiting here. He used to go out at night quite often, though. I'd sometimes see him walking down the lane at sundown."

"Was he a fit man, Tom?"

"Fit as a fiddle as far as outward looks are concerned. He was tall, with premature gray hair and a sober face. It looked to me like he could climb the peaks and be right at home."

Gavin sipped his coffee, savoring the heat and slightly bitter aftertaste. "Only he didn't make it home one night."

"No," Tom agreed. "He didn't."

Taking the time to enjoy another sip, Gavin regrouped his thoughts. "I was wondering if you've seen, either recently or in the past, a wolf pack near here, Tom? Maybe you've heard them?"

"As a matter of fact, I have," Tom said. "For the better part of the past three months I've heard howling in the hills. I'm sure you, as a ranger, know that gray wolves disappeared from Colorado when the last ones were hunted and killed in the forties."

Gavin nodded. "I do know that."

Tom went on. "I heard that they've been reintroduced

to some states, but not ours. They can travel great distances, though, so they've been expected to get back here eventually."

"And you're hearing them."

"Can't miss them. Even ears as old as mine can pick up their yowling."

Gavin shifted in his seat. "Have you reported this to the other rangers or the wildlife guys?"

"Not yet. But I did hear in town that several years ago a gray male was sighted ten miles from our border, so I assumed he'd made it and brought along his kin." Tom leaned forward in his chair. "Are you checking on those wolves for the Parks and Wildlife guys?"

"Yes, and also for my own curiosity. Skylar Donovan, the doctor's daughter, said something to me yesterday about her father chasing a wolf. She thought he might have been after a wolf when he fell."

"Seems a reasonable explanation for a city man spending time away from civilization, especially given how close to the road those animals seem to be. Maybe he wanted to see one up close."

"How many of them do you think there might be, Tom?"

The old man scratched his forehead. "Well, there's more than one wolf, for sure. I'm guessing more than two. Each of them has a distinct sound. And I've seen a lot of torn-up animal carcasses around."

Gavin was distressed over that news. He'd been roaming these hills, too, and he'd seen those carcasses for himself. But there were no reports of wolf sightings in the databases he regularly checked. And that was a good thing. If the wildlife guys came in to inspect the area, not only would his search for the monster that put the *Were* in *werewolf* have to be curtailed, he'd have to find someplace else to spend time with his own issues each time a full moon came around.

"So, you're worried for the doctor's daughter?" Tom's question brought Gavin out of thought.

"She mentioned wanting to see that wolf killed, if in fact it played a part in her father's death. I'd hate to see her try to find it. She's alone out here."

"And she's a city girl," Tom said.

Raising his mug to his mouth, Gavin spoke over the rim, "A feisty city girl."

"Maybe I should report the sounds?" Tom suggested.

"Can you postpone that until I take a better look around?"

Tom smiled. "Do you fancy a fur rug?"

Gavin hid a grimace as his internal wolf gave an indecipherable whine. "No. Nothing like that, Tom. If there's a pack, I'll report it. I'd like to see a gray, that's all. I'd also like to make sure the Donovan girl doesn't do anything silly, like trying to hunt the ones you've heard."

He got to his feet with a longing glance at the mug in his hand. "Can I keep this if I promise to return the mug later? I truly believe you make the best damn coffee in the state."

"Sure." Tom beamed. "Stop in anytime for more. I always have a pot on."

"I'll do that."

The old man shook the hand Gavin offered, and smiled.

As Gavin hit the road, his worry doubled. If the old guy thought there was more than one wolf in the area, then more people than himself would be on the lookout for a pack and soon know what roamed here.

He hoped Tom would honor his request to keep the news to himself until Gavin found that big abomination again, this time more prepared to deal with it. Gavin knew he'd have to hustle on this matter before Skylar took it upon herself to return to a forest that hid one of hell's furry minions. And before he'd have to confess to being one of them.

Chapter 10

"Clutch, gear, gas."

Skylar thanked the heavens that the motel sat on the edge of town, giving her plenty of room for a steep learning curve in stick shifts as she hit the road in Harris's Jeep at a scant thirty miles an hour. Busy Miami streets near her home in Florida weren't made for sticks or four-wheel drive. Florida was all about sleek and flashy convertibles and automatic transmissions. Torn seats and muddy tires weren't allowed.

Things got better as she cruised along, though, and she tried hard to place her surroundings in a landscape that looked totally different in the daylight. Last night her attention had centered on Gavin, and on what followed them from the hillside, with no thought for the road.

Still, her sense of direction didn't desert her. After taking a bend or two, a few miles out from town, she got her bearings.

The first stop on today's agenda was a visit to the care-taker's place. Though her father hadn't mentioned the man, other than jotting down his name and phone number on a note she'd found by the cabin's kitchen sink, along with the word "watcher," she recalled seeing Tom Jeevers's house on her drive in from the airport. She was sure she could find that house now if she took her time and followed her nose—a saying her father often used to keep his daughters on track with whatever they were doing.

And damn…besides missing her father, she'd missed a call to Trish, who must surely be frantic by now.

"Damn. Damn. Damn."

What she did not need was her big sister coming to the rescue. She wasn't going to share the contents of that trunk in the cabin's attic with anyone, especially after being on the mountain and feeling its heaviness for herself.

She wasn't going to share Gavin Harris and what they'd done last night, either. Some things were just too private and confusing to talk over with a family member who gen-erally, at least on the surface, had her shit together. All the shit that counted, anyway.

Plus, she still felt confused about her father. Now, more than ever.

Gavin Harris's rush to get her away from whatever walked around out there last night had worked. Having her mind led elsewhere by the way he'd mesmerized her body made temporarily forgetting the other things easy. But the eerie feeling of being followed, and of Gavin's swift retreat from what he might have found on that mountain, came back to haunt her now.

"Lord, he is talented, though," Skylar muttered as she stepped harder on the gas pedal, realizing how absolutely absurd it was to crave a man she'd really only recently met.

At the mere thought of Gavin, the ache between her

thighs throbbed with renewed interest. She would see him one more time to give him back his car.

She looked at her watch. Fifteen minutes had gone by, so the road she needed should appear right about *now*.

Making a sharp turn around a stand of trees, Skylar saw a green mailbox with the Jeevers name painted on it. She pulled into the yard and looked at the house before turning off the engine.

The house looked nice. Well kept. Tidy.

No one came to meet her when she got out of the car. No one answered when she knocked on the door. Undaunted, Skylar walked to the side of the house to find a window to tap on, but the windows were too high in the walls, due to the dramatic drop off of the ground from the front of the house to the back.

The yard behind the house also sloped downward at a steep angle toward the forest beneath it. Skylar shielded her eyes from the sunlight and stared through a lattice of fragrant pine branches, hoping for a better look at the stunning view of the valley. She spotted a small building down there, barely visible beneath those trees.

"Mister Jeevers?" Calling out, Skylar carefully made her way toward that distant building on uneven footing. "It's Skylar Donovan. I believe you knew my father."

Receiving no answer, she hesitated, thinking seriously about going back, and about getting to her own cabin to search for more clues dealing with her father's possible strange mental malady. But she was already here and trespassing on another person's property, so she went on with a nagging suspicion that Tom Jeevers was probably somewhere around, tinkering with the kind of tools most men living apart from town were likely to possess.

She reached the building on the slope. It was small, maybe twenty feet by twenty feet, and made of concrete blocks expertly painted to look like the logs covering the house perched on the slope above it. The roof was some kind of green corrugated metal. There were no windows.

It was quiet under the trees, save for the wind in the branches.

"Mister Jeevers? Are you out here? I'm sorry to bust in like this, but I'd like to talk to you."

Nothing.

Honestly, she didn't belong in another man's backyard.

It was as she turned to leave that she caught sight of the door to the building, open a crack. From the handle dangled a long, thick chain. On the ground beneath the chain lay the broken remnants of a fist-sized lock.

But that wasn't what set her teeth on edge.

Through that small opening in the wall came a putrid smell that triggered her gag reflex. Skylar knew what this awful odor had to be, though she'd never smelled anything like it before.

It was the stench of death.

Gavin found Skylar's cabin's door unlocked and figured she must have left it that way the night before, planning to return.

He went inside.

He looked around, and as far as he could tell, the front room didn't look disturbed. He took the time to look at several landscape paintings hanging in carved wooden frames on the walls and the handful of trinkets strewn on the mantel perched above a fireplace of worn gray river rock that took up one whole corner of the room. There were no photos or anything of a truly personal nature that reflected the cabin's last occupant, or his daughter.

Skylar didn't actually live here, though.

The bedroom was another matter. Gazing at the open

bedroom door, Gavin suffered a sudden pang of acute physical longing for the woman who'd been sleeping there.

He tossed his head. How would he get any work done if he missed Skylar already? *Missed* being a completely inadequate word for what he was feeling. Though he didn't really know her, he did know every sleek, sexy inch of her body, having explored as much as possible with his hands and his mouth before and after discovering its fiery internal depths.

He would never forget being able to get to a place of such incredible intimacy and abandon so quickly, and he silently thanked Skylar for getting him through it unscathed. Problem was, now that he'd experienced such freedom in the bedroom, and with her, he wanted more of the same. *An endless supply.*

His body twitched with the memory of their sometimes rough coupling that had utilized every surface in the motel room. The wolf remained quiet today, allowing Gavin room for reminiscing because it also wanted to remember, though that kind of quietness was odd behavior for the wolf this close to a full moon.

Several steps brought Gavin closer to the cabin's bedroom door. Questions appeared in his mind with each stride. What was Skylar's life like in Florida? What did she do for a living? Was she a teacher, secretary, CEO, or a doctor in her own right? He should have found those things out by now and also should have asked her why her father might come all this way to play with the wildlife.

Why wolves, though? Why did Dr. Donovan come to this state, and this area in particular? The bad news was that he'd come to the right place for that kind of search.

"Well, all right." The house seemed fine, so there wasn't a sufficient excuse for him to stay. The desire to be in a place where Skylar lived, if only temporarily, couldn't be

condoned. Neither could setting one boot inside that bedroom just to get a whiff of any lingering scent.

He'd wait for her outside.

Turning back to the front room, Gavin hesitated as the
glint of something shiny, caught in a beam of sunlight coming in the window, captured his attention. Doubling back to
the table near the couch, he picked up the object and stared.

"Well, I'll be damned," he said, studying a gold, diamond-
encrusted ring nestled in a blue velvet box. There was no
mistaking the purpose of a ring like that.

His heart took an unexpected dive that made him want
to sit down. Skylar neglected to mention being engaged
and hell, he hadn't thought to ask.

Disappointment coursed through him. He honestly believed that theirs might be a connection with the potential
for growth, despite his personal issues and everything he'd
thought about those issues for the past two years. At least
he'd hoped so, against all odds and as ridiculous as that
hope might have been.

Placing the ring back where he found it, Gavin straightened. Then he noticed the note paper beneath the box. It
wasn't addressed, and he had no right to read what was
on that note.

He turned his head to look at the gun resting on the
seat of the chair. Skylar must have dropped it there before
traipsing after him up the mountainside, thinking to play it
safe and keep from accidentally shooting him in the dark.

Thank heavens for that small favor.

Sick over finding the ring, he picked up the gun, an old
revolver, gauged its weight in his hand and turned it over.
Skylar had said the gun was loaded.

He spun the chamber and dumped the ammo onto his
palm. A ripple of shock ran through him. The weapon
was loaded, all right. With unusual ammunition. Make that

highly unusual ammunition. Bullets made of silver that felt like fire on his open palm.

Silver bullets were meant for hunting a specific kind of animal.

His kind.

Dumbfounded, he stared at a metal that, according to ancient lore, could take down werewolves with a single bullet, though no resources he found provided an explanation for why this might work when other metals didn't.

Some sources believed silver to be like a solid dose of moonlight that, if buried deep within werewolf tissue, would be too much for a beast to take all at once.

Other sources proposed that silver, long used medicinally, would work its way to the heart through the bloodstream, trying to heal a system that could no longer be fixed, taking out both host and wolf at the same time.

Yet there were plenty of arguments citing the silver-bullet theory as being hogwash, and stating that a bullet was a bullet, no matter what it was made of. If struck in the right place, a crucial place, any bullet might take down man or beast. Spots like the head, or a direct hit to the heart…

A beating heart like his, which had already taken a blow from a diamond ring…no bullet necessary.

Gavin reloaded the gun and replaced it on the chair, wondering as he looked to the front door if Skylar knew anything about the special bullets or if she'd merely found the weapon among her father's things without looking closely at the ammo inside it.

He thought back.

"I have a gun," she told him. "I know how to use it."

So, what else did she know about?

Who was the lucky guy with the ring?

He ran a hand through his hair and then pinched the

bridge of his nose to ease the ache building behind his eyes as he remembered more of their conversation.

"I think my father might have been chasing a wolf when he died."

New meaning about that struck Gavin with the force of a hammer falling from the sky. This was Skylar's father's gun. These were Dr. Donovan's silver bullets. Chances were that Papa Donovan hadn't been chasing just any old wolf out here if he had purposefully bought those custom bullets. A werewolf had been his target. And there were, as far as Gavin knew, only two werewolves here.

Screeching noises roused him… The sound of a car driven around a tight curve by someone in a hurry.

"Skylar."

Smelling the hot tires with his overworked wolf senses, Gavin headed outside, alerted by the sound of a car door being forcefully kicked open.

She was there, as if he'd conjured her. Skylar faced him across the small yard, her face as white as parchment paper. "I think Tom Jeevers might be dead," she said, holding on to the car for support.

Chapter 11

Gavin was by her side quickly, easing her from the car and into his arms. "What? What did you say?"

"At his house. In the back. Bad smell. Really bad."

Gavin held her firmly. "I just came from there. Tom was fine."

"He wasn't there. I found another building."

"What other building?"

"The one behind the house, under the trees."

"The shed?"

Skylar's eyes pleaded with him to believe her. "Get help."

"Okay. You'll come with me," he said. "Get back in the car."

She did as he asked without question or argument and sat quietly as he got in beside her.

"Tell me what happened."

"I don't know what happened."

"You didn't go inside to look for the source of the odor?"

Stricken by that idea, she shook her head. "Not so brave now, huh?"

What was left of Gavin's wounded heart went out to her. She was seriously shaken. Her tension transferred to him as though a lightning bolt had been trapped in the car with them, with nowhere else to go but back and forth between the two.

"Did you see anyone?" he asked.

"No."

"Are you all right?"

"Out of breath, that's all. Scared for him. For Jeevers."

"Why did you come here, instead of heading for town?"

"I left my phone here, and this was closer."

That wasn't the entire truth. His uncanny connection to her suggested there was more. She must have known she'd find him at the cabin. Maybe she also knew he couldn't have stayed away. He believed that she'd chosen to run to him, instead of in the opposite direction.

Heat continued to flush the skin on the back of his neck. Gavin's forearms tensed as he turned the steering wheel, fighting an impulse to pull over and kiss the woman beside him, no matter how dire the situation might be.

There was no way for this connection, this bond, to be make-believe. Skylar either trusted him or wanted to. By being together, by joining their bodies in an exquisite physical union, and maybe even before that, they'd assessed and discovered each others' worth. One soul sought the other, finding solace in their new companionship.

"You're engaged," he said after using his radio to make a call, though his mind should have been elsewhere.

She glanced at him.

"It might not be a good idea to leave valuable things lying around where anyone could find them," he added. "I saw the ring. The door was open, if that's any excuse. I wanted to make sure everything was okay since we left in a hurry last night."

The conversational turn didn't seem to unsettle Skylar. She said, "If it still meant something, that ring would be on my finger."

"Must have been a recent decision?"

"Fairly recent, but ancient history now."

"But you brought it here?"

"To send back."

Maybe that was on the note he hadn't read.

"I'm sorry." Gavin heard the relief that gentled his voice, and figured she'd pick up on it, too.

"I'm not," she said, gazing at him.

Gavin pulled the Jeep over with a sharp twist on the wheel. Unfortunately this wasn't anywhere he could have been alone with Skylar, but in Tom Jeevers's front yard.

"Stay here, okay?" he said, hating to leave her.

She nodded.

Out of the car, and with his radio in hand, Gavin strode to the house and knocked. Receiving no answer, he skirted the perimeter, stopping short when Jeevers met him in the back.

"Harris?" Tom said. "Back so soon?"

Gavin lowered the radio. "You're all right, Tom?"

"The question supposes that something might have happened to me in the past hour?"

With a glance behind him at the car, Gavin said, "Good. Glad to see you're okay. Would you mind if I have a look at the building in the back, Tom?"

"Why would you want to see that?"

"I've had a complaint about a bad smell."

Tom's returned gaze was one of surprise. "Bad smell?"

"I'd like to investigate, Tom."

Tom's brow furrowed, adding to the creases already

ingrained in his deeply tanned skin. "Well, I suppose it's okay to take you down there now that he's gone."

Gavin tilted his head. "Now that who is gone?"

"Doc Donovan."

"What's he got to do with the building behind your house?"

"He rented it to keep some of his things in."

"You decided not to mention that this morning when we spoke?"

Tom shrugged. "I never saw him use it. As far as I knew, after moving stuff in a few years back, he never came here again."

"You haven't looked at it in all that time?"

"My knees aren't what they used to be, and that hill is steep. There aren't any windows in that structure, and he put a lock on the door. What would I have looked at?"

"I'd appreciate it if you'd show me, Tom. I just need a quick look around."

"All right. I was going to have to bust that lock eventually, anyway, since the doctor is no longer with us. I'd thought to tell his daughter about it while she's here. Hang tight and I'll find some bolt cutters."

As Tom wandered toward the back door of his house, Gavin walked down the slope, only discovering that the little building he'd assumed was a shack was something slightly bigger once he got close to it. The painted camouflage was good. The smell emanating from it was as awful as Skylar had described.

It was an odor having nothing to do with what had been stored here. Something had died.

Gavin tightened his grip on the radio and paused by the door to stare at the dangling chain. The unmistakably silver chain, lightly tarnished with age and weather, and composed of huge interlocking links.

Waves of apprehension washed over him as he reached for the door. He'd made it through a night of sexual gymnastics with a woman, fearing the worst in himself, but he doubted that facing what this building held would be nearly as easy.

Hearing footsteps behind him that he recognized, Gavin pivoted to block Skylar's approach. It just wasn't in her nature to be left behind. He'd have to remember that.

"Do you ever do what's asked of you?" he challenged in a rough voice devoid of any of the kindness his lover might need at the moment after a discovery like this one.

"Hardly ever," she shot back.

"You can't go in there. I won't allow it, Skylar."

"You're going inside?"

"I have to. Tom's okay, and up at the house, so whatever this is requires my attention."

"I think this might have something to do with me."

"Why would that be true?"

"My father has been here. I'm sure of that."

"Why would you think so?" Gavin pressed.

"I just do."

He didn't have time for this. Puzzles would have to wait and so would enigmatic women. This building was surrounded by an atmosphere of violence, and it reeked of death. Skylar had been right about that, too.

"Could be that an animal wandered in and got stuck when the door partially closed off its escape. Rotting elk carcasses can smell like this as they decompose," he explained, though his crystallizing senses told him a different story.

This was no elk stench. The odor struck a chord that made his inner wolf squirm.

Inching the door open, he held his breath and crossed from the light of day into the building's ominously dark interior.

* * *

For once, Skylar didn't move. Between the stench of the place and the expression on Gavin's face, she felt frozen solid. Her muscles and her vocal cords were completely useless.

"Got them," a very alive old man she assumed must be Tom Jeevers shouted from the hill above them.

She watched Gavin back out of the building. He looked to her and then to the man heading their way before again fixing his gaze on the radio clasped in one of the same strong hands that had given her such pleasure. When his eyes found hers, he said, "You'll need to go back to the car."

She wanted to do as he asked. She really did. The chills spreading over her like an icy contagion were the cold fingers of premonition, warning that she might not want to find whatever was in this building. But her shoes were glued to the ground.

Tom Jeevers slid down the last of the slope to stand beside them. He held a large tool she recognized. Bolt cutters.

After taking a lingering look at her, he noticed the lock on the ground and the open door, and made a face.

"There's a light switch inside on the right," he said to Gavin without introducing himself to her. "Shoulder high. I'll show you."

Gavin stepped back to let the man pass and then followed Jeevers into the building when the lights came on.

With no desire to actually see what that room held, and after hearing muffled exclamations from both men, Skylar swayed on her feet. Passing minutes slowed to a crawl. She put a hand to one ear to stop the ringing sounds about to drive her mad. She wasn't a coward. Was not.

Although neither man emerged from what she currently designated as a house of horror, it was crazy to think that a dangerous fate had befallen them, too. What could they be doing in there? Why were they taking so long?

She wanted to shout out those questions.

Covering her nose with the top of her shirt, she planted one foot in front of the other. Finding the nerve to shuffle forward, she reached the door. Nobody stopped her when she entered. Her fear gave the building a sinister cast, though sinister would have been putting things mildly.

Four steps in, she froze again. Gavin and Tom Jeevers stood in the center of a large open space, unmoving after all that elapsed time, their faces contorted with horror and disgust.

Skylar quickly saw why.

The floor was gray concrete. Walls were padded with extra layers of insulation for soundproofing. Chains with medieval-looking manacles hung from the closest wall, bordering a huge floor-to-ceiling cage that took up most of one corner. The cage's bars gleamed with silver flecks in the light from an overhead lamp. Its door hung open.

Her first impression was that someone had built a torture chamber inside this building behind Tom's house. The awful smell told her that someone had used it.

Strong arms caught her when her legs gave way. Gavin—his pallor as gray as the concrete, his expression grim.

"Tom, can you explain this?" he said.

The older man shook his head. He also looked ill.

"This sits on your property," Gavin said.

With her head pressed to his chest, Skylar felt the rumble of Gavin's voice when he made that charge. His heart was racing. His shoulders continually twitched as if, like hers, his instincts told him to run.

"How could you not know about this, Tom?"

"It wasn't my place to interfere," Tom finally managed

to croak. "I didn't have a key. I never saw anyone come in or out."

Aware of Gavin's gaze shifting to her, Skylar raised her chin. Feelings of terror shot through her when she read what lay behind Gavin's intense blue gaze.

"What about your father, Skylar? You told me you knew he'd been here."

She eyed the cage. Her breath squeezed out to form a reply to his question, but another question took precedence. "What kind of animal would that cage hold?"

"A big one," Gavin replied.

"I was wrong. My father couldn't have been here. He would not have allowed this. He was a doctor, and he was kind."

"Could he have discovered this place and been helping whomever or whatever he found here?"

"Yes. That must be it, and why I thought he…" She couldn't finish that sentence, frantic now for a way to explain this scene when her heart and head each maintained different fears.

That cage was built to hold a large animal. A strong animal. For what purpose, though? What about the chains on the walls?

Those chains weren't low, or anywhere near the floor. They'd been attached to the walls with industrial-sized iron rings and placed high up, spread far enough apart to restrain something bigger than a human.

No.

Not that.

She was going to be sick, and fought off a whirl of vertigo. Her father couldn't have found and trapped the kind of creature he'd been seeking because they didn't exist. Even if they did, he could not have kept one here.

He wouldn't have dared.

Unless her father's plan was to keep a dangerous creature locked away from others. Keep it from harming others. Study it closely.

No. That can't be it, either.

Those manacles would eliminate wolves and other typical four-legged predators.

"No," she repeated aloud, helpless to explain this room. Any attempt to address her father's motivations without the facts to back them up might damage his pristine reputation and all the good he'd done. He couldn't speak for himself, and she refused to judge her dad by the way things looked.

She was trembling so hard, Gavin pulled her closer. But she felt a change in him. He was unsure about her now, and about what she'd said about her dad.

She wanted to shout "werewolf" and be done with it. Get that out in the open and let these men decide how crazy she was. But was she crazy? Had her father been nuts, too, or merely a damn good hunter to have bagged a beast? Was there a chance her father's mad mind assumed some other poor animal was a werewolf?

As more awful theories piled up, Skylar dug deep into her thoughts. If her father *had* trapped a werewolf, or any other kind of animal for study, there would be written evidence of that work. She'd have to search to see if such a diary existed in order to find out what had gone on in this dreadful place.

"Charging my father with knowing about or abetting this kind of activity gets us nowhere if all we have to link him to this place is my hunch that he'd been here before," she said.

"He rented this building from Tom." Gavin's voice was as grim as his expression.

"Anyone could have done this," she insisted. "The lock was broken."

Transferring his attention to Tom, Gavin said, "She's

right. If Donovan hasn't been here in a couple of years, room for blame is left wide-open."

"We don't know what actually went on here." Tom looked to Skylar as he spoke.

"That smell tells us something did," Gavin said.

Her lover slowly distanced himself from her. His hold on her loosened in a way that suggested he might believe her a part of this, or think that she could have been tainted by her father's deeds.

She spoke again. "What happened to being innocent until proved guilty?"

"Nothing happened to that," Gavin said. "We've all had a nasty shock and we're searching for meaning."

"They might think I did this." Tom Jeevers headed for the door. "I'd better call it in."

Skylar pointed to the radio in Gavin's hand. "Aren't you going to use that?"

"I already have."

That meant others were on their way here.

"I need some air," she said.

Without another word, Skylar left the room. On her own, with only seconds to spare before Gavin might follow her outside and before other members of the law arrived, she leaned against the corner of the building on legs that felt like rubber, allowing the tears of shock and fright and blatant disgust to pool in her eyes.

Wet-faced and shaky, she blinked slowly when a shadow behind her blocked the sunlight. She didn't need to guess who it was.

Chapter 12

"Can we talk?"

Skylar whirled to face him.

"Before the others arrive?" Gavin added.

"I don't know anything about what happened here," she said.

"Then tell me about silver bullets. The bullets in your gun."

She looked at him with her lips parted for a shout she didn't let loose. "I believe the only way you'd find out about that might be called trespassing," she said.

"As I said, I had probable cause to enter your house."

"Such as?"

"Searching the premises for intruders, since we were gone all night."

"Is that all?"

"No. Actually it was just an excuse to wait for you. I wanted to be there when you arrived."

His confession made her look away.

"You have secrets." He spoke softly, not caring to distress her further.

"Obviously, my father is the Donovan who kept secrets," she said.

"Can you talk to me about that, Skylar? Will you?"

"It wouldn't help this case."

"Why not?"

"He was good at what he did and spent his entire professional life helping others. These things…" She waved at the building beside them. "These things aren't indicative of the man I knew. They're far removed from what I know about my father."

"Did he come here to get away from his work?"

"Yes. Dealing with mental patients day in and day out began to take a toll."

Gavin absorbed this news slowly. "He wasn't a general kind of MD?"

"He's a…" She paused before starting over. "He was a psychiatrist."

"At a hospital facility?"

"Yes."

"A mental hospital?"

She nodded. "One that housed patients with extreme mental deficiencies."

Gavin thought he was starting to see a pattern that might lead to answers to some of the problems they faced. But he couldn't yet connect the dots. What he knew pointed to Skylar's father as a suspect in whatever went on behind Tom's house, though at the moment they had no real idea as to what that was.

"We haven't found anything illegal here yet," he said tentatively, disliking that fact. "No proof of illegal activity to go on. For that, more evidence needs to be gathered."

Besides, Gavin inwardly added, if he told anyone of his suspicion that a werewolf might have been caged here, he stood to be laughed out of town.

For him, the chains and silver cages made it a foregone conclusion, though. The fact that Skylar's father rented this place from Tom incriminated her good old dad in something unspeakable, as did that gun with the silver bullets.

Silver chains, silver cage, silver bullets.

All this silver business rubbed him the wrong way, as did the picture Skylar painted of her father.

"You do realize that withholding information might prove a fatal mistake?" he said, carefully moderating his tone.

He found it unimaginable that anyone might have trapped that gigantic monster from the mountain here. How the hell could that have been managed? Even if the hunter had used tranquilizer darts made for taking down elephants, the beast would still have to be transported to this location.

And damn it, he was a sucker for the damp green eyes now looking into his. He wanted to kiss the tears from Skylar's beautiful, innocent face. She made him want to believe she knew nothing about her father's intentions.

He brushed the drops of water from her cheeks with his thumbs, allowing his fingers to linger on her too-pale skin.

"If I ask you something personal, will you answer honestly?" Gavin willed himself to keep some emotional distance from the woman who'd taken hold of his soul so quickly and easily.

Long lashes briefly cloaked her eyes. "I'm not sure. Right now I'm not sure about anything."

Gavin lowered his voice. "Did your father have an

agenda for those silver bullets, or were they only collector's items?"

"I haven't found the answer to that question, though I've been wrestling with it since I arrived," she answered earnestly.

"You knew about the bullets, then?"

"I found the gun and the bullets in a trunk in the attic of the cabin."

Gavin blew out a breath and blinked again, thinking *Holy hell*. Skylar's father might actually have known about the thing in the woods, or thought he did. And that beast might have been right here, either of its own accord or held against its will by Skylar's dad.

Had the elder Donovan actually succeeded in capturing and chaining up the monster Gavin so desperately wanted to find? Could Donovan, at least for a time, have kept that monster captive here behind Tom's house, right beneath Gavin's nose?

Some pieces of this puzzle were lining up, and the pattern he saw suggested that Doc Donovan was a werewolf hunter.

Had the monster managed to get loose and go after its keeper? Maybe Donovan let it go?

Gavin rolled his shoulders as he speculated about the doctor's body being discovered torn to shreds and missing a face. His muscles tensed with the memory of being torn apart on that same mountain.

Theories about revenge would make a horrible kind of sense if life mimicked the pages of horror novels and monsters possessed the ability to think like human beings. Could this be a case of a beast reaping revenge on its tormentor, like in the Frankenstein story?

Wasn't he after the same thing in his own hunt for that big beast? Revenge?

If Skylar's father had succeeded in trapping the creature in this building and it somehow got loose, possibly showing complex thought processes…heaven help the man who'd dared to cage it.

Gavin felt the rightness of his reasoning, but could he prove any of it? Talk about it with anyone? As far as most people were concerned, the only monsters running around hurting other people were low-life human criminals.

If he mentioned any of this, he'd be considered a candidate for Dr. Donovan's mental ward.

"I'd like to know more about your father," he said when the silence had stretched for far too long. "You said he kept secrets. I want to hear what you know about those secrets."

"So you can pin what we've found here on him?" she countered.

Think carefully about what you say next, and how you'll explain what you're about to propose.

"Skylar." Gavin took his hand from her face. "Is it possible that your father believed in the lore of old European legends?"

She shook her head, unwilling to hear more. He could see she resented this kind of personal intrusion.

"Do you have any idea what silver is used for in those legends?" he pressed.

She remained mute, but he couldn't let this go.

"Could your father have brought a wolf here?"

Feeling her mounting tension, Gavin's excitement began to stir. Skylar knew something, all right. She was trying to hide her conclusions from him. Once again, her eyes met his, and the electricity sparking between them scored his soul. The look on her face was sad and lonely and startlingly defiant.

He reached for her without thinking, desiring his hands

on her, whether to offer comfort or demand her compliance with his line of questioning. With his cheek buried in her soft, silky hair, he posed the final question, holding her tightly in case she tried to avoid what was coming.

"Did your father believe in werewolves?"

Sirens in the distance broke the silence that followed his question. The woman in his arms struggled to break free, perhaps tortured by what he'd suggested.

She probably thought him crazy for proposing such a thing. Her heart banged in her chest. Small rattling quakes ran up and down the length of her spine. But he didn't let her get away from him, because he was badly in need of her answer.

"Skylar," he said. "Is that why he came to Colorado? To hunt wolves, hoping to capture a special one?"

When she tilted her head back, Gavin noted the fear darkening her eyes. After seeing this place, she'd be afraid to speak further about her father. He didn't blame her, really, especially after he'd mentioned the seriousness of withholding information.

Who would believe it, anyway? he wanted to shout, *Other than me?*

"Werewolves?" Her voice was hardly more than a whisper. "Yes. I think he believed in them."

Skylar's reply set off tiny explosions in his overworked mind. Hell, was Skylar's father at the center of this?

The noise of the sirens told Gavin that two law enforcement vehicles had arrived. He heard doors slam. Calm voices carried on the wind. When Skylar struggled again, he let her go.

"You don't have to be here," he said.

"They'll want to speak with me eventually. Better get it over with."

Skylar set her shoulders and walked past him, looking

young and small from behind…and fragile and burdened as she marched to face what came next.

Gavin could have told her this wasn't the end, and that it was only the beginning of the nightmare.

Chapter 13

The interrogation was shorter than Skylar expected. When they freed her to go home, the sheriffs, accompanied by a couple rangers, headed down the hill to see what this nasty business was all about.

She couldn't stay there, near that shed, so she started walking in the direction of her cabin. It was either that or wait for Gavin, who might be some time yet, and would certainly have more questions about her father's secrets.

She was aware that Gavin's thoughts were turning her way, though he was nowhere in sight. The more time she spent with him, the more the bond between them deepened.

It was getting too dangerous to keep holding back some serious family issues. She knew that now. The damn word haunting her was the word Gavin had brought up—*werewolf.*

Is that why he came to Colorado? To hunt wolves, hoping to capture a special one? he'd asked.

Stumbling on a stone bordering the road, Skylar fought off the rise of her temper. Reason told her it would be best to leave Colorado, go home and forget about this place. Put the cabin up for sale with all her father's things in it and move on. Lose the dreams. Lose Gavin Harris.

Pausing long enough to glance over her shoulder, she repeated "Lose Gavin," aloud, testing both the idea and her resolve.

Right then the idea almost seemed doable.

Almost.

Her stubborn streak just didn't agree. Neither did the spot deep inside that wanted his touch so desperately.

What would her father have thought about Gavin, so different from her ex-fiancé? Her dad hadn't liked Danny much. Gavin already showed more stability than the edgy companionship she'd shared with the cop, a relationship that had resembled a positive relationship on only a superficial level. Even after saying yes, she'd known that no woman should settle for superficial when her heart wasn't truly with the program. She'd learned this lesson the hard way.

While Gavin...

Gavin, her handsome, virile lover, kept her on the verge of something she didn't dare name, in a completely different way. He was strong, capable, gorgeous and smart. Around him, she felt safe, but also as if that sense of safety might be temporary, with the future some kind of wild unknown.

The looks. That voice. Hell, yes, she was undeniably attracted to him. Probably too much. He pulled her wildness out and into the open, exposing that side of her. Her shakes and quakes weren't all signs of weakness, but an effort to control the secret longings she felt building up inside.

Yet Gavin had spoken the dreaded word that plagued her. The word she hated most at the moment. *Werewolves.*

Confused, flustered, Skylar thought about going back to Tom's house to quiz Gavin about what silver bullets were meant for.

It was going to be a conversation straight from hell.

As luck would have it, she didn't have to turn around or wait long for him to find her. Recognizing the sound of the Jeep's engine, she planted herself in the middle of the road, ready for the next showdown.

One look at her face—the set features, the lips forming a straight line—told Gavin that Skylar wasn't going to jump into the car without an argument.

Too many things left unsaid had created a tension between them that stretched their connection to the breaking point. The accusations he'd made regarding her father might have seemed absurd to anyone else, yet apparently weren't crazy to Skylar.

Why?

Cutting the engine, Gavin got out of the car thinking that if he remained on his side of the vehicle, chances were the woman eyeing him so intently might feel less threatened. Though he wanted to search the trees for the monster able to eat its way out of that silver cage, it was still daylight. He kept his attention on the woman in the road.

"Want a lift?" he asked casually.

"I don't think so." Her voice sounded clipped.

"Want to talk?"

"Do you?" she countered.

"Yes, I do. But why don't I drive you home, and we can leave the talking for later? Get you off the road?"

"You think I don't know what you're dying to say? I can hear your unspoken questions from where I'm standing."

"You've had a shock," Gavin said.

"Understatement," she tossed back.

"Your father didn't necessarily have anything to do with that place."

"Do any of you actually believe that?"

"At this point, and as I've said, any evidence is circumstantial at best. They'll have to go through that place with a fine-tooth comb to dig up more, and that will take time. Please let me drive you home."

She shook her head to reinforce her decision to remain on the road. "You brought up werewolves."

He nodded. "Yes, and you went along with it. I find that not only fascinating, but strange."

"How so?" she challenged.

"You didn't laugh at the word."

"It's not funny."

"No, but it probably should have been funny. That's the point." Gavin rested both hands on the roof of the Jeep. "Are you searching for proof that your father wasn't off his rocker? Because now those law guys are going to try to discover that same thing."

It was clear that some of the fight had gone out of her when she said, "He couldn't have hurt anyone in a place like that."

"You'd be the one to know."

She glanced around uneasily. "You're right. We shouldn't talk here."

"If you don't want to go to the cabin, we can go someplace else."

Gavin waited her out, trying to read in her expression what she needed at the moment to help ease the shock of seeing that building and imagining what it might have hidden.

"What were you doing at Tom's?" he asked.

"I was going to thank him for watching over Dad's cabin."

"That's all?"

"No," she admitted. "I was looking for information."

"About what?"

"My father, and what he did here in Colorado."

Some of the iron in her tone returned as she added, "Shall I repeat my protest about him not using that awful place?"

"No need. I'm sure no one could believe their father capable of that."

Having successfully defused another potential argument, Gavin waited to see what Skylar might say next. She might want a fight, but he wasn't going to let her have it.

"If my father had lost part of his mind, other people would have noticed. The rest of his family, all of us, would have heard."

"One would think so," he agreed. "Especially if he worked in a hospital where anomalies are noted on a daily basis by people trained to see them."

Skylar's hand moved to the door handle. "I can't explain about the gun."

"Though you admit to knowing what silver ammunition is supposedly for."

Her face fell. "Yes. Wolves. Not just wolves, though. Imaginary wolfish beasts."

Gavin shifted his stance to hide the degree of his surprise.

"Okay," she said. "Believing in werewolves isn't normal behavior. I get that." Looking directly at him, she asked, "Is it?"

Unwilling to answer that question, Gavin blew out a breath. He sure as hell couldn't confess.

"What will those guys in uniform assume when they investigate the room back there?" she asked.

"They will assume that a lunatic has escaped from an asylum."

He was wrong about her face not being able to get any paler. Skylar's shoulders slumped as she opened the door. It took minutes for her to get into car. When she did, she sat as far away from him as possible.

Tonight, he thought, gazing at Skylar with regret and a gigantic knot in his gut. *In a few hours, when the full moon rises and the wolf takes me over, no explanations would be necessary if you were to see me. And that might actually hurt you more than it hurts me.*

Gavin felt the intensity of her heated gaze. For once, he wanted to shape-shift right then and there to put an end to the misery they'd face sooner, rather than later. Get it over with. Let her know that her father might not have been loony.

As if revealing his beast would put her mind at ease.

Chapter 14

The man beside her drove in silence. Skylar wanted anything but distance, but the terrible find had created even more distance between them.

Skylar figured it was past noon. Time had been suspended after her discovery of that shed. She wasn't able to shake off the latest round of chills or ditch the feeling that she was about to step off a cliff.

She kept wondering, as she had for several nights now, if madness might be contagious, because the answer to that particular question seemed more important after today's events. Although she supposed true madness defied the use of logic and reasoning, her brain now hurt.

She refused to link her father to that building behind Tom's house. It just wasn't possible.

When they reached the cabin, she got out first, walked up the steps and turned at the door. "You never got that lemonade."

From a few paces behind her, Gavin said, "Don't you think we're going to need something stronger?"

She gestured him inside. "You're in luck. No self-respecting Irishman with a name like Donovan would fail to know how to stock a bar."

"Funny," Gavin said, pausing on the threshold with a glance in the direction of the bedroom. "I didn't put Donovan and Irish together until you mentioned it."

"Yes, well, we don't really know much about each other, do we? Other than how well our bodies fit together."

Skylar headed for the kitchen, vowing to keep as far away from the bedroom as possible until they did find out some things. She honestly wanted to know more about the man in her front room, even though her body needed more of what he had to offer.

Before this she'd thought of Gavin as a distraction to keep her mind off her father's death and off those exotic dreams about a creature on the hillside. She wasn't sure when that changed, but it had, probably due to Gavin's gallant impulse to protect her from whatever danger he perceived in these mountains.

That, and the incredible sex.

They might have become lovers for the wrong reasons, but did that have to stand in the way of getting to know him better now?

Gavin was at the window when she returned with glasses and a bottle of whiskey. She felt his reluctance to deal with the things needing to be said.

"What are you always looking for out there?" she asked.

"It's habit. My job is to watch for things out of the ordinary."

She handed him a glass when he turned. "Well then, maybe you can fill in a few missing details for me."

She moved the gun from the chair to the table so that he

could sit down if he wanted to. With their attention on that gun, and the silver-bullet issue hanging over them like a dark cloud, Skylar went on. "My first question for you, in what will be a lengthy interrogation, is this—why are you drinking while on duty?"

She hoped her weak smile might break the ice, and watched some of his tension ease. Obviously, he'd expected a more serious discussion after everything that had happened in the past several hours. She was saving that.

"Just a swig to calm the nerves," he said. "I've never really developed an appreciation for this stuff."

"Neither have I." Skylar poured the amber liquid into their glasses. "But what was in that shed would get to anyone."

His nod of agreement caused strands of his hair to fall forward, curtaining his angular cheeks, adding a rugged air to his chiseled beauty that made Skylar's breath catch in her throat.

She knew his outline. She had seen it before, and not just in the motel. In her dreams, the being she had the hots for wasn't merely a man. Was Gavin Harris actually more than he seemed, or had she gone off the deep end again to even consider such a question?

He studied her as if he were attempting to see where this benign conversation might be going. She dared to say what was on her mind, gripping the glass so tightly she feared it might crack. "The moon is full tonight."

His eyes were riveted to hers.

"Will you be going after the wolf we heard out there? Does more light mean that you might actually be able to find it?"

Without waiting for his reply, Skylar poured a few more drops of whiskey into their glasses, needing something to do with her hands. She took a swig and made a face as the burn slid down her throat.

"Everything comes back to one word—*wolf*," she said. "You told me last night that the wolf out there on the mountain is a special wolf."

Gavin set his glass on the table, breaking eye contact. "It's a dangerous one, yes."

"Earlier, after discovering a horrible scene at a neighboring house, what came to your mind was again the word *wolf.* Did my father believe in werewolves, you asked. Am I to ignore the connection between those words, or that you brought them up?"

Tiny movements in the muscles of Gavin's forearms took her attention there, to the smooth bareness exposed by his rolled-up cuffs. She'd had her tongue on that skin in the night, and he had believed in returning the favor in kind. His mouth had traveled over every inch of her, bringing out far more in her than just shivers of delight.

Steel willpower kept her from looking to the bedroom doorway now.

"Please, Gavin. What have wolves got to do with any of this?"

Why, in my dreams, are you there?

Gavin moved to stand beside her. Taking the glass from her hands, he spoke with his mouth inches from hers. The delicious warmth of his breath raised her pulse and increased her anxiousness.

"We're speculating about the wolf," he said. "And I'll admit to being unable to think when I'm this close to you. All I want to do is take you inside that bedroom, Skylar. You're like an obsession, or a very bad craving. But I'll warn you now that you probably don't want to get to know me any better than you already do because I'm not permanent relationship material. I'm involved with the danger around here, and I seek it out. Today, and especially tonight after the sun goes down, I'll be absent. I can't protect you if you stay in this cabin."

His words were like a spray of those damn silver bullets. He felt the same as she did and craved her the way she craved him, yet he'd just clarified his position on having a relationship without answering her questions.

"Protect me from what?" she pressed. "What do you think is out there that might hurt me?"

Her heart sputtered when she looked into the eyes of the man who had freed her from old hang-ups and taboos. Even with all the strange things going on, she'd have passed up necessary information for one touch of his hand on her bare back, and for that hand to render her mindless.

She saw that same wish mirrored in Gavin's blue eyes, expressive eyes that were flecked with gold, wide-open, and told her how much he hungered for her.

Maybe she was in need of both wildness and safety at the same time. Yet Gavin was the one who had been watching the cabin, and admitted as much. Had her dreams been some sort of precognition about meeting the kind of man she needed in order to be the woman she wanted to be?

Or was something more mystifying going on?

Could dreams affect reality? Be her reality?

His breath on her face stirred her inner restlessness. His nearness fed the wildness aching to be released. There was no way to explain how badly she wanted to be satiated, moved, licked and loved by this man. In just two days, life had become so much more interesting and complicated.

But the word *wolf* stood between them. And something felt off, if only by a fraction.

Blowing out the breath she'd been holding, Skylar grabbed hold of Gavin's shirt. "Tell me," she whispered.

"Tell me why you were watching this cabin, and why you walked into my yard."

"Skylar…" He tried to interrupt. Maybe he wasn't able to follow her thread of thought.

Any minute now she would have to confess that she'd conjured him up out of the stuff of her dreams.

I have to be sure, don't you see?

"How do I know you're you, and not some kind of…" She didn't finish the statement. Wasn't able to. She knew how it would sound.

"We don't have time for this," he protested, his breath mingling with her breath, his lips touching hers when he spoke. "I'm not sure what you're asking."

"I'm asking for the truth and for a starting point that might explain all of this."

"Are you talking about what happened at Tom's?"

"That, and more. This. You and me." She lowered her voice. "And the wolves."

He blinked and set his jaw. Skylar's next thought, as she closed her eyes, was to hope she wasn't dreaming now. Because that would mean the man beside her wasn't real and that she hadn't yet woken from sleep.

"I've never been crazy," she whispered to Gavin as she reached for the buttons on his clean, pressed shirt. "But I feel crazy now."

He didn't protest when she placed her palms against the fabric covering his chest. His skin felt hot through the cotton and pulsed with a heartbeat as hard and fast as hers.

"Please prove me wrong," she said, expecting him to tear himself from her grasp and run the other away. It's what most men might have done. Danny had.

Gavin's hair brushed her cheek when he shook his head. The dark strands felt like satin.

"I'm trying to understand. I'm sorry," he said. But he remained close.

"Werewolves," Skylar whispered. "Tell me why you brought them up."

Her emotions were running rampant. She needed an outlet. Giving in to the lure of his mouth, Skylar pressed her lips to his, finding solace in his taste and his heat. She felt Gavin fight his need to join her on the floor. But another blistering round of sex wouldn't solve anything in the end, and only postpone the answers to these same questions.

Hell, was she awake now?

Her hands glided over Gavin's incredibly taut stomach. She backed up a few inches. "My father had secrets, and I'm asking if you do, too. I need to know if you're part of my father's hidden world, my dream world, or if we're all merely insane."

She paused for a breath. Her hands stopped moving.

He didn't speak, either to explain or condemn, and he didn't touch her back.

She went for broke. "I see you in my dreams. I think I hear you call to me at night. I feel you near me, even when you're not. You've been haunting me since I arrived, when that was ridiculous because I hadn't yet met you."

The man beside her continued to stare, showing no reaction to what might have been the ravings of a madwoman.

She rushed on. "That cage had heavy silver-coated bars. You questioned my possession of silver bullets and asked if I knew what they were for. You're thinking that my father may have trapped a wolf in that shed, in that cage, and that it might have been a mythical beast. And because he may have tortured it and the cage is now empty, that animal is not only angry, but could be out there somewhere, loose."

She had one last thing to add, one more long-winded thing to say.

"I might be completely out of line and in need of treatment at the hospital where my dad worked because I'll dare to tell you right now that if that cage held some kind of super wolf of the type you called 'special,' and if you can imagine how it might react to being caged, then you'll understand why I'm beginning to believe that same beast might have killed my father."

She took in a much-needed breath. "And because I might believe that, you must understand why I can't be sure that any of this, including what you and I have done, is more than a fraying filament of my imagination."

Gavin's eyes danced with bright golden flames as he leaned back with his gaze locked to hers. Slowly he began to unbutton his shirt. Pulling the edges open, he let her see all of him from his chest to his belt.

"This is me," he said. "Take a look, Skylar."

His chest was wide. His abs were magnificently muscled. Yet he wasn't perfect, and maybe that's why he'd wanted to make love to her in the dark.

Crisscrossing his flesh, stretching from a spot above his heart to his third rib, ran two parallel scars: thick white jagged lines that looked as though they'd been drawn by a child with a marker.

Skylar looked up again to meet his eyes.

"Danger comes with the job, and I've had my share," he said. "This is what I've been warning you about."

The injuries were close to his heart. The scars didn't ruin his perfection, though; they served to bring more attention to the tight golden skin surrounding them.

Dear God, what kind of madness had she let Gavin see?

"Who did this to you?"

"I fought off a wolf," he replied.

No. Her voice sounded faint. "That's why you're going after it."

"That's the reason, yes."

Special wolf. That was his special wolf. Not anything sinister. Just an animal.

"You think it's out there now?" she asked.

"There aren't many wolves around, so there's a good chance it's the one I've been tracking."

He'd been hurt badly, and she'd made him expose that. Skylar wanted to look away, give him space, but didn't. Couldn't. He was so damn beautiful, so masculine and sculpted. This was the body she'd shared herself with last night, and she wanted to do the same now.

She swallowed hard. "Could my father have been killed while chasing that wolf?"

"I didn't know your father or the circumstances surrounding his death. But I do know that once an animal has tasted human flesh and gotten away with it, that animal has to be found and put down."

"Because it will go after someone else?"

"Usually it will."

Skylar let that sink in. Old questions resurfaced, but with a new focus.

"Hypothetically, if a wolf had been kept in the cage in that room and gotten loose, would it be smart enough to want to go after humans? Any humans, and not only the one who caged it there?"

"I don't know. Maybe," he said.

She had answers. Some answers, anyway.

She touched the scars gently, and felt his skin quiver. "Does it hurt?"

"Not anymore," he said, watching her fingers move over him.

Skylar knew he was lying without truly knowing how. With her hand on his bare skin, their bond solidified. By making love and succumbing to their night of passion, they truly had united on an inexplicably deep level.

In her defense, who wouldn't assume that a connection this deep and sudden must be make-believe?

"Somehow," she said, removing her hands, "the scars suit you."

He pulled his shirt closed. "I have to go now. I have to check in."

He had to leave, and she'd have to let him go. Enough truth had been exposed for one day.

Gavin didn't want to talk about being mauled by a wild animal, and she couldn't make him. Nor could she divulge more of her father's secrets, not when she didn't know what those secrets were.

Neither of them was ready to confront the uncanny sense of being fully connected to each other. They were, in essence, still strangers on one level, and yet so much more on another.

And Gavin, just five minutes ago, had made it plain that he wasn't in the market for a serious relationship.

When he turned for the door, she followed him into the yard. The sun was only slightly past its highest point in the sky, so there were plenty of hours to fill before sundown.

He stopped by the gate before swinging it open, looking every bit the handsomely rugged ranger whose presence tugged at her body and her soul.

"Will you take that motel room again tonight, Skylar, if I ask you to?"

"I shouldn't expect you to visit me there?"

"Not tonight."

He sounded regretful about that. So was she.

"A full moon makes animals more restless," he added. "Hopefully I'll find the one I've been searching for."

His sad smile melted Skylar's heart. She wondered what

lay behind the expression, if it was a memory of the terrible hurt he must have endured from that animal. Or was it his reaction to the way she'd come unglued in front of him?

"Will you do it, Skylar? Go to town? Stay safe?" He issued the request in that velvety voice she already knew so well, the voice that heated her skin and fevered her insides.

"Yes. I'll go," she lied, hoping he believed her.

Chapter 15

"I've been calling you and am now approaching frantic mode," Trish said when Skylar checked her messages, all ten of them. "If you don't call me back right away, I'm calling the Colorado authorities and booking a flight."

Curled up in the corner of the couch, Skylar punched in her sister's number, hoping her voice would sound normal enough to prevent Trish from making good on either of those threats.

"I'm here, healthy and..." she said when Trish picked up. She had been about to add *sound of mind* to that checklist, when that was pretty far from the truth.

"It's about time," Trish shouted. "Where the heck have you been?"

"The power went out last night. I spent the night at a motel in town and just got back."

"That motel doesn't have a phone?"

"I'm sorry, Trish. I really am. Things happened so fast, I didn't think to call."

"What other things?"

"Everyone here is busy tracking some kind of rogue animal. One of the local rangers came by last night to suggest that with no lights here I might be better off in town."

"Well, glad to hear you exhibited some sense." Trish lowered her voice. "Did you show the ranger the gun you found?"

"As a matter of fact, I did. But they want to capture the animal, not shoot it dead."

"Did they get it?"

"I don't believe they did. I haven't heard about it if they have, anyway."

Silence.

"What kind of animal is it?" Trish eventually asked.

"Some kind of wolf."

"Well, thank God it isn't a bear. Does Colorado have grizzlies?"

"I really don't know," Skylar replied. "In any case, I don't venture far from the yard, except when I have to."

That should just about cover it, Skylar thought. Out-and-out lies had a habit of multiplying.

"Is the power back on?" Trish asked, evidently satisfied with the story for the time being.

"Yep. I'm making tea and about to go through more of Dad's things."

"Find anything interesting yet?"

Hell... Now she was keeping things from her sister, the way their father had kept things from them. This made her uneasy, and it was unfair. Yet she felt the secrecy was necessary if she hoped to keep Trish off her back for a while longer.

"Just the gun I've already mentioned. Dad really didn't

have many personal items stockpiled. Mostly clothes, trinkets, a few small trunks, kitchen items, several paintings by local artists and some really strong whiskey."

Trish laughed. "I take it you tried this whiskey."

"I did and couldn't choke it down. Guess I'm not Irish enough for that degree of sensory attack."

"That may turn out to be a good thing, Skye. Sure you don't need help or want company? I've finished with my case and wouldn't mind a break."

"This isn't a task for two, Trish. But I do have a question. Have you ever been here, to this cabin?"

"Nope. I'm pretty sure none of us knew exactly where it was located until Dad's partner at the hospital told us the address. Dad seemed to confide in Dr. James quite a bit. Too bad he didn't do the same with us."

Trish took a drink of something, swallowed and spoke again. "Well, that's water under the bridge, isn't it? I spoke to Dad's partner last night and voiced my concern about you being MIA. She asked if I'd like her to fly out to meet with you and help with Dad's things, and she urged me to say hello to you when you eventually turned up. She'd like to see Dad's cabin and offered to take it off our hands if we sell."

"Great. But really, Trish, this shouldn't take me much longer. I might be home next week, and I'll say hello to Dr. James then. Believe it or not, I'm actually starting to enjoy the scenery and fresh air."

"Truly? How odd for a city slicker," Trish mocked. "By the way, is there anything you'd like me to do here? Take care of your mail? Return some of those gifts before you get back, so you don't have to?"

"Thanks, but no thanks. I'll take care of all that later."

"Skye, you sound…"

"What?"

"Better. You sound better. So okay. I'm just offering to be available."

"And I adore you for that. I really do. Later, then?"

"Later. And please don't scare me again," Trish said before disconnecting.

Setting the phone down, tired of withholding the emotion rolling through her, Skylar headed for the attic, where she'd search those trunks for her father's missing paperwork— paperwork she sincerely hoped wouldn't be there. Especially papers having to do with wolves and keeping living things locked up in cages—sort of like what went on in her father's mental asylum at Fairview, with its comfortably padded cells.

Ah, well, Skylar thought, climbing the narrow stairs to the attic. *This is real. No dream. So what were you doing here, Dad?*

Gavin drove faster than he should have, unwilling to slow down, pressed by the speed of his thoughts. Skylar was behaving strangely. She said she'd heard him call to her at night. What did she mean by that?

If she heard sounds made by the demon in the hills, it meant that the beast had been close to this area for some time, and that he'd been right in guessing it was close.

This whole scene was getting stranger by the minute. Skylar's talk of dreams made no sense, and staying with her hadn't been an option. After seeing that awful room at Tom's and being surrounded by silver this close to the full moon, his nerves were jumpy. Now, he added worry to the mix—worry that Skylar might put her life at risk by going after the wolf she thought her father might have been chasing. Worry that she might find Gavin Harris instead, in his other, less appealing incarnation.

He didn't see how he could go on with his search when he also had to carefully watch Skylar and keep her safe.

Skylar Donovan was causing him to rearrange his agenda. She alone had seen his scars, his battle wounds, evidence of his tryst with death. And yet she hadn't found them ugly. Her touch had been unexpectedly tender.

There should have been no scars at all. If the white lines on his chest hadn't disappeared after two years, they likely never would.

He had been branded with the mark of the werewolf. And he still felt the heat of Skylar's touch. Her warmth helped to lessen the old aches. If he closed his eyes, he could almost feel her with him now.

Emotions swirled inside him, casting for a place to land when he remembered how badly Skylar had needed him the previous night without being coy or afraid to show it. With her help, he had prevailed over his fear of the wolf inside him. In loving her, he had successfully compartmentalized his wolfishness.

He had loved Skylar Donovan to within an inch of her life. After their athletic give-and-take, was it any wonder he craved her now, or what he might give for a rematch?

He glanced up at the sky. Only hours remained before sundown, and his hunger for Skylar left him torn. If he lost this opportunity to find the big bad wolf and return the favor of a fight, everyone in these mountains would be in danger for another month or more. Only when a full moon rode the sky could he find the added strength he gained by merging with his wolf. By uniting with his wolf, he'd be able to continue tracking the beast.

And if he lost Skylar in the meantime…

If she were to be harmed…

The human half of him would wither and die.

He stopped the car so abruptly the brakes squealed. Above the sound, the pounding of his heart was audible.

Gavin weighed his options as if he actually had some.

Skylar was important to him, but ridding the world of a fanged demon with the ability to create more like it had to take precedence.

Whichever way he looked at this, the woman he had first seen half-naked on her porch was going to be a pain in his backside and get in the way, either intruding physically or in his thoughts.

His hands were, at that very moment, itching to turn the wheel and head back to her. The impulse was nearly as strong as his imminent transformation.

The only way he could see to break the spell he was under would be to present himself to Skylar after dark, coated in fur, and send her running home to Florida. And if he did so, how many people would come after him then, knowing who and what he had become?

Having found the room behind Tom's house, the sheriffs would be on the lookout for anything off base and out of the ordinary.

He was stuck.

Glancing in the rearview mirror, he thought he could almost see that furred-up hell demon's bloody mouth smiling.

There were four trunks in the attic. Since she had already been through the first one, which had produced the gun, Skylar moved on to trunk number two, pressed tight against the back wall.

Standing up in this cramped space wasn't doable, so she crouched on her knees. Light came in through one small window near the eaves, and there was a bulb on a wire overhead.

This trunk by the wall, like all the other trunks, was locked. But the locks weren't going to stop her. She'd opened the first one by applying leverage with a metal garden stake.

"Lock-picking is now officially added to the résumé," she muttered as she stuck the metal stake between the two posts of the small padlock and twisted with all her might.

This one didn't break. Undeterred, she backtracked downstairs, determined to see this task through as quickly as possible. She picked up the gun, already familiar with its dark, cold weight.

In the attic, she carefully aimed at the lock and squeezed the trigger, unconcerned about the potential damage to the trunk.

The blast echoed loudly in the small space, kicking her back a step. The lock was shattered by a specialized silver bullet that might have cost a hefty sum and was a big reminder of the need to see what other kind of secrets this trunk held.

It took both of her hands to open the lid. The trunk was filled to the brim with papers and the kind of notebooks her father often scribbled in.

"Bingo."

Psychiatrists were predisposed to write down everything, in detail, and she'd been counting on this, though she found touching the notebooks difficult. She worried as much about what the notebooks might hold as what they might not.

"Please," she said aloud over the ringing in both ears. "Don't let any of this prove his guilt."

Minutes passed before she gathered enough courage to begin. Reaching for the notebook on top, she opened it to the first page.

Chapter 16

Gavin found cell phone service on the high point in the road, and pulled over. He cut the engine, thinking it safer to keep his research on Skylar's father to himself for the moment, rather than using the computers at any of the ranger substations strung across the area.

He planned to find out everything he could on Dr. Donovan, and why the man's daughter had confirmed Gavin's fears that her late father's activities could have had something to do with werewolves.

Unfortunately, there were a lot of Donovans with the word *doctor* in front of their names when he searched, and he didn't know Skylar's dad's first name. He focused on their home state and hospital facilities housing mental wards.

There were too damn many of those, too. He'd have to narrow the search field.

He typed *Skylar Donovan* and *Florida* into the browser,

sure her name wasn't a common one, and sat back to study the screen when the information came up. He'd never asked Skylar anything about herself, other than her relationship to her father and that blasted cabin, and he regretted that now.

But—

"Holy hell," he whispered as he began to read what filled the screen.

What struck Skylar about the first few notebooks was the rather disturbing fact that her father had chronicled the lives of several people in the area, here in Colorado, as if they'd been his patients.

The details her father had put on paper dug deep into other peoples' lives. It was possible he acted as doctor here, too, and helped the locals with their problems. Maybe that was a good thing and the data he collected helped him to recall the sessions.

She didn't recognize any of the names. The symptoms seemed to cover a wide range. Where were these people? Who were they? She'd seen only a few cabins and homes scattered here and there along the route to town, and Gavin told her most of those people had been gone for a while. She skimmed pages as well for the word *wolf* without finding it. She read faster and faster, her stomach feeling queasy, as if some part of her knew what had to be here and what was coming.

Dad...she wanted to shout.

Could a man who liked to plant flowers possess the ability to chain any living thing to the walls in a secret room? Could the same man who kissed his kids good-night have hidden a dark, sadistic streak?

Final question, Skylar promised herself.

If she was the most like her father out of all of his daughters and was currently in school studying to be a psychiatrist, like him, wasn't she the perfect candidate to understand her father's potential dark side that might have included a belief in werewolves?

She reached for another notebook, opened it and stared at a line scribbled in red ink:

They don't lose their minds. Not completely.

Skylar rocked back on her knees, a strange sense of premonition streaking through her. She forced herself to read on.

I don't know if there might be more than one of them. But the world cannot be trusted to know of their existence. No one else should be deceived, as I was, when the outcome of that deception remains unclear. She is my responsibility.
I do what I can, but she is angry, and I'm tired.
The goal is safety…at all costs.

Skylar turned the page, found only one other paragraph.

Imprinting remains and the connections seem to change the body at a cellular level. It's as if one soul readjusts its perceptions to include another as part of itself, and each soul leaves a mark on the other. Is this to last forever?

Frantically, Skylar flipped to another page. Was her father writing about the clutches of madness?

Possibly criminals and people already on a downward slide could take advantage of the added strength and inflict real harm on others. Those are the ones the world has to watch for.

There was nothing else. No explanation for those cryptic statements. Skylar tore through several more notebooks and the contents of an unlocked trunk with no luck. There was nothing like the first few paragraphs, which read like a personal confession but didn't actually clarify anything.

More of them?

The world can't know of their existence?

Imprinting?

What the hell did any of that mean, and how had her father been deceived?

Was he writing about an obsession with a patient, or his obsession with…a wolf?

It was too much. And too little. Skylar put her head in her hands and stared at the floor, knowing that her knees wouldn't support her for much longer and that she needed rest almost as much as she needed answers.

Judging by the light from outside filtering into the attic, she could tell that not too many hours had gone by. Returning downstairs meant imagining Gavin with his shirt open, his bareness vivid enough in her memory to be permanently etched there.

She went down the ladder, feeling confused, trying to gather her strength. She looked at the front door, wondering if people could imprint, and bond forever.

Gavin Harris wanted her and wished to keep her safe, but they'd glossed over the dream issue and how he'd managed to step out of those dreams in order to knock at her door.

Chance? Fate? Did precognition actually work through dreams and random passages in notebooks? She'd been afraid to push for an explanation from Gavin, and her father, who would have known about dreams, was no longer able to help.

Placing the gun back on the table, Skylar went to the window to take in the view, picturing Gavin out there after dark, chasing a wolf bent on attacking humans. If she whispered his name, would Gavin hear her and realize that she needed to find out about the wolf as much as he did? Maybe more?

Would that wolf's body show evidence of having been trapped in a cage? Tortured? Were the articles in that building used for some other purpose?

Had her father been guarding something?

She leaned heavily against the wall, thinking.

She could go to the motel, as Gavin suggested, and get far enough from the cabin to allow herself some peace of mind without thoughts of moons or cages. Gavin would know where to find her. Possibly he would come to her later and they...

They could...

"Obsessed," she said aloud to put an end to the thought of what they'd do together. "Obsessed by a dream and a ranger."

In reality, Gavin was doing his job. The forensic people working on that room behind Tom's house would exonerate her father. Surely other people collected silver bullets for a reason that had nothing to do with killing.

Skylar moved back to the table and picked up her phone. She skimmed through her contacts for her father's partner. Dr. Jenna James. She moved a finger toward the button to place the call but didn't touch it. What would she say to her dad's long-time acquaintance, the person he'd worked beside on a daily basis and spent more time with than he spent with his family?

What kind of message would her call for help send to another psychiatrist?

Pressing the phone to her cheek, Skylar could see through the window that the yard seemed completely normal. Flowers still bloomed in raised beds. Walkways were lined with mulch. Her father had taken the time to garden and keep up this cabin.

Actually, she thought now, *maybe I do need help.* Self-diagnosis wasn't an art form. She'd make that call to Dr. James, just not quite yet.

In the meantime, she'd keep the tarnish from her father's legacy by putting the word *werewolf* to rest. She'd hope for Gavin to find the wolf he sought and take care of it tonight, once and for all. She would call for a ride and go back to town in search of the sheriff's office, to see what else they might have found at Tom's place.

She took a deep breath.

Hoisting the phone, and after glancing again at the gun her father had more than likely kept around just for protection and nothing weirder than that, Skylar placed the dreaded call to Florida—to Fairview Hospital, her dad's former place of business—praying that Dr. Jenna James *wouldn't* pick up on her personal line.

"You booked him?" Gavin asked at the station.

"We've brought Tom in for an interview," Jim Delaney, the sheriff on duty, replied with bureaucratic discretion.

"Can I speak with him, Jim?"

"Professionally, or on a personal matter?"

"Personal."

"He's in room two."

"Is he a suspect for placing any of that stuff in the building behind his house?"

"It is his house, Harris."

Gavin held up both hands. "We've all known him for years."

"Yep. He's a fixture around here. So we'll let him go after one more round."

"Okay," Gavin said, relieved. "I just need a couple minutes."

"Be my guest. Professional courtesy, right?"

"I appreciate the leeway here, Jim."

Gavin found room two and nodded to the officer sitting in a chair outside the door. "Permission granted," he said. The officer nodded.

Tom sat behind a table, looking tired. Gavin sat opposite him. "Hey, Tom. Anything I can get you?"

"A free pass out of here would be nice," Tom replied.

"I'm sure you'll be out of here soon. They need to cross all the t's before opening the door."

Tom sat back, his face a mass of weary lines. "What kind of a person would create a place like that?"

"I'm not here to ask you about it. You're probably tired of addressing that issue, so you can relax. I'd like to talk about something else."

"Such as?"

"Skylar Donovan."

Tom's face sobered further.

"You told me you hadn't met her yet when we spoke this morning. Isn't that right? But you didn't introduce yourself when you met her."

"I was quite busy, as were you," Tom said. "Besides, who else could she have been? They have the same eyes, and the same kind of bearing. I recognized her right away."

Gavin nodded. "She looks like her father?"

"Only somewhat similar."

"If you hadn't met Skylar before, who else in the family have you met? I'm asking because I read some things online a few minutes ago that sparked my interest in the family, beyond what might or might not have happened here."

"I don't rightly know any of them," Tom said. "But I did see a woman with the Doc once, though only from a distance."

"Not Skylar?"

Tom shook his head. "Tall. Reddish hair that was long and wavy. A real looker."

"Where did you see them?"

"On the Doc's driveway when I drove past."

"Then it could have been anyone, I suppose. Maybe even someone stopping by or asking directions."

"None of my business," Tom said. "Nice hair, though. I remember thinking that."

"Do you recall when this was?"

"Had to be over a year ago. I drove that road weekly to Sam Martin's place back then, before Sam passed on."

Gavin stood up. "Well, thanks. Rumor has it you'll be out of here shortly. I'll stop by your place tomorrow to make sure you got home okay."

"I'll put the coffee on," Tom said.

Gavin felt a slight sense of accomplishment as he headed back to his Jeep. Of course, that woman Tom had seen with Skylar's father could have been anyone, but it could just as easily have been a doctor from Donovan's hospital in Miami. Fairview Hospital. According to their online photos, a certain Dr. Jenna James had long auburn hair.

From that photo, Jenna James seemed to be young, and quite stunning. Not at all what he would have expected from a colleague of Donovan's. The woman had a long list of medical initials trailing after her name. But from what he'd found in his search, most of the doctors at Fairview kept out of the limelight and the news, often taking a backseat to Skylar's father, whose full name was Dr. David

Donovan. Although Jenna James was a full partner in the directorship of Fairview, her bio was curiously low-key.

He didn't want to think about what the internet had to say about Skylar's personal history. Not yet. He needed time to digest some of what he'd found. For now it was enough to know that, according to some archived newspaper articles, Skylar, just six years old at the time, had lost her mother. She'd inherited a fortune from some other relative at the same time and, along with her sisters, invested a good chunk of that inheritance in the hospital her father had helped build.

And here was the real kicker: Skylar's mother had been a patient at Fairview.

Skylar couldn't have known her mother very well. What did kids remember from when they were six, anyway? Also, he'd found nothing about Greta Donovan's death.

Gavin's list of interesting information about Skylar and her father was growing, but it had to wait. The approach of darkness rustled across his skin like a stiff breeze. His hands kept fisting on their own, fingers curling, forearms cramping. His spine cracked when he turned his head.

It was almost time to find the monster, face it and take that beast down. That was as necessary as returning to Skylar as soon as possible to kiss her, speak with her, take her to bed.

Dreams, she'd said. Dreams and watchers and werewolves.

After today's shock, and after being recently unengaged and orphaned, Skylar would need company and reassurances that things were all right. He planned to give her that. He knew how being alone felt because he hadn't seen his parents since his close call with death in these hills.

He glanced again at the darkening sky. Maybe there

was time for him to see Skylar, touch her, hold her one more time.

Just in case.

In case he wouldn't be returning from his meeting with the giant furred-up devil. In case he never got to kiss Skylar Donovan's sweet, succulent lips again.

His Jeep was parked down the street. Having only one hour at most before sundown was cutting things too short. Still, the depth of his need directed his next step.

"I have to see you, Skylar," he said, jogging to his car.

Chapter 17

Thanking her lucky stars to have reached Jenna's personal voice mail instead of Jenna herself, the message Skylar left was short.

"Skylar here, Dr. James. Trisha said you wanted to see my dad's cabin, and that's fine with me. I'll be in Colorado for a few more days and would like to speak with you, just to connect with someone normal. I have a couple quick questions to ask you. You now have my number. And thanks, both for the condolences and for taking care of the things you did for Dad."

She disconnected and lowered the phone.

Speak with someone normal? Did she really say that to a psychiatrist? One bad thing about the current world of non-face-to-face communication was that messages like the one she'd just left couldn't be taken back.

She paced from window to window and across the wooden boards of the porch. Antsy didn't even begin to describe her current state. She searched the sky for a hint of how much time was left until the sun set, unable to shake the idea that if she were to close her eyes, she'd feel insanity's fiery breath on the back of her neck.

The quiet gave way to a sound that paused her pacing. There was a car on the road. Not just any car.

She ran. For him. There wasn't any way to put on the brakes. Gavin was coming back to her, and she wanted him with every fiber of her being.

He stopped the vehicle when he saw her, and stepped out. She stopped three yards away from where he stood, with her pulse thundering.

"What happened?" he asked soberly.

"You came back," she said.

He closed the door and walked toward her, his body sending out an aura of need similar to hers. Bless him, he hadn't returned for any other reason than his desire to see her. She read that in his face.

She was in his arms before he slowed down. She was breathing in audible rasps as she brought her face close to his.

He spoke first.

"I'm not sure what this is." His whisper was hoarse as his lips skated over hers. "I can't seem to stay away, and I don't even care."

He lifted her up with unsteady hands, and Skylar clung to him by wrapping her legs around his waist and her arms around his neck. When his mouth covered hers, heat flashed through her like lashes of flame.

She kissed him back, returned his sensual attack with one of her own, and he groaned with an earthy satisfaction that sounded like relief.

Skylar wasn't sure how they made it to the cabin. She was tuned to him, ready for him, willing to take him on and take him in. If she had her way, the ground would do just fine for what they were about to do and, as always with this guy, the sooner, the better.

Her ranger had other ideas. Holding her tightly in his arms, he put a boot to the half-open door and walked through. That was as far as they got. She was on the floor, on her back, with Gavin's long length covering her and his mouth never leaving hers.

He kissed her greedily, deeply, each move of his mouth a ravenous feasting. Skylar tore at his belt and pants. He kicked off his shoes and helped her remove his clothes, then hers, in the dim, waning light. This time, he allowed her full access to his lean sculpted body, scars and all, because he was as ready as she was for this union.

An inch of space was too much distance between them. Their bare bodies slammed together as if they were two parts of a whole needing to be reunited.

They seemed to be enacting a kind of sensuous war, their actions falling somewhere between an all-out sexfest and hungrily making love. There was no clear-cut delineation of the unevenness of the relationship. Even the edges of the room blurred as Gavin pressed her arms above her head and settled himself between her naked, pulsing thighs.

Then he was inside her with a slick, heated slide that drove a pleasurable groan from her throat. Buried deep inside her, he paused, shuddered and closed his blue eyes.

But he didn't hesitate for long. Before her next breath, he rallied with a quick withdrawal followed by a second perfect thrust of his hips. Straight and true, that plunge touched her innermost need, tickled her core and spawned shuddering intense physical longings for him that Skylar could barely contain.

If she'd thought they had done it all in that motel room the night before, she'd been wrong. This level of rugged intimacy was new, different and meaningful. This was something else altogether.

Gavin held her in that place where white-hot sensations and riotous emotions met in a kaleidoscope of light and feeling. A place where there wasn't enough air in the world to breathe in and there would never be enough time to keep this up.

Another thrust of his hips and a second hesitation forced from Skylar an outward cry of startled emotion.

Then he moved just once more.

And that was all she needed.

Feelings burst open, ran riot, exploded inside her. She came with a dizzying, room-spinning climax that went on and on until Skylar clawed at her lover with her hands and nipped at him with fierce teeth. But he didn't register any of the damage she inflicted. Her little attacks didn't seem to bother Gavin Harris at all. He was there with her and at the same time curiously absent, Skylar realized when the world eventually stopped revolving.

He shook, holding off his own satisfaction, and the effort took all of his concentration. One giant quake rolled through him after another. Withholding this last bit of himself seemed important to him, as if it were a task to be mastered.

All the while, his vibrant blue eyes stared into hers.

"No," she protested, breathless, hardly able to speak at all and seeing in his expression a hint that he might leave her now. "Don't go. You don't have to. Not tonight."

His sad smile reminded her that she'd only heard him laugh one time, and she longed to hear that laughter now. His muscles were tense, his voice strained. "You have no idea how much I want to stay."

"You're with me right now."

His sadness was devastatingly potent. "I have to go. I'm late already and feel the night closing in."

"But you'll come back," she said hopefully.

The fact that he didn't reply left her anxious.

"You don't have to go," Skylar insisted.

"I do. Please understand that I have to."

"Why? Wolves only come out at night? Is that what you mean? If you have to find one, this is the time?"

"Yes. That's what I mean. The one I seek will be out there."

"To hell with that," Skylar argued. "Being together like this is important to me. You'll never know how much. Tell me I'm not the only one who believes there's something to this. To us."

"You're not the only one. Hell, Skylar. But I've told you. I've warned you about me, and that I also have needs that lie beyond this moment."

"You've told me no such thing, other than to mention revenge against an animal that hurt you and might also have hurt my father."

He touched her forehead with a warm finger and tucked a strand of hair behind her ear—gentle actions, tender moments before a dreaded separation that made the idea of that separation a whole lot worse.

"Then I'm coming with you," she said.

"I can't allow that."

"If there's a wolf or a pack out there, surely other rangers can help us find it," she pressed.

"Us? No. You need to go into town where it's safe."

She stared back at him. "You truly believe that same nasty wolf is still here, and near the cabin, don't you? That's the big danger you perceive for others and for me. Not some madman, but a damn wolf."

"A man-hater," he corrected, whispering in a way that

made Skylar's scalp prickle. "And as dangerous as they come."

He slid off her and braced himself on his elbows without looking away or losing eye contact.

"You're either brave or stupid to go out there if something you consider to be that lethal is on the loose." She spoke her mind without using a filter. "Especially tonight, under a full moon, when everyone is restless."

Skylar felt him stir, and regretted the turn in the conversation. There had hardly been a time when the idea of the wolf hadn't been in the room with her in this cabin, either openly or in hiding.

"Then you'd stop me from taking my best shot at finding it?" Gavin asked.

"I…"

Could she say what she was thinking? Skylar wondered. Or were secrets to remain secrets?

"I don't want anything to happen to you."

His eyes softened, adding fine creases underneath. Seeing that softness tugged at her heart.

"The best way to help me is for you to remain safe, so that I don't have to worry about you. Can you do that, Skylar? Will you get to safety?"

"I said I would."

"You didn't mean it."

She wondered how he knew that.

"So," he began, using her words to further his argument, "does arguing about this make you brave, or stupid?"

She answered that question honestly and the best way she could. "It makes me determined."

"No," he corrected. "I'm determined and have some of the skills to back that up. You are a liability, like…"

He didn't say the rest of what he was thinking, so she did.

"Like my father was, or might have been, being a city man and out of his element here?"

He sighed heavily. "Yes, if he actually was chasing wolves in these mountains."

"How do we find out what my father did or didn't do? What he knew, or believed?"

"We know that he must not have thought what he was doing that last evening was dangerous, otherwise his gun would have been found in his hand, not here in this cabin."

Skylar found the flaw in that reasoning, though it didn't help much.

If her father was delusional and if werewolves had been his target and his reason for being in Colorado, he wouldn't have believed he needed those silver bullets the day he died because ten days ago the moon hadn't been full. No full moon meant no werewolves, supposedly...if Hollywood got that right.

The horrible, nonsensical element to all this overthinking suddenly left her feeling sick. She'd come full circle back to werewolves.

"My father fell, and there doesn't have to be anything sinister about that tragedy other than how things ended up," she said, testing out her voice and trying to believe that theory.

"Did you think there was something sinister going on?" Gavin asked.

After glancing at the window, she said helplessly, "Yes. But that's my problem."

Yet, she thought, if there was no magic key in the word *werewolf*, why had Gavin brought it up behind Tom's shed? Was he just trying to gauge her mental state?

Wait just a damn minute.

Was there something in the way he was looking at her?

Shit. If he wanted to know about her mental state, did that mean he knew something about her mother?

Could he possibly know anything about that?

If he did, would Gavin be wondering if the whole family might be off its rocker? Like the jokes, did he believe that psychiatrists took up the profession because of their own numerous issues?

Damn it, hadn't she, for the past few days, wondered that same thing about her father and herself?

What else did he know?

Had he found out that she studied about psychiatry in a school near Miami? That she'd taken time off to get married, and more time to come here to finish her father's ties to Colorado?

"Skylar?"

She heard her name, and a sound beyond it from somewhere outside. Familiar heat began to battle the onset of chills. Her body convulsed, automatically responding to the provocative quality in Gavin's tone.

Something inside her shifted uncomfortably, in need of more heat.

"Skylar," Gavin repeated with concern.

Through a flutter of her eyelashes, Skylar saw again in fine detail the man so close to her. The wide shoulders above a broad muscular chest. The thick torso, narrow waist and hips. The dark hair, worn long and those brilliant light blue eyes. Every detail about Gavin Harris mirrored what she'd imagined her dream lover would be.

Yet Gavin was only a ranger. A man, not a werewolf.

There were no such things as werewolves.

Holding up a hand, she crawled out from beneath her lover, embarrassed, and no longer trusting her own conclusions because the merging of her dreams and reality continued to mess things up.

There were no werewolves; therefore, either someone had pushed her father over that cliff, or no one had, and his fall was an accident, as officially stated. She would have to accept that and also accept that she'd gone to bed with a stranger because of a dream.

On her knees beside Gavin, she asked with a stern authority, "Do you know about my mother?"

It pained him to answer. She saw that. He didn't really know the nuances of what she was asking, or why, but his answer was important to her.

"Do you know about my family's trouble?" she pressed, looking anywhere but in Gavin's luminous eyes.

"About your mother's commitment, yes," he replied. "I know about that."

Quickly chilling again, Skylar got to her feet and reached for her clothes before turning for the door.

Gavin was beside her. "Skylar, what the hell just happened?"

"I'm going to town like you wanted, if I can use your car."

She wouldn't look at him now, couldn't allow herself to see either the hurt she might be causing or the relief that might show on that face. This man might like to bed her, but he'd gone too far by investigating her family's personal history behind her back.

Gavin Harris, the very definition of eye candy and so unbelievably talented in the sack, might believe that mental illness was not only contagious, but that her father had actually tortured some poor animal in that shed behind Tom Jeevers's house.

And if he believed that, he wasn't worth a damn.

While she…with dreams of moonlight and mountains and the erotic allure of Otherness…

Well…

It came as no surprise that she was a goddamn fool.

When she glanced back at the man holding on to her arm, he looked as perplexed as she felt.

"It's okay." She spoke as she dressed. "It's getting dark. Go. Do your thing. You'll know where to find me."

He let her go because he had no right to keep her back. Besides, what more was there to say when he knew about her mother?

Skylar got to the Jeep quickly and climbed in. When she looked up again, Gavin was nowhere in sight. The gorgeous bastard hadn't even blown her a kiss.

By the time she reached for the keys in the ignition, darkness cloaked the yard. Stars were already starting to appear since there were no clouds.

Her energy was gone, and her queasiness had returned. Swallowing was difficult, her breathing forced. She couldn't stand the idea of getting through another night with her disturbed thoughts, not after veering so far off track. The truth was that she didn't belong here and was sorry she had volunteered to come.

She started the engine, threw the gear shift into Reverse and stepped on the gas. Beyond the dirt driveway, she gunned the car around a sharp bend in the road.

There it was. *That damn moon.* Shining as if it had every right to be the darkly mysterious thing some people presumed it to be. Light streamed across the tree tops, silvery and almost magical, though it only served to highlight a new emptiness inside her.

She felt like closing her eyes to regroup. She could have used a few deep breaths and more alcohol. *Something. Anything.*

She just couldn't go on.

Pulling the Jeep to the side of the road, she cut the engine and sat back. Listening to the quiet beyond the open window, she inhaled air as if she were oxygen starved.

Then she began to pound on the steering wheel with both hands, continuing the tantrum until her hands were sore and throbbing. Giving in to the emotional turmoil eating away at her insides, she slumped forward with her head in her hands.

Chapter 18

It wasn't okay. Nothing was all right, and that was putting things mildly. Whatever Skylar might do next was out of Gavin's hands, yet he hoped her word meant something.

Close one.

Too close.

He now fought to hold on to the human in him. With Skylar tripping his emotional switches, he felt the moon's presence through the roof. That moon called to him right now. *It's time*, the silver seducer whispered. *Don't fight.*

He stood in the front room of the cabin, ignoring that invitation and listening to the sound of the car taking Skylar from him in the nick of time. His blood thickened in his veins. Though moonlight couldn't reach him here, his wolf pounded at him from the inside, seconds away from a major meltdown and about to be released one notch at a time.

Volts of supernatural electricity charged through him, causing a claw to spring from the tip of the middle finger of his right hand. It was, he thought, appropriate, and a stiff universal gesture to the whole ordeal. More claws followed until all ten fingernails had been replaced, and his hands could now be considered lethal.

Nowhere to hide.

Angry at the way he'd let Skylar go, he swiped the razor-sharp claws across the legs of his pants, cutting through the cloth and into the meat of his right thigh. Pain was necessary to his thought process. The scent of the blood trickling from his wound helped to replace Skylar's seductive perfume.

It's time.

Apprehension twitched his shoulder blades. His mouth felt dry. The wolf's perceptions came flooding in on an adrenaline-laced tide to prepare him for action.

He wanted to call Skylar back. Hold her. Comfort her. Any fool could see that's what she needed. But the moon could no longer be ignored. His body was about to meld man and predator, blurring the lines of both, and there was nothing he could do about it.

He stepped onto the porch with a last look behind. Vaulting over the steps, he leaped to the ground, doubling over as the wolf clawed its way up his windpipe and his flesh began to split.

Pain.

An all-too familiar agony.

Christ, he hated this part.

Five seconds passed, then eight, until more muscles got with the program, stretching, rounding as they molded into larger shapes. His legs quickly joined in, filling up the extra space in his pants while neck vertebrae separated with a sound like bombs going off.

His ribs cracked apart as they expanded, making his heartbeat soar in an effort to keep up. The scars on his chest burned, each one brutally painful, barely tolerable. He covered them with both hands to press back the sting, trying hard not to drop to one knee.

But he withstood this. He had to. It was always the same checklist, in the same order: hands, arms, shoulders, hips, legs, back and torso. His face came last, its delicate bones unhinging before shifting its angles to rearrange into an alternate pattern without so many recognizably human features.

As a final insult, a light dusting of hair the consistency of fine fur sprang from his skin. Not thick hair, or enough of it to cover him completely, yet enough to leave him slightly shaggier and a little bit like some kind of throwback to a darker age.

He growled and coughed. Straightening at last, Gavin gave a loud feral roar. With one more glance to the driveway and the road beyond it, he took off toward the hillside where one creature preferred to rule as if it were the king of beasts and could do whatever the hell it pleased.

And that, he confirmed with a deep, guttural growl, just wasn't acceptable.

Skylar told herself that she was stronger than this and shouldn't condone her jumbled mental state for one second longer.

She wasn't really invested in any kind of relationship with Gavin Harris after just two strange days. On the contrary, he'd warned her not to expect a relationship with him at all. A guy couldn't be expected to be more honest than that, except when it wasn't the truth.

Gavin had lied about this, of course. Every look, move, kiss told her he wanted more.

The motel in town seemed like a terrible place to hide out until morning. At the cabin there were several more things to go through, though the thought of doing so didn't seem as exciting as before.

As for Gavin researching her family...truly, she hadn't seen that coming. The fact that she knew nothing about Gavin seemed much too one-sided now and was a problem she'd have to solve. At least this time, during her hasty exit, she'd remembered to scoop up her cell phone. Finding service was another matter, though, and possibly meant driving until she found reception or heading for the hilltop above the main road where service wasn't blocked by the mountain.

Who would she call?

Trisha would come here to help get the cabin packed up if she asked. Her big sister's presence would also keep Skylar grounded and keep her addiction to Gavin under control, if that's what needed to be done.

An addiction. Yes, that's what this is like.

Every cell in her body urged her to go back to the cabin and follow him or try to pick up his trail.

Some part of her brain refused to be turned away from thoughts about those damn wolves and how her father had ended up.

But Trish was in Miami and hours away when help was needed now and, really, was already overdue.

Though the light on the phone beamed when she tugged it from her pocket, it was a false bit of hope. There were no service bars.

"Damn it."

Skylar reached for the keys dangling from the ignition— Gavin's keys—wondering what kind of man chased away a woman he was so obviously interested in by providing her with the means for escape. No branch of law enforcement she knew of allowed civilians to borrow their vehicles, yet she'd been behind this wheel twice. She understood about his work, and that he had an agenda, but...

She turned her head sharply, senses snapping to alert.

A glance in the rearview mirror showed no cars coming, yet she was sure something passed behind the Jeep in a blur of black-on-black.

Gavin felt exceptionally fleet, though his muscle mass rippled beneath the density of its new heft. This dangerous physical reprogramming left him feeling much the same inside, with different shadings of Gavin Harris on the outside, and a whole new love-hate relationship with his body.

Growls bubbled up from deep inside him with each stride. Though he couldn't speak without human vocal chords, the fierceness of the rumbling sounds he made got his point across just fine. He was angrier than ever and resolute in his determination to see this task through.

Where are you, beast?

Can you hear me?

The moon over his head followed him through the trees with the rapt intensity of a searchlight. If he stopped too long in a place hidden from that icy silver light, he'd shift again in reverse, so he was careful to keep to the open portion of path.

Skylar...

My lover...

He swore. It was best not to think of her. He couldn't be sure about completing this dangerous objective if he kept her in the forefront of his mind.

But some weird fluke of nature allowed him to think he could hear her thoughts, and if she were to call to him again, the way she had the night before, he feared what he might do.

You really shouldn't have left me, she'd said, and he had returned to her, to that motel, as though compelled to do so.

He felt the fear she refused to show. Her disjointed thoughts were increasingly difficult to separate from his. He couldn't get her scent out of his lungs, her taste out of his mouth. One small distraction, like picturing her naked, and he might miss something crucial out here, ending things too quickly in the monster's favor.

He was smart enough to realize that his life had taken a turn for the better the minute he'd laid eyes on Skylar Donovan. After cursing himself and his situation for two long years, barely hanging on to see this task through, all it took for his heart to lighten was seeing her on that porch.

Suddenly a reason to continue living beyond his search for the monster presented itself. There was a reason to live, to protect and to love while he could, in any way he could.

Meeting Skylar had done that.

His senses snapped back to the path. The night smelled like danger and carried an unsettling vibe. Things were too quiet.

Skirting a mound of moss-covered granite, Gavin stopped, curtailing a growl. The monster he sought was here, all right, somewhere close by.

He roared his approval and stood his ground, waiting for the inevitable, daring the creature to find him. But it didn't appear. Its scent grew stronger but then quickly began to fade. Though that abomination's presence clung to Gavin's skin like a second coat of fur, it obviously had other ideas about where to focus its attention.

Gavin jerked his head to the path behind him, fear welling up.

No. Not that.

Not her.

Don't you dare go after Skylar!

He ran, following the scent of wet fur, his heart exploding in his chest, but he didn't get far before his senses screamed for him to stop.

He was hit from behind, hard, and flew sideways. His left shoulder smashed painfully into a tree, but he rebounded quickly and spun around. Ramming was this sucker's MO…

He saw nothing. Not even a leaf moved.

Damn you, beast.

He ventured a step, stood still and upright, and was hurled forward by an unseen force so strong, moving so fast, he didn't even see a hint of it coming.

But he knew what this was. He'd been in this same situation before.

His nerves fired up. His chest hurt like hell from the pounding inside it. His head swam with fear and remembered glimpses of a semi-invisible opponent. He didn't like this game. Didn't appreciate anything about it, or how much stronger the beast was. But he'd be damned if that beast would be allowed to go anywhere near Skylar.

Gavin lunged forward, saw a shadow streak through the brush and gathered himself. As the shadow passed to his left, he leaped again, catching the moving bit of darkness squarely, and hearing its eerie, echoing howl of anger.

The monster turned, lashed out with a lethally clawed, five-fingered paw. Gavin ducked, but felt the claws part his hair above his right ear. Whirling around, he struck at the beast with both hands, his own anger giving him the strength necessary to tag a moving target.

The beast rallied, swiveled and roared. Using its swinging arm as a bat, it connected with Gavin's stomach, momentarily doubling him over.

But not for long.

Gavin was up on his feet, angry, ready for the next round. Yet all was again silent around him, and there was no monster. It was as if he'd made the whole thing up.

Chapter 19

"Miss Donovan?"

The voice wasn't familiar and, therefore, didn't register as Skylar slammed herself back against the seat wondering what the shadow was.

"It's Tom. Tom Jeevers," the man approaching the window said. "Are you all right? You've been sitting here long enough for me to reach you from the fire access road."

Skylar turned her head, attempting to regulate her breathing. It was only a man, not a people-hating, flesh-eating wolf in the rearview mirror. "Tom?"

"Is there something wrong with the Jeep?" he asked, looking past her. "Where's Harris?"

Feeling silly for imagining she'd seen something, Skylar rallied. "He's in the hills, searching for a wolf."

Tom nodded his gray-haired head. "Sent you to town, did he?"

"Yes."

"And you're heading that way now?"

"I stopped to listen to the night."

"It's a fine time for that," Tom agreed. "Best time to get a walk in, too. With no cars on the road to bother me, I can think, take my sweet time and breathe. After today, I needed a breather. I don't suppose that you, being from a busy place like Miami, would understand that?"

"I do understand. The quiet takes some getting used to, though," Skylar admitted. "I tend to want to fill it with something, like most city people do."

Tom placed both hands on the door. "Well, I won't keep you."

"Tom?"

He waited.

"Did they find anything today?"

She didn't have to explain what she meant. He said, "Not yet. Not that I know of. I'm just glad they didn't keep me in town. I'm not one for being cooped up after all these years out here."

"I'm sorry." She said this sincerely. "I'm sorry my father had anything to do with that shed."

He nodded and started to turn. Skylar held him up again. "Gavin thinks the wolf out here is dangerous. You will be careful?"

"Oh, don't worry about that. No self-respecting alpha would bother with an old bag of bones like me, I'll bet. I hope Harris catches it, if he's so inclined, though I like to see animals run free, doing what they're meant to do."

"This one hurt him," Skylar said. "I think his search is personal."

"Really? I hadn't heard that." Tom sounded earnest.

"Well, it's none of my business," she said. "So I'll be careful on this road if you will."

Tom stepped back as she got the car running and

shifted into gear. He stayed by the side of the road until she pulled out.

Cruising down the road, Skylar watched in the mirror as darkness quickly enveloped Tom Jeevers. She sincerely hoped he was right about that wolf not bothering an old man who, though spry enough for someone in his eighties, probably couldn't outrun a jackrabbit for half a city block.

She drove slowly, deciding how far she'd keep up the pretense of running away before turning back. It wasn't just stubbornness that formed her decision to ignore Gavin's warnings, but a pressurized feeling of absolute necessity. Something was going on out here, and her dad's cabin was part of that mystery.

She drove around one more bend in the curvy two-lane road before jamming on the brakes and white-knuckling the wheel, robbed of yet another crucial breath.

She was not mistaken this time. Something moving very fast had crossed the road, nearly colliding with the Jeep and forcing her to a standstill with her heart again racing.

Deer? Mountain lion? There and gone in a flash?

Seeing no hint of any animal, Skylar rolled up the window and eased the car forward, steering to the right far enough to find room for a U-turn.

She'd go back and pick up Tom, take him home. Her second brief sighting of that animal left her hyped, wary and aware that Tom might not have been the blur she'd seen a few minutes ago. More than one potentially dangerous creature might be on the prowl tonight.

"Gavin," she said aloud, heading back the way she'd come. "Be careful."

The Jeep crawled forward as she rounded the bend. But though she searched, Tom Jeevers was nowhere in sight. Then again, he probably knew these hills well enough to find an alternate trail.

The cabin, on the other hand, was easy to find in the dark. When she climbed out of the car in her dad's driveway, she paused to consider why all the lights in the cabin were blazing.

"How did I know you'd return?" Gavin said from beneath the porch overhang, with a sharp eye on the woman who was the second reason his body battled him mercilessly from the inside out.

"Probably because you would have done the same thing," Skylar replied.

"You're messing with me, Skylar, and putting yourself at risk."

"I have a right to do so, and didn't expect you to be here."

"Which would have made this worse since you'd have been here alone."

"I wouldn't have been here at all," she argued. "I was planning to go after you."

Gavin didn't dare rub his forehead, or lift a hand. The claws pushing against his fingers stung like a son of a bitch. Despite the cover of the porch, the moon still ruled him, and any respite was temporary.

The only other time he had repeatedly shifted back and forth from one shape to another on the same night was right after the attack that had left him hurting.

It was the wolf's turn, and they both knew it.

"It sounds crazy," Skylar said, coming no closer to him than the base of the steps. "And I can't explain it to you or even to myself in a way that makes sense. I have to be here, not in town. I have to help you find whatever is out there."

She waved a hand at the hillside. "It's as though my entire existence depends on this."

"Depends on what, exactly?" Gavin asked.

"I don't know. It's a feeling. A gut feeling that something isn't right, and that I can find out what that is if I try."

"And you think you'll find an answer on the mountain tonight?"

"Yes."

Gavin let a beat of silence pass while he studied her.

"You'll do no such thing," he admonished gruffly, pushing off the wall and fisting his aching hands. His chest was throbbing. Facial muscles tingled wickedly as if they, too, might betray him, shift out of order if necessary, if he didn't get with the program and stay there.

"Help me do this," Skylar said. "Let me go with you."

"I can't allow that."

"Why not?"

"I'm responsible for what could happen to you."

"It's a wolf, Gavin, and I have a flashlight and a gun if you think those things would allow us to find the sucker."

Gavin's throat seized, warning him that he had precious little time to debate this with Skylar and not that many words left. The fact remained that he couldn't lead her, escort her or follow Skylar up the blasted hill. He couldn't take two steps off this porch with her watching.

"Please listen," he began. He had nowhere to go now except to a very bad place. If Skylar started for that path, he'd have no choice but to reveal himself to her. He was out of options and would protect her with his life, no matter what shape he was in. Hell, she might faint if she saw him, and that would be that.

No, he amended right after the thought. Skylar wouldn't faint. She had probably never given in to a weakness like that. *Not you, my fierce lover.*

"I can't take you up there, Skylar." He willed her to accept what he was saying and back down, just this once.

"Then you won't go, either?" she countered.

"It's my search, my fight. Not yours."

Zeroing in on something in his tone, she took a step forward.

"I've read about your family," he said, hoping to deter her from approaching by using the personal information he'd discovered earlier that day. Hoping she would storm off again and let him be.

"I know you've had your share of issues, Skylar, and that your mother wasn't the only Donovan to spend time at Fairview."

He watched her hands and arms go rigid, and he hated hurting her. Skylar's pretty face was set and surrounded by clouds of shiny golden wheat-colored hair that he wanted to run through his fingers. Her lips were bloodless.

"I know you were there also," he continued, coughing to get that out, hanging on to his human shape with the sheerest thread of willpower. Between the moonlight and the woman across from him, his emotions were in upheaval. "And I know you're studying to be a psychiatrist like your father."

"After spending time in the loony-bin to see how the other half live, you mean?" she said.

"How long was it, Skylar? How long were you there, in that Fairview place?" He eased back on the gruffness with that question, and it cost him. Spasms cramped up his throat.

"Didn't your internet search divulge that information?" she challenged.

"I didn't pursue an answer. I thought…"

"One week." Her face was expressionless. "I was there for a week when I was six years old because I wanted to see my mother and wouldn't take no for an answer."

So, your stubbornness isn't anything new, he thought.

"What did you do?" Gavin took an involuntary step

toward her, absorbing the pain of his burning thighs and shins that came with his new proximity to the open sky.

"I broke in," she said in an emotionless tone. "Sneaked in, actually, right under their noses, when visiting my dad. Then I tried to let her out."

His brow furrowed as he pictured that. "You tried to get your mother out of the hospital?"

"Yes."

"When you were only six?"

She didn't bother to answer that question, realizing it was a rhetorical outburst on his part.

"Wouldn't that be impossible?" he asked, battling to speak through the tightness in his throat. "And why would you be able to stay there at all? Why would they allow you to stay?"

"They couldn't stop me, Gavin. They couldn't get me out, once I'd gotten in. *She* kept me. Somehow my mother sensed I was near and she fought at the right time to get out of her room. When she found me, she kept me with her, threatening to hurt me if anyone came close with the intention of taking me away."

"Are you saying that no one managed to help you get away from her?"

"After the first round of coaxing and threats and drugged darts, they didn't even try. By then, I suppose she'd built up a tolerance to the drugs. Not wanting to see harm come to me if they pushed too hard, the staff waited out the standoff."

Gavin ran a hand through his hair, fighting off shivers severe enough to visibly move muscle. The moon called but he couldn't respond. Not yet.

"No one would leave a little girl in a situation like that," he said. "They could have shot her with something. Helped you."

She smiled wanly. "I thought of that long afterward. But I believe it became a test. She behaved with me there, as long as they left us alone. I was a calming factor that made her more or less amenable to her daily regimen, such as it was."

"How did you escape?" Gavin's forward momentum took him to the top of the steps.

"She finally let me go."

"And then what?"

"She died."

"Did they...?"

"I don't know if they accidentally had a hand in that."

Gavin closed his eyes, unwilling to imagine the story that Skylar had just told. Or that her father had allowed it.

"I'm so sorry." He shook his head.

"I'm not sorry. It was my goal, and I achieved it. My sisters never saw her there, never knew her. They couldn't even conjure up her face."

"And you can?"

"Yes. I can. I remember her eyes."

His voice no longer sounded anything like him, yet Gavin went on talking. "What about your father and the part he played in this unusual scenario?"

Though the rigidity of Skylar's lean frame hadn't relaxed, she answered him. "I don't remember much about his actions, and I can hardly picture him there. My mother didn't want him near us. He and I never spoke about it afterward, and went on as though my time at Fairview never happened. But I do realize that it had to have been his decision to allow me to stay as long as I did. That for my own safety and hers, he temporarily caved to my mother's threats."

"You don't hold that against him?" Gavin couldn't help but ask.

"Not for one day."

This woman knew nothing of revenge or retribution, then, and Gavin envied her that innocence. She was here to pack her father's things and to find out why he died, without any thought to that other time in her life.

"That was personal information, and not in the news," she said. "How did you access it?"

"I'm tied in to a few special archives."

She fell quiet.

He had started to sweat, the result of his ongoing fight with the moon.

"Skylar, what was wrong with your mother?"

The slow, sad smile that lifted her pale lips as she answered him gave nothing of her feelings away.

"I once heard my father describe her condition as a form of lunacy, but of course that didn't really explain anything. Right after she released me, Dad said my mother's sick mind made her believe she was a…" She swallowed and finished the statement. "A wolf."

The word, and the way she said it, made Gavin bow his head in disgust. Then he wondered if he might be imagining this conversation because out of all the women in the world he could have been attracted to, it turned out to be the daughter of a woman who thought she was a damn werewolf.

Lunacy. Christ! That was an old term applied to sick people who, it was believed, were strangely affected by the moon and in very specific ways. He had looked that term up, as well as all the others he could find relating to the effects of the moon on human beings.

"That's why you thought your father might be chasing wolves," he proposed, looking closely at Skylar. "To conduct more experiments?"

"If that was his plan, he never mentioned it to me or to

any of my sisters. The sad fact is that none of us have been close to him for some time. He distanced himself from his family years ago, preferring to spend time at the hospital and here, alone."

"What about that partner you mentioned? The one who identified him after the accident?" he pressed. "Was that person at Fairview when you were?"

She shook her head.

His hands were rising as if he'd reach for her despite his own pressing problem. *Screw the wolf. To hell with the moon.* He hurt for Skylar. He ached for what had happened to her and for what she'd been through. Yet she seemed just as courageous now as she must have been as that six-year-old kid.

He couldn't touch her, didn't dare get closer to her. Skylar didn't need to experience another inexplicable example of madness from someone close.

"It's not just a wolf out there," he said before thinking about the effect of his statement, or how it might sound to the woman he craved more than the moonlight.

She continued to stare back at him.

Tired of having her call ignored, the moon sent a beam of brilliant light that reached the tips of his boots. His toes tingled, and his shoulders rolled on their own, without any conscious thought on his part to ease the icy needles stabbing him between his shoulder blades.

Have to go. He had to get off this porch and away from Skylar. He was no good for her. She had escaped from that past only to hook up with another goddamn lunatic. How was that for irony?

Gathering himself, Gavin jumped forward, knocking Skylar toward the railing, bending over her and hearing her breath whoosh out. With his face inches from hers and the rest of him already starting to change, he whispered, "Stay here. I'm begging you."

In a single fluid bound, he turned and bolted for the cover of the trees.

Chapter 20

Skylar pushed off the railing and stood up, convincing herself that it didn't matter if Gavin knew about her childhood and the things she'd never told anyone about her mother.

If a lover with the potential for madness in her genes didn't turn him on, well, she'd get over it, and get over him.

She would have thought more of Gavin Harris than that, though…and also that after confessing to him that she never took no for an answer, he'd believe that she would stay away from that hillside tonight.

There was a mystery to be unraveled in these hills, its allure strong enough for her to discount the danger. Getting out there, though, was hard. She felt ill. Her body seemed heavy. Her stomach growled again, protesting the lack of food.

Groping for the wall, she stood up straighter. Still winded from the surprise of Gavin's closeness, she managed to haul herself up the first step, and then she turned to look at the path leading into the trees.

Gavin must have gone that way.

Only an idiot wouldn't get that he didn't want her to follow.

Stay here. I'm begging you, he'd said.

Yet it seemed to her that he was too adamant about keeping her away from that path, and that he might be hiding something, rather than just wanting to keep her safe.

What didn't he want her to see?

Steadied by a couple deep breaths, Skylar climbed the rest of the steps to the front door and looked inside. The gun was on the table where she'd left it. Going in, she picked it up and retraced her steps to the porch.

"Am I certifiable to believe that if I find that wolf, I'll know what Dad was after and what went down?"

Who will answer that question if I can't?

Steeling herself, and with the gun in her hand, Skylar jogged toward the path, hampered by what felt like a two-ton weight on her shoulders and a slight drag in her suddenly aching left leg.

Gavin let his anger rip through a series of growls as his second transformation of the night happened in record time. The shift completed as he hurled himself up the steep, tree-clad slope.

Only a slight hesitation at having to leave Skylar behind marred his stride.

Small nocturnal animals darted out of his way, recognizing the threat. Night birds protested from the tree tops. Somewhere to his right a pair of owls hooted. All this activity showed that the beast he sought wasn't yet in this area, though it wouldn't have gone far. This was its territory, just as it was Gavin's. They both seemed to return sooner or later to the familiarity of home ground.

He reached the granite outcrop without becoming short

of breath, and he scrambled to the top of the old stone pile.
From there he looked out over the trees below, thinking he
saw lights winking near the base of the mountain.

He could not afford to concentrate on those lights.

On top of his granite perch, he roared, waited, dropped
to a crouch. No responding roar came.

The monster had not found its way to Skylar's cabin,
as he'd feared, though Skylar wasn't safe from its reach.

Skylar.

His heart thudded in response to thinking her name.

*Look what obstacles you have risen above to become
the woman you are today. But I can't help you find what
you seek. Look at me. You crave the love of a dark-haired
man, not what I have become.*

A sudden sound brought him to attention. It wasn't close,
but the birds had stopped chirping.

He leaped from the rock, landed in a crouch with a hand
in the dirt and his head lifted.

About time you showed up, beast, he thought, rising
slowly.

Skylar stumbled again, not sure what was wrong with
her legs. This time she went down, falling to her knees,
tripped up by a rock or something else unseen. Her hands
and knees stung when they hit the hard ground.

She stayed there a moment, cursing her clumsiness and
looking around. The path beside her was lit from above by
a potent shaft of moonlight resembling a searchlight. The
ground was visible in front of her for five or six feet, but as
she breathed in the smell of her surroundings, that ground
began to undulate in waves similar to a desert mirage.

Before she could get up, a wave of vertigo hit her. The
trees and everything else nearby began to spin as if caught

in a cyclone, though not one single leaf fell. Uttering an oath, Skylar didn't make it to her feet.

Hers weren't the only sounds, she realized, taking those night noises as a sign that no evil predators roamed nearby waiting to chew off one of her limbs. There was no other choice but to wait the dizziness out.

The gun was no longer in her hand. She must have dropped it when she fell, and the weapon was difficult to see in the dark. Also, her left foot was bare. She'd lost a shoe, and wouldn't get very far without it.

Don't panic. This will pass.

Problem was, the dizziness didn't fade. The vertigo stubbornly messed with her equilibrium, and made her stomach tighten.

"Damn."

She muttered another stream of choice four-letter oaths that went from bad to worse as a sudden piercing pain between her shoulder blades nearly stretched her flat out in the dirt. Closing her eyes made the world turn faster and tied her stomach into knots. Her forehead dampened from the strain of maintaining her composure as more pain seared behind her eyes.

Her heart beat fast from the shock of the fall and her inability to get up. The thump of her pulse filled her head and her chest, sounding like the drum section in a large brass band.

Soon other body parts caught the beat, drumming, hammering loudly. Her guts heaved up in protest. Her muscles quivered.

Uncontrolled body twitches turned into quakes. Quakes became shudders strong enough to tip her sideways. Having nothing to hang on to, she dug her fingers into the dirt.

She wasn't sure if any illness could strike this fast and this hard without any kind of warning. But the ridiculous dizziness seemed as though it was going to hang on and overtake her here, alone, on the mountain. Her body was betraying her big-time, and just when she needed to get on with her search.

Though impossible to fathom, the pain from her shoulders spread to her back and arms. Nerve fibers caught fire. She couldn't lift her head.

Her hands felt oddly tight and strangely hot. She pulled them from the ground and shook her head in denial. She was hallucinating. Her fingernails weren't really growing and sharpening into points.

Those aren't my hands.

Those hands had claws.

She had to shut her eyes as the fire of fever flashed through her and her stomach again turned over.

What's happening?

She heard a voice, a deep male voice, speaking from somewhere close by as if addressing her silent question.

"Give in," he instructed, his voice a lifeline in a turbulent sea of pain. "Stay calm. As calm as possible. Fighting increases the pain and slows down the process."

Process? What process?

Heaven help me!

"Skylar. Trust me," the familiar velvety voice continued. "And may the devil take me now if I've done this to you."

Fighting to stay conscious, Skylar touched her face, smelled blood, felt something warm trickle down her cheek. But this wasn't real, she told herself over and over. It was only part of some new dream.

Someone moved beside her, casting a shadow on the ground. Beyond the scent of blood, she recognized this new scent. *Gavin.* Not a stranger. Gavin had found her, and would help.

Strong arms covered her as her ranger's body curled

around her body from behind. He tried to lift her up, but his tight hold increased the level of her pain.

She screamed in agony, feeling as if she were being turned inside out. Sizzling blue-white bolts of internal lightning fried her nerve endings.

Beside her, Gavin grunted and swore. She heard the unmistakable crunch of bones breaking. Had Gavin broken his arm in his attempt to lift her? A sickening sound, like wet meat slapping the ground, followed.

Swear to God, she couldn't stand much more.

Fear began to take her over, revving her system for flight. Adrenaline spiked as she cried out again and made an effort to stand. Gavin caught her to him, shaking and speechless, locked in the throes of some kind of physical torment of his own. When his body jerked a final time, he let loose a low rumbling growl that reverberated in her chest as if she'd made it.

And then he hoisted her into his arms, high off the ground. Holding her tight against his chest, he lurched sideways, out of the moonlight.

Chapter 21

"Gavin, I'm sick," Skylar said as he made for a spot deep under the cover of trees that would block the light.

He'd morphed back to his human shape so that she'd recognize him and not be scared. But he wasn't able to maintain that shape.

He hurt like hell.

His arms, wrapped around Skylar, were again furred-up and thick with muscle. His rib cage, pressed to her right shoulder, made nightmarish popping sounds as he moved. The wolf he'd merged with didn't give a fig for decorum and priorities. According to the wolf, Skylar Donovan smelled way too good to let loose.

She shook in his arms, her body contorting every time his did as if mimicking something it was supposed to do, and following his lead.

He chanced a closer look at her.

Skylar's beautiful face was deathly white. Her teeth

made bloody indentations on her lower lip. More blood pooled on her cheek, a harsh contrast to her pallor. Long, fair lashes fluttered, and he waited for her eyes to open, dreading that moment, hating it in advance. But she cut him a break for which he was eternally grateful.

Her body pulsed in time with his, one tremendous boom after another jerking them both. She always felt light in his arms, but she was also a weighty part of the same darkness that consumed him.

Out of the moonlight, her blue shirt seemed dull. Her jeans were torn on one knee. He set her down carefully, regretfully, against a tree, and moved away from her, unable to explain any of this to her without a voice.

"Gavin…" she whispered.

But his mind was nearly beyond being able to deal with her rationally. The beast in him wanted her desperately because Skylar was going to be like him. Soon.

Skylar was close to shifting tonight, and wolf recognized wolf. No doubt about it. She was about to shed her skin and become like him for the first time. She was experiencing her first taste of what the moon could do to her, and Gavin, stunned by this, despised himself.

The blame was his. In some way, he'd done this to her. She suffered the consequences of his sleeping with her and being so attracted to her that he put her safety in jeopardy to satisfy a man's physical cravings.

In his defense, resisting her had never been an option. Skylar looked and tasted like the mate he'd feared he'd never find. Both he and his wolf chose her because of needs so intense that nothing could have kept him from her.

She didn't know any of this.

Skylar was innocent.

"Vertigo," she said, exhaling in staggered breaths.

She called this travesty vertigo when in reality what

happened tonight was a life sentence of unbelievable pain and torment: of living on the fringes and never feeling normal again.

I am so sorry.

I can't take it back.

Don't you see?

Under the cover of the trees, his body felt as if it were being crushed from within. Imploding with a pressure almost too much to bear. He supposed another shift might kill him this time.

He had to run: get away from Skylar and allow his wolf the room it required. But another monstrous entity also roamed here tonight, and Skylar, weakened and hurting like this, was fair game.

He wasn't the human she expected to see, and yet he didn't dare deny the moon her wicked brand of revelry—the moon that demanded payment for every rebellious transgression, such as denial.

"You won't leave me here, Gavin?"

Without a voice, he couldn't comfort her or shout at her for being so damn stubborn about doing whatever she pleased. How many times had he warned her about staying inside?

Now look, he thought.

"Are you okay?" Her voice shook with concern for him.

Damn it, Skylar. I don't deserve your concern. I did this to you.

He really was sorry. God, he was. He would have given anything to take it back.

You'll be all right for the time being if you stay in the shadows, my beautiful lover, he wanted to say out loud. *Your transformation will be postponed.*

But for how long? She couldn't stay here all night, a

prisoner of the moonlight, and he didn't see any way to get her home.

"I heard something break," she said.

Shaking his head was an action she didn't see with the tree blocking her view. And he couldn't manage more. He was very close to giving everything away.

"I'm sorry." Her voice was huskier now. "I think the spinning might be easing up. In a minute I might be able to stand. I can try."

In the silence following her remark, Gavin heard her draw several more rasping breaths. When his wolf whined, the sound emerged as a guttural growl of fury.

"Gavin? What was that?"

He thought seriously about stepping clear of the tree and allowing her to see him. But that wasn't doable. Skylar didn't deserve the knowledge that the man she'd given her body to that very day was a werewolf.

God. Skylar.

She might damn him from this night forward and be justified in doing so. Skylar would surely hate him if she knew he'd done this to her in some way that he still remained ignorant of. Especially since she'd need him more than ever.

No way could he go after the other monster that had done this same thing to him. He wasn't going to let Skylar tackle this transformation from woman to wolf alone. The memory of the trauma of his system rewiring for the first time tormented him still.

Damn moon.

"Something's wrong, isn't it?" she ventured. "You're not okay. What is it? Are you still there, Gavin? Hell, what a pair we are."

Gavin dragged all ten claws down the bark beside him, relishing the minor punishment wood slivers provided. Pretty soon Skylar was going to distrust the silence and come after him, crawling if she had to. He saw no way out of this, but to let her.

And then a ferocious roar, like the sound of a rolling earthquake, shook the darkness around him.

The terrible sound drove Skylar to her feet. Not quite ready to stand on her own, she clung tightly to the tree beside her.

"What the hell was that?"

The sound turned her insides to putty. She felt like death warmed over and was now covered in chills.

If the wolf Gavin chased made that sound, they were screwed. The damn thing howled like an animal on steroids.

"Gavin. Tell me you're here, and that you heard it."

He could have gone, she concluded when he didn't reply, but she didn't think so. She was certain she felt him nearby. That sense of him should have been suspect, she supposed. It was strange how she'd felt Gavin from the start, before seeing him in the garden that night and before ever setting eyes on him, as if she possessed some special kind of ranger radar.

She took a tentative step away from the tree and held out both hands for balance. A second step moved her inches closer to where she thought her handsomely rugged ranger silently waited. Despite whatever it was that kept him from speaking to her.

One more step toward the path that was still drenched in moonlight, and she thought she might make it. But she was broadsided by a moving mass of darkness with the force of a wrecking ball.

Knocked over, but instantly free of the heavy weight of the thing, Skylar rolled to her side and scrambled to her feet. Another roar, this one fainter, yet very close, raised chills on top of chills on the back of her neck.

"Gavin?" she shouted. "Be careful. Something is here."

Snapping her head around, she backpedaled to the tree and pressed her back to it, wishing she hadn't lost the gun. The spinning was gone now and she felt mostly normal, wide-awake and completely alert.

"Damn you," she said to the man so obviously avoiding her. "I know you're there. You can stop this shit, and either pick up my gun or help me find it. I'm fairly certain you can't fight that wolf with your bare hands."

Another growl made her turn to face the trees behind her. Peering into the dark, trying to separate that cloak of darkness from anything that might be hiding within it, she missed the closer threat.

By the time she noticed she was no longer alone beside her tree and that her companion wasn't Gavin, it was too late to scream.

Chapter 22

Some kind of creature faced her, standing upright on two legs and partially resembling the shape of a human.

Stunned by the creature's appearance, Skylar geared up for a sprint, high on adrenaline, wondering how far she'd get.

The thing didn't move. Nor did it attack. It stood there, watching her like the predator it probably was. She sensed something else beyond the entity in front of her, and was too shaken up to want to acknowledge that this creature might have brought a friend.

"Gavin," she said, inching back farther, hoping he heard her and was ready to do some damage to whatever this was.

In response to her voice, the big creature turned its head to look at her, and a fresh round of fear spiked through Skylar that was so potent and senselessly enlightening, she staggered sideways.

Can't be. It's just a mistake. This creature heard me and responded to the sound.

Her gut told her a different story, though, as it clenched. Her body knew what her mind refused to comprehend. She'd sensed this presence, experienced this scenario in her dreams.

No!

This creature couldn't be Gavin. Yet how many times had she questioned the immediacy of her attraction to the ranger, and her feeling that he'd stepped from those dreams and into her current reality?

"Gavin," she whispered, shaken, extremely anxious and again questioning her mental state.

"Gavin, is that you?"

Another roar came from the surroundings in reaction to her voice, but the creature in front of her didn't make that sound. The werewolf turned and stood rigidly with its back to her, its huge body as tense as hers.

Her fear filled the air with a crackling tension that seemed tangible enough to touch before it scattered like spores in the wind. More fear gripped her throat, making speech impossible, stapling her in place though she was desperate to get away.

Brush north of the path rustled. Skylar covered her mouth to muffle a scream. The werewolf—damn it, that's what it was—dropped to a crouch, its body hunched and ready to spring to meet whatever caused the sound.

And if a creature like the one in front of her feared what was out there, how awful must that other thing be?

In a moment of suspended silence, her worst nightmare stepped onto the path and into the moonlight with a full coat of black fur that shone like polished obsidian.

God...

This was a real monster, and as different from the werewolf beside her as the werewolf was from humans.

The world had just come unglued.

The monster's coat rippled in a nonexistent breeze, over a massive chest and long appendages. Nearly twice the size of the creature beside her, its wolf-shaped head perched on a thick, muscled neck. An elongated muzzle protruded menacingly beneath deep-set eyes. Its mouth hung open to reveal a full set of needle-sharp teeth.

Skylar's knees went weak at the sight.

The black beast lifted its massive head and sniffed the air. Those terrible eyes looked in Skylar's direction with an intense focus that pinpointed her location in the shadows.

Skylar shook so hard everything around her moved. *Run*, she told herself. *Try to get away.*

But Gavin…

Was that Gavin in front of her, suited up in his own fur coat and rising to cut off the bigger monster's view of a woman whose legs no longer worked properly?

Neither of the incredible creatures budged in a face-off that lasted minutes. Low warning growls bubbled up from the throat of the one Skylar hoped wasn't actually Gavin, those growls as scary as anything else in this fantastical scene.

Undeterred, the huge black monster remained still, with its head cocked to one side as if it might be calculating a next move or considering her presence. It continued to zero in on her, ignoring the creature barring the way.

And if that wasn't strange enough, under its intense scrutiny, Skylar began to burn with an unfamiliar heat. A burn so hot, it felt cold. She gazed on the scene with a new awareness, as if layers of her senses were being peeled back to reveal a freshly kindled power for seeing what was in front of her.

The darkness around her lightened, dulling shadows from black to gray. Shafts of moonlight that she hadn't previously noticed dappled the ground around the creature

she felt sure stood guard over her, highlighting a musculature that was magnificently alien. But what good would
that kind of muscle do against the larger beast?

She didn't want to find out. She had to run, and couldn't.
She wanted to speak, though no words came. The black-
coated monster didn't move from its circle of moonlight.
Only its coat shuddered, catching and reflecting the moonlight each time the beast took a breath.

Finally, the werewolf beside her lunged at the larger
creature, kicking up leaves and dirt that flew in all directions. When the dust cleared, Skylar saw only one creature
standing. The werewolf she thought might be Gavin was
also looking around in disbelief, because no evidence of
the black beast remained.

Gavin glanced over his shoulder once at Skylar and then
bolted after the monster that had knocked Skylar down and
returned, drawn to her like a moth to the flame.

He knew now by the monster's actions that this area was
no longer safe for her.

But why hadn't it attacked? Taken what it wanted right
there? Surely his own presence hadn't made a difference.

If he could have gotten Skylar out of there that minute,
put her in the car and driven straight to the airport, she
might possibly have had a chance. But that wasn't an option.

"Not tonight. Not like this. Not for you, Skylar."

Moonlight ruled their shapes. His shape, and soon hers.
Gavin again faced the dilemma that was tearing him in two.
Find the monster or stay with Skylar. Run after the beast
maker, or help a new beast be born.

His pulse raced. As dire as the situation was, he couldn't
resist Skylar. As a human female, she'd been a knockout to
his senses. With wolf added to the mix, she was a real phys-

ical need, an urge heeded by every cell in his body that told him she was his mate and that werewolves mate forever.

He found himself circling back to her. Skylar Donovan was so very important to him.

Needing a voice, he darted beneath tree cover not far from where she still stood, and began the shift in reverse. Listening to the sounds of his body retracting, feeling his skin sucked inward with a sting and a hiss, and nearly unable to breathe, he caved to the pain and pressure that made him utter one last growl.

Halfway through the shift, and with no more time to spare, he moved toward Skylar, his body close enough to human in shape for her to recognize his outline.

"Skylar." He cleared his throat, swallowed back a howl of distress, and began again. "Skylar, we have to get out of here."

Her voice rang with relief. "Oh, thank God. I thought you were gone. I thought…"

"No. I'm here. Listen to me. That fiend touched you. It now knows your scent."

She swayed on her feet with one hand on the tree while she listened to him without interrupting.

"That creature kills and maims, showing no mercy. If it was the same monster your father ran into out here, you can see how easily an accident could happen. If your father chased it, sought it out or knew of its existence, he'd be one of the very few."

Gavin searched for the strength to go on, afraid he might not find it. The pain burning through him was bad, the worst ever, and he had to rise above it.

He backed up, his transition nearly complete, his ears ringing with the mind-numbing pain of far too many shifts and a body currently uncertain of which shape to maintain.

"You don't have to believe me. Trust what your own gut tells you. Do you know what ran you down?"

"Yes," she said without moving, without running to him. "A werewolf. It was a damn werewolf."

Gavin shut his eyes. "Yes."

"And so are you," Skylar said, surprising him when he'd been pretty sure nothing more ever could.

She didn't elaborate. Maybe she couldn't. But she knew.

"There's more." He spoke through gritted teeth, already agonizing over what to say to her next.

"Impossible," she argued, shaking her head, scared to hear anything else. "There can't be more."

Gavin strode forward until he was near enough to catch Skylar if she collapsed, and close enough to fill his lungs with her familiar heady scent. She didn't back away from him. Her eyes searched his as if she saw him clearly.

"You aren't sick," he began.

She cut him off. "I'm better. Fine. We can go home now."

He held up a hand to calm her and shook his head. With a tight check on his emotions, ruled by an aching heart that pained him more than his body did, he said, "You're not okay, Skylar. You have to get from here to there." He pointed down the hill. "And that trip is going to prove more difficult than anything you've ever attempted."

Her green eyes widened. When she brushed strands of golden hair back from her white face, he would have given a year of his life to kiss her fear away.

Dried blood caked one of her cheeks, from where she'd scratched herself with something a whole lot worse than a fingernail. The wolf in him wanted to lick that wound, along with the rest of her, and make her forget they'd started this conversation. The man wanted to console her, ease her into the next phase of her life, and didn't really know how to do that.

"You're not sick," he reiterated, starting over.

It's time. Say it. Do it. Tell her.

"You're like me."

He watched her face crinkle in distaste and sensed her refusal to believe him.

"Do you understand, Skylar?"

She shook her head. "I'm not sure what you are. I know the term because we've spoken the words. And I've dreamed…"

The sentence went unfinished as her mind turned his information over, seeking a recognizable pattern in non-sensical data. Then she looked up and into his eyes.

"Why?" Her voice rattled up from deep in her chest. "Why are you doing this? Talking to me like this?"

"Why aren't you running away?" he countered.

Her eyes never left his. That gaze seemed to touch his soul.

"You don't have to stand here, Skylar, but you do have to accept what I'm telling you as the truth. You've seen what I am. Trust, me, this is not a dream."

She didn't faint, collapse or have a fit. Skylar Donovan presented to him the bold front he'd seen before, and he loved her even more for that strength now. He prayed she wouldn't hate him after this night was over, if she made it through.

"I'm no werewolf, if that's what you're suggesting," she stated adamantly.

"Go ahead, then. Step into the light."

She looked past him, shuddered, and again met his eyes.

"I'll take you," he said. "I'll hold your hand. Hell, Skylar, I'll carry you if that's what you want. But unless we wait until morning, which is a dangerous plan with that abom-ination hovering so close by, or we slide down the hill on our asses, avoiding the trail and keeping to the trees, we have no choice but to face this."

"Face what?" she asked in such a way that he knew she wanted him to spell it out for her. She wanted to hear her new life sentence without him beating around the bush.

"If you step into the moonlight, you will change." His heart pounded out the beat of his distress. "You aren't human. Not anymore. And if I've caused this, you can use those silver bullets on me and I'll welcome them. But only after I help you through this first shift and if you make it through this night."

Her teeth were chattering. "You're full of shit," she snapped, sidestepping him, walking on unsteady legs toward the moonlight.

She dared to step into that light. Bathed in it, letting its silvery phosphorescence flow over her, Skylar turned to face him with a triumphant look on her face.

Seconds later, she let out a gasp of horror and surprise.

Chapter 23

The threat to Skylar's sanity continued with the sensation of spiders crawling over her face. Spiders quickly became icicles, prodding painfully at her forehead and her cheeks— little jabs, sharp and insidious, here and there.

Standing frozen in the moonlight, the world around her became a tornado of revolving darkness, light and stars. An uncomfortable vibration rumbled deep inside her that began to spread outward and soon took over her arms and legs.

She cried out against the onslaught of pain accompanying that vibration, and fought back with her hands, tearing at her face, her stomach and her hips, fearing this was real and that she wasn't going to wake up.

Her body was in a state of upheaval, getting ready to die one part at a time. That's what this felt like. Dying.

Screams slipped through her lips as the discomfort became real agony that quickly began to escalate. Still, she wouldn't give in, refused to give up her fight. She didn't really want to find the werewolf.

And now…

Now she was becoming one, if Gavin had told the truth. Her tainted body was being restructured, rewired against her will. Something insidious was short-circuiting her genes to make her like the creature ruining her sleep night after night. Only here, in reality, there was so very little she could do about it.

Not true. Not happening.

In the moonlight she felt naked and terribly, horribly, exposed. Skylar remembered a fleeting explanation her father had given long ago to a child searching for meaning. "Moonlight is poison to people whose genetics are damaged," he said.

How the hell did he know that, way back then?

Profound, deep-seated grief over that memory undermined her determination to stand upright. The last of her energy drained away with the promise of an upcoming shift.

If Gavin was right, she was turning into her father's worst nightmare. Her worst nightmare. Any minute now, she'd be like the thing she imagined her dad had trapped in that cage…and as crazy as her mother. A wolf now resided inside her body, and the moon was that wolf's release switch.

Ready. Set. Go…

Through the whirl of pain she opened her mouth to whisper to the moon, "Come and get me, you bitch!"

And in the end, what will this moon madness produce?

"A she-wolf," the man with the velvet voice supplied from the sidelines, as though he'd heard the question.

Hearing that term from the familiar voice brought on the sweeping undertow that threatened to drag her under. Skylar fell to her knees fighting to stay conscious, only slightly aware of the man yanking her upward.

* * *

Removing her from the light and getting Skylar the hell out of there wasn't going to work, Gavin discovered as he pulled her up from the ground and into his shuddering arms. The only question now was whether being close to her would worsen her pain, or ease her fright when she got a good look at him.

Skylar. He ran a careful hand over her face, traced her quivering lips as his claws extended. His bones screamed bloody murder. The ability to speak disintegrated when there were so many things to tell Skylar, who was well on her way to the kind of breakdown he remembered.

She shook violently because the thing inside her was trying hard to get out. Like Skylar herself, her wolf wouldn't take no for an answer. Nevertheless, the danger of being in the open with a murderous rogue nearby left Skylar vulnerable.

He felt for her, hurt for her and wanted to take back everything they'd done together if that would fix this. He'd go his own way if allowed a do-over. He would leave her alone, and none of this would happen.

The sound of her back hitting the tree sickened him, but she flailed against his protective hold on her arms. Without a voice, soothing her wasn't an option.

Careful not to scratch her with his claws, Gavin readjusted his hold as she thrashed and squirmed. Swearing silently without the pleasure of hearing those oaths, he applied more pressure to her shoulders, pinning her in place with as much force as necessary to restrain her ongoing gyrations.

Skylar, listen.

They were back to the first time he uttered those words, and he had to settle for thinking them and sending them to her silently with the hope she'd catch on.

Breathe. Stop fighting. Letting it in is the only way to survive this.

Timing was crucial, and time had run out. Above the noises Skylar made deep in her throat, Gavin sensed the approach of the moment he dreaded. The beast he'd sought for so long was on its way back, and he wasn't ready for a showdown. Skylar wasn't in any kind of shape to fend for herself, and he'd have to let her go in order to face the nightmare.

The smell of the abomination was its calling card: damp fur, aged menace and the iron odor of blood, probably from whatever it ate for dinner. Gavin spun around and turned his back to Skylar, leaning into her, shielding her and willing her to be silent, though her soft cries were evidence of her discomfort. He growled his displeasure over the return of such a beast and studied its approach with a stern, unwavering gaze.

Silently, stealthily, as if floating above the ground, the stalker moved in without getting too close. It appeared as a blur of dark between the trees ringing the area where he and Skylar stood, acting as if it might be content to toy with the senses of the werewolf it had created.

Gavin didn't buy the delay or the silence. And he sure as hell wasn't going to be deterred from guarding Skylar.

Anger made his growl a sharp warning. His racing pulse provided him with a sizzling new adrenaline-sparked energy.

The delay was in his favor. While the beast lingered on the outskirts of the area, Gavin hoisted Skylar into his arms. Though she fought like a wildcat to be free and face her own demons, Gavin held her as if her life depended on it, since it probably did.

He walked into the light, felt the slap of moonlight sucker punch him and the agony of the accumulated physical strain of winking back and forth between man and Were without fully landing on either choice for long.

Hit over and over again in relentless waves by the pain of the reverse shift he wanted so badly and couldn't manage— the one that would enable him to speak to Skylar again— Gavin ran, slid, leaped down the hillside, utilizing every bit of effort he could dig up and a whole lot of concentrated determination to turn his back on and gain some distance from the abomination behind him.

Time suspended in the effort to reach the cabin. Not certain how he made it to the front yard, or why Skylar's struggles ceased as he hit the porch, Gavin skidded to a halt beneath the overhang.

Safe?

God, were they safe?

His heart stuttered with surprise when the front door opened on its own. He stumbled back in shock. A woman stood in the doorway, a woman he vaguely recognized from bits of data stored in the back of his mind.

Barring the way into the house, she spoke in a low-pitched, authoritative voice that contained the power of a command. "Go on, wolf. I'll take it from here."

Chapter 24

Who the hell was this?

The stranger in Skylar's cabin made him freeze in place.

Go on, wolf?

As if he could leave Skylar, no matter how bad he felt or looked at the moment? This intruder was facing a werewolf as if that wasn't scary at all.

The next reverse shift wasn't going to happen, however much he wanted it to. Possibly a built-in defense mechanism had come into play to keep this woman from recognizing him in the future. Either that, or since he'd abused the whole shifting thing, there might be a chance he'd have to stay in this frigging furred-up shape forever, his human shape lost because it had surpassed the limits of what a human body could endure.

He stood on the porch, holding Skylar for what seemed like eons. He was furious, not sure why this auburn-haired woman didn't run for cover when confronted by a monster.

She appeared to be calm and in full control of her wits. Her heart didn't race. She didn't scream or wince. The beautifully constructed face showed no hint of fear or revulsion. When she'd spoken, she'd sounded unemotionally rational.

"I'll take it from here."

Gavin homed in on that, desperate to understand what was going on.

"Why don't you bring Skylar inside and then do what you need to do," the woman suggested, testing his patience. No smile on her lips. No joke. All business.

"We both understand that if she comes inside, Skylar will feel better. Isn't that right?"

Gavin continued to stare without loosening his possessive hold on Skylar. Let his lovely lover go through this alone? *Don't think so. I caused this. It's my fault.*

"If I take the time to explain my presence to you and make introductions, it's going to be worse for her. Do you want that?" the woman asked, looking directly at Skylar, limp in Gavin's arms.

No, damn it. That's the last thing I want.

"Good." She moved aside, making room for him to take Skylar inside.

He wanted to take that step, but couldn't make himself do so, caught in a stranglehold between a nebulous, twisted-gut feeling that told him he needed to do as this woman suggested, and his inability to relinquish his lover.

"Please," the woman said. "I'm a doctor of sorts. You can trust me. I knew her father."

This was a friend of the Donovan family. That's how she knew Skylar's name. Still, how did that make her so inured to his shape?

As he stood there weighing his options, Gavin caught a new scent that made his heartbeat ramp up to a new high.

You're a wolf.

She nodded.

Gavin moved past her into the cabin, accepting that against all odds of finding another moon freak, wolf also tainted this woman's blood. The scent was heady. Different yet unmistakably there. Not only that, she had a full grasp on what the curse meant and how to deal with it, which led him to believe she'd been a werewolf for some time.

Not alone. Not the only one.

"Not by a long-shot," the newcomer confirmed with a blank, expressionless face.

Though the door remained open, the cabin felt cramped and claustrophobic as he laid Skylar on the leather couch. Skylar's face was ash-gray. She seemed short on breath and made wheezing sounds as if her vocal cords were seizing. Noting those things made him feel ill all over again. Sicker than usual.

It will pass, Skylar.

He looked to the auburn-haired she-wolf and added, *Hopefully it will pass.*

Skylar's overwrought body shook the couch. His body shook just as hard, rattling the table beside her. Sweat gathered on his forehead from the effort it took to stand here under this roof without moonlight calling the shots. The damn light outside beckoned to him.

But there was no hint of a transition back to his human form under the shelter of the roof. Not one crack of bone or sting of a claw retracting.

Hell, could he really freeze in this shape? Forever?

"I don't want to tell you what to do," the she-wolf said, coming up beside him, her presence a startling reminder that he might soon have the answers he'd been looking for all this time. "But it's clear you're in trouble and that what you need is out there, in the night."

What I need even more is right here.

Gavin needed to get that point across.

"Skylar needs my help now," she said, reading his thoughts loud and clear in yet another unexplainable anomaly he had no time to question. "Let me attend to her. Trust me to do that."

Gavin couldn't handle another minute indoors. Pain tore through him like a silver-tipped arrow going all the way through.

I can't go.

"You have to, for her," the newcomer said with a solemn finality that Gavin actually believed.

He had to trust this wolf, he supposed, because there was nothing he could do to help Skylar, and he felt so ill.

"I will take care of her," the woman said. "I promise."

The growl he offered in acceptance of her offer emerged as both a thank-you and a threat.

I will be back.

"Tomorrow," she said. "Don't return tonight. It's best she doesn't get close to you while you're like this after you've imprinted. Her body will want a shape she doesn't fully understand how to reach and isn't ready for."

Hellfire, he wanted to shout. *Who could possibly be ready for this transformation or believe it could possibly be a part of reality?*

The woman across from him waved at the doorway.

She's stronger than you think, he added in this strange thought-reading process. *Skylar is strong.*

"Strength will help, but there are no guarantees she'll survive this if the light reaches her now, as you well know. It's up to the body and its willingness to adapt. Being near me in this human shape will calm her down enough to postpone the transition."

Postpone?

"Wouldn't you have wanted an explanation first, before your first change?"

Yes. No. Hell, how do you know all of this?

"That's a story for another time."

You said "imprinted." What is that? What did you mean? Tell me this one thing.

"You've mated. Found each other. Bonded. Yes? With us, imprinting is a fierce emotion, and it lasts forever. Your wolf senses hers now. That's why you're not changing back, even though you're near me."

He nodded as if that mystical remark made sense because the depth of his feelings for Skylar had been immediate and overwhelming. But did this imprinting business mean that Skylar couldn't escape from him if she wanted to, and vice versa?

"Please," the woman standing beside the door repeated. "You should go."

He had no other option. His body was telling him that. With a relief bordering on madness, Gavin rushed back through the open doorway, hating the separation from Skylar and questioning this stranger's trustworthiness, but he was no good to anyone like this. The she-wolf had arrived in the nick of time to help Skylar, and who could have predicted that?

The situation had changed. There were now four werewolves in this one tiny area—which made him wonder how many more Weres there might be, worldwide.

He had hurt the very person he wanted so desperately. Would Skylar forgive him?

Moonlight welcomed him as if they were the lovers here. In the open, away from the cabin, the silvery light caressed him with cool fingers, misty palms and chilled lips. That touch dripped over his face, flowed over his shoulders in a beastly, otherworldly cascade of instructions that eased his tremors somewhat.

It's done, then.

He prayed that Skylar was in good hands. He demanded that outcome from the moon. Because the only way to get on with this night was to believe Skylar would survive, and that he would be free to hunt down the creature at the center of their spiraling universe. The monster out here was Gavin's ground zero.

Raising his face to the moonlight, he breathed it in. He opened his mouth, tasted the light on his tongue, swallowed it down as greedily as if it were Skylar's breath.

"I surrender."

With the wind in his face and the light prodding him on, Gavin bolted up the path using all his strength, intending to find the demon whose third generation included the lover he could still feel, phantomlike, in his arms.

"Skylar, can you hear me?"

The question sounded very close and soberly demanding, but nothing was wrong with her hearing. In fact, Skylar heard everything—the clock on the mantel, the stranger's breathing, insects outside, wind in the trees, the drip of a faucet, and louder than all that, the irregular boom of the thunder inside her chest.

She also heard something else with her brand-new, sharply acute awareness: the same mesmerizing call that had plagued her from the beginning, from her first night here. His call. Gavin's voice…so strong and sexy and persuasively clear, it was the voice of a lover whispering her name while on the verge of physical penetration. Like the gasp of sound Gavin made as he slid into her blistering heat.

Gavin.

She opened her eyes, blinked. A woman's face filled her

field of vision: a light-skinned angular shape punctuated by high cheekbones and large golden-green eyes. Dark coppery hair with a fringe of bangs surrounded the almost too exquisitely perfect features of a woman in her early thirties.

"You're safe now, for the time being," this stranger said in a voice Skylar easily placed because she had listened to it on a recording earlier that day.

"It's Jenna," that voice said. "I came as soon as I could catch a plane."

Jenna James. Doctor. PhD. Her father's partner. The psychiatrist who worked with her dad at Fairview Hospital and seemed much too young in person to have been a colleague of the famous Doctor Donovan's. This was the female cohort the Donovan siblings had been jealous of for the past few years. Their father's confidant, and closer to him than his real family.

"Why?" Skylar struggled to ask, her voice gruff, her mouth as dry as sand. "Why are you here?"

"Your sister mentioned being worried about you, and that, in turn, worried me."

Skylar vaguely remembered Trish mentioning a conversation with Dr. James, though that seemed so long ago.

"How… How did you find me?"

"I've been here once before and often spoke to your father by phone when he stayed here."

"Then you were the only one who did."

The faint, persistent thrumming in Skylar's skull threatened to drive her to the medicine cabinet. She reached up to cover her ears, remembering the claws as soon as she lifted her hands. But there were no claws on her hands at the moment. The room didn't revolve the way the night sky had.

Her dizziness had waned. She didn't feel quite so sick now, though the shakes continued as did the chills.

"Do you understand what's happening to you?" Jenna

asked seriously, in a tone that demanded an equally serious answer.

"No."

Gavin had used the word *wolf*, but that could also have been her imagination, like the claws and everything else going on. Case in point, how could she hear Gavin's voice now if he wasn't here? She believed he was calling her name over and over as he placed more distance between them.

How could she explain to anyone else about what she'd seen out there, or thought she'd seen? Especially this woman, who delved into peoples' minds on a regular basis.

Skylar tried futilely to get up. Dr. James held her down with a firm hand on her shoulder, though there probably was no way Skylar could have managed, anyway. Her limbs just weren't behaving. She felt boneless and unsteady. The knot in her stomach was the size of a plate.

Her dad's partner sat on the low table next to the couch, eyeing her levelly. Jenna James's questions were professional, direct, and got right to the heart of the events that had transpired over the past couple of days.

"Do you realize what your friend is? What he has become?" she asked.

"Do you?" Skylar countered, her voice slightly surer, the ache behind her eyes increasing as she remembered the way Gavin had looked in the moonlight. The Gavin that wasn't Gavin, with added height, molded muscle, and the constant rumble of deep-seated growls he'd used to ward off danger as he carried her to safety.

Gavin was a werewolf, and her dreams weren't just dreams. He had leaped right into her reality as if she possessed the power to make that happen. And he had made sure she was safe before rushing back outside for what? To do what? Hunt another wolf? Be what he needed to be?

What kind of danger lurked on that mountain that made Gavin show such concern for her well-being? The stalker they'd avoided last night? His fear over whatever walked under the full moon tonight had been pronounced and contagious.

While she...

No. She wouldn't think about the claws. If she avoided those kinds of thoughts, maybe they'd go away.

Where are you, Gavin?

"Don't," Jenna James instructed coolly. "Don't call him back. He needs to be away from you tonight. If you care for him, let him go."

If she cared for him? Hell, she thought of nothing else but him. She was possessed. He'd gotten under her skin.

"There's something out there with a dark heart," Skylar explained, clasping her hands and then unclasping them, afraid to look down.

"Yes. I know," Jenna said.

Skylar looked at her. "How could you possibly be aware of anything happening in this place?"

"I'm in on the secret," Jenna replied. "A few of us are. And now, so are you."

Jenna stood up and moved to the windows, checking to make sure all four were closed and covered. Why? Skylar wondered. To stop something from looking in...or to keep her from looking out?

Neither explanation mattered, she supposed. She felt the darkness outside as if some of it had flown in on her wake. Night coated her lungs, producing the rounds of icy chills that arrived without any sign of giving up.

Although four solid walls surrounded her, and Jenna James's cryptic remarks about secrets and about Gavin resonated in the closed space, Skylar felt moonlight seeping through the roof.

She sat up abruptly and turned to face the door, scared, sensing that moonlight wasn't the only thing trying to get in, and this other thing was an entity that ate up moonlight as if it were candy.

"What's happening to me?" Skylar pinned the doctor with a direct gaze that defied the fear building up inside her. "Tell me what you know."

Chapter 25

When her father's partner turned from the window, Skylar put a hand to her forehead without worrying if she might see things like claws on her own hands. It was far too late for that.

Jenna James was here. The woman's pale skin was radiant in the light from the one lamp in the room, as if it glowed from within. Most of her red-brown hair, long, shiny, streaked with gold highlights, was worn pulled back from her face so that every sharp angle on that face was prominent. The problem with Jenna, Skylar realized, was that she looked too alive to be human.

Something else. The psychiatrist's body pulsed in the dim space as if her skin cocooned something living beneath it. This was also the way Skylar felt, with the knot in her gut continually twisting.

Nothing normal about this.

"What are you?" Skylar asked, firing off that question

on the tail of the previous request before the doctor could open her mouth to answer.

Jenna's smile seemed wan. "I'm Were, Skylar. A woman and a wolf share this body. Somebody's worst nightmare, I suppose, if they knew. But most people don't."

"I'm guessing my father knew." Skylar's teeth still chattered, but she couldn't clamp them together and talk at the same time, and this was information she needed badly.

"Yes," Jenna said. "David knew."

"About you?"

"After a while."

Skylar thought about the paragraphs in the notebook in the attic. "Did you two have a thing going on?"

Jenna shook her head. "Nothing like that."

"Then why would he come here to chase wolves when you were right next door?"

"I'm not sure he came here to chase them, Skylar. I think your father might have come here to protect them."

"Protect them?"

She really didn't want to be here with Dr. James. She didn't want to speak about any of this, especially to her father's confidante. But this woman had known her father well, and she'd seen Gavin. Seen what he was, what Skylar, on some level, even now refused to believe he could be.

Werewolf.

And since this wasn't a dream and couldn't be her imagination, facing the details of being fully awake became a necessity.

"A Were," she said, testing the word, finding it foreign. "Then you're like Gavin?"

Jenna shook her head. "Your friend and I are enough alike to seem so at first glance."

"You'll need to explain that, but first, tell me why the blinds are closed."

"For your safety. Tonight the moonlight is not your friend, Skylar."

"What about you? If you go outside, will you change?"

Skylar couldn't believe she was asking a question like that seriously.

"I can withhold the desire to shift when I want to, after years of practice."

"Desire?" Skylar latched on to that. "You want to change shape?"

"For me, it's natural, while ignoring and withholding a shift when the time is right isn't."

"But he has to change shape. Gavin has to. He didn't seem able to control it."

"Gavin. That's his name?" Jenna looked to the door he'd exited out of. "Yes. Your friend is new to the trick and has to heed the moon's call or face the threat of being driven mad by the body's push to reshape itself."

Oh, Gavin. It isn't as if you could have told me. I do understand that, at least.

"Why him? Why mad?" Skylar asked. "How are you different, and what am I? Where do I fit in?"

Jenna's voice remained calm, though her expression wasn't truly reassuring. "Your mate was bitten by a were-wolf, which made him become what he is. When the virus, passed along through saliva or a mingling of blood, enters the bloodstream, not by choice, but by an act of violence from someone who purposefully passes it on, imagine the surprise of the recipient when the first full moon comes around."

Jenna came closer. "I was born Were. I wasn't bitten by anyone. For me, being Were is a genetic pattern passed down from parents also born Were, just as their parents were before them."

Skylar wanted to throw up. There seemed to be guidelines for becoming a werewolf. There were viruses and people born into families from a secret alternate bloodline.

Why didn't the damn shivering cease? She was chilled to the bone.

She had to speak, had to know more, yet moving her lips seemed momentarily impossible. Rallying, forcing herself to get a grip, Skylar asked, "How far back can all that passing on of the pattern go?"

"As far back as anyone can count, and then further than that. Before the Flood, and the dawn of civilization."

Needing to get to the bathroom or outside to be sick in private, Skylar moved her legs at last, finding them rubbery and useless. She wasn't going to get away from this. Had to face what was happening.

"He didn't lose his mind. Gavin helped me," she said, more frightened in the relative safety of the cabin with this werewolf doctor than she had been on the mountain when she fell. This woman put people in monitored rooms if they sounded crazy, yet was it possible that Jenna didn't hear how nuts she sounded at the moment?

"More," Skylar said shakily. "Tell me more. How many of you are there?" The question rang with the sound of rising panic.

"More than a few," Jenna replied. "Quite a lot, in fact. We have to stay vigilant to keep forms of the virus from diluting further as it's passed on from rogue bite to bite. The world as a whole doesn't know about us. They can't know. So we police ourselves as much as we can."

Skylar doubled over with her hands on her stomach. Her insides were roiling. She spoke without looking up. "Tell me this. What kind of werewolf would bite another person and make them a werewolf? How does that work?"

"Good guys wouldn't bite. Not for any reason. It's forbidden."

Skylar hated the image that sprang to mind. If Gavin became a werewolf because of a bite, he must have come across a bad guy, and now he had to deal with the strange new direction his life had taken.

She remembered how she'd first seen him up close, in the yard, kneeling by the hose, and how she had absurdly looked for signs that he might be a creature like the one in her dreams.

The thought that there could be such things as werewolves made her wonder if it was possible she could have known what Gavin was before meeting him, and if some people possessed wolf radar. Had her father possessed it, or did knowing Dr. James make him aware of the flaws in nature?

What had he written in that journal she'd read?

They didn't lose their minds.

Gavin had dragged her from the mountain with her safety in mind on two occasions. He did this because he maintained his wits, like Jenna said good guys did. Gavin's human brain stayed in control while wolfish parts took over his body. And once upon a time, he'd been bitten by somebody or something. The scars on his chest could be tied to his ordeal.

"So, what kind of creature did this to him?" she muttered beneath her breath. Who turned him? Was it the stalker she thought she'd heard following them on the mountain? That thing in the trees Gavin had shielded her from?

Could her father have met that same thing?

Damn it, had her father been bitten? Is that what this was all about?

She looked up to find Jenna sitting beside her. Their eyes met. Skylar's stomach whirled.

"Was my dad…?"

Jenna shook her head, seeming to understand her un-spoken question. "No. He wasn't one of us."

Okay. All right. Jenna's answer brought a little relief.

"If someone…" She drifted off, staring into Jenna's gold-rimmed eyes before starting again. "If someone were to chase werewolves, it would have to be on a night when the moon is full. How else would anyone recognize a were-wolf?"

Jenna held her gaze. "Most Weres require a full moon to shift. All of those possessing diluted blood do."

Skylar remembered a former breakthrough on that line of thinking, and used it now. "Then Dad couldn't have been after werewolves when he died, since there was no full moon at the time. I thought…"

Jenna encouraged her to go on in a warm, sympathetic tone. "You thought what?"

"I thought someone pushed him or hurt him on that hillside."

Would she ever look at this place the same way after tonight? Skylar asked herself. The answer was a resound-ing no because she was afraid of this night, this room and the next question moving through her mind. So she back-tracked, saving that question.

"And," she said, "your conversation with my sister made you worry about me, why?"

"I've been worried about you for a very long time. Your father didn't want you here. He didn't want you or your sis-ters anywhere near this place."

"He made that quite obvious," Skylar concurred.

"There was a reason."

"Protecting wolves? You're going with that as an ex-cuse?"

Jenna smiled sadly.

"Gavin didn't bite me," Skylar said. "Yet you both think I'm facing a change."

"You are facing a change."

"Explain to me how that fits in with the rules were-wolves have." Skylar rushed on. "If I go out there again, you're saying that I'll shift?"

"Yes. Eventually. You'll meet that fate in what we call the Blackout phase. It's the first rewiring phase of a body's imminent rearrangement. It's best if you don't do that to-night without a full understanding of what's about to take place."

"Why postpone the inevitable, if that's true?"

"Because if Gavin didn't put the wolf in you, we need to know who did, and what that might mean."

Skylar managed to get to her feet, swayed dramatically and sat back down. Her voice was faint. "You do realize how ridiculous this sounds?"

"I do. But I believe you know the truth already."

"I don't know anything." Skylar glanced longingly at the door, wishing Gavin would come through it. "Why is it called a Blackout?"

"The virus changes the body at every level, takes over, forming new neural pathways and messing with cell struc-ture. It's a terrible ordeal, Skylar. I won't lie about that. It causes a loss of consciousness from which some people never awaken."

"Did that happen to you?"

"Yes. For Weres like me, from a family of Weres, it's only slightly easier and more like an awakening, a firing up of the process, rather than a complete restructuring."

Skylar's stomach tightened again, as if something inside her clenched over this knowledge. "Then he went through it." She looked at Jenna. "Gavin went through the Black-out."

"There is no escape clause."

"And I'm going to go through it, though we don't know why. What happened to me out there tonight was just the beginning."

When Jenna nodded, Skylar sensed the woman was hiding something, not willing to tell all.

There was so much more to learn, though. So many questions were in need of answers. The sickness Skylar felt demanded she address the one question nagging at her. The one she couldn't avoid any longer.

It was an awful idea, born of a darkness that could only get worse if the question was answered.

Jenna had admitted to being worried about her for a long time. A call from Trish had brought the doctor here to Colorado the same day. What would make Jenna do that?

She took in a breath and braced herself on the couch, fighting a rising sense of panic.

Opening her mouth, Skylar released the dreaded words, along with a long, exhaled breath.

"Was my mother a werewolf, Dr. James?"

Time seemed to freeze as the silence grew. She had to fill that silence, had to speak the next part of the question and complete the thought. Her lips parted. Sound came out.

"Not just a locked-up delusional lunatic," she said, "but a real, claw-wielding Were?"

Chapter 26

The forest reeked with the smell of Otherness, as though the creature Gavin chased had marked off a specific territory. The problem came from the fact that the area afforded panoramic views of Skylar's cabin through the trees, from all angles.

Gavin faced a second problem. He craved another scent so badly, he nearly turned back at each bend in the path. Her scent. Skylar's. The woman whose essence was imprinted on his soul, according to the mysterious woman helping her.

He spun around and dropped to his haunches, trying to duck the feeling of being too close to the beast, to the kind of danger that could make bloody threads out of a young woman's dewy flesh. It was possible the beast he sought could avoid being found tonight, but what about next month or the month after that?

Had it shown itself tonight because of Skylar's presence, noticing the wolf in her? Did it want a piece?

Gavin refused to ponder that possibility, and yet he realized that the best thing for Skylar would be for her to go back to Florida, removing herself from this threat. If she left, though, was there any way to predict how far the imprinting might stretch to accommodate a long-distance relationship? Would that relationship disintegrate as she traveled away from him, state by state?

What would happen to their connection when Skylar discovered that her new werewolf self was due to something he'd done to her?

Forever. The woman in the cabin said werewolves mated forever. That thought seemed as monstrous as the rest of the werewolf thing, and still there was no getting around it. Nothing was to be done about any of this, except to stick to the original plan, which went so much deeper now that someone else was involved. Someone he cared deeply about.

Someone he ached for.

Gavin straightened and resumed his pace with his senses wide-open and his skull tingling from the effort of not thinking about Skylar. The world had become much more complicated in the past few days and he'd have to deal with it one problem at a time. Safety came first. Hers, and others'. Mostly hers.

This creature could not be allowed to infect anyone else.

Moonlight lit the forest with a clear silvery light that felt like liquid on his skin and tasted like particles of stardust. The light he now dreaded fed his energy, refueling his body with each step he took, but at the same time it stripped his humanity from him, and left him unsound.

As he neared a rock pile forming a ledge overlooking the valley beneath, Gavin stopped, breathing hard, not from physical exertion, but simply to take more scents in. He wasn't alone. Every sense told him that. Red flags were waving in his mind. The air felt dense, thick, in a way even brilliant moonlight couldn't penetrate.

Turning in a slow circle, hands raised, claws long, lethal and ready for the upcoming fight, he let a growl rip that transposed his anger into a sound the monster in the shadows would surely comprehend. Then he growled out an invitation for the damn thing to come out and face him.

Hair on the nape of his neck bristled as his shoulders began to undulate. The scars on his chest, as if recognizing the creature who'd made them, burned once again with an icy-cold fire.

Gavin wished for a voice, so he could to fling oaths at the night. Settling for a low disgruntled roar, he waited, watched, listened, as he studied his surroundings.

He heard it finally…a sound not meant to be an announcement. He spun toward the rocks with his heart pounding.

I might not make it back, Skylar. And I am so very sorry.

Low vibrations punched through his gut as if he'd swallowed an engine idling in neutral. Wildness began to gather and swirl inside him like a volcano about to erupt. His view of the landscape sharpened. Neck muscles stiffened.

Taking down this beast would soften the blow of his own possible demise. He might be a broken man, but as a werewolf, there'd be nothing to stop him now, short of death.

He rolled his massive shoulders, relishing the spark igniting his mounds of muscle. When the sound he both wanted and dreaded came again, he leaped to the rocks, growling a response. *I know you're here.*

Branches moved to his right. Leaves fluttered down. A spot of shadow began to grow, getting larger by the second, filling the space between the trees.

You really are a monster. The world has no place for the likes of you.

When the beast stepped clear of the greenery, dark-furred, long-muzzled and twice the size of anything Gavin could recall, it stopped long enough for him to get a good long look before ambling forward at a gait that felt to Gavin like death approaching in slow-motion.

"Yes," Jenna said, seated by Skylar, her face showing none of the fear flooding through Skylar at the moment.

Yes?

Had she heard correctly?

Yes, her mother was a werewolf?

Damn it, think back.

She'd been a child when she demanded visitation with her mother. Only six years old. Some of those memories, tucked away because they were too painful to dig up, came back now with the force of an unleashed tide.

Windowless cell. Men in white coats. The hole in the door that food passed through. A mattress on the floor.

More memory, burning like fire…

Her mother's fuzz of dark hair, shaved close to her scalp. The wildness in her mother's gray eyes that came and went, but mostly stayed, scaring a young girl who was determined to stick it out and be with her mom for as long as she could.

Cold concrete floors. Hushed voices. Foul smells. The sense of her mother holding back a raw, raging power.

Skylar repeated her question to Jenna James out of necessity. "My mother was…a werewolf?"

As she waited for a further response, Skylar found breathing difficult. Because that had to be the right answer, didn't it, and a possible source of her own condition? This doctor had treated patients at Fairview, though not long enough ago to have known her mother.

And if Gavin hadn't done this to her, someone else must have.

Love bites. Nips of her mother's teeth on her hands and arms. Little endearments that didn't seem strange to a child who craved motherly love and knew no better.

Could that have done it? Made her what she had supposedly become?

Faced with this new dilemma, those days inside Fairview's walls became suspect, and the world continued to tilt on its axis.

Like mother, like daughter?

Maybe no bites were necessary, and her mother had passed her the genes? Could having only one wolf parent produce a genetic Were like Jenna?

God...

Had her father known about his wife's condition?

How far back did her dad's information and interest in werewolves go?

She shook so violently, her teeth rattled. When Jenna reached out to her, Skylar warded her off with a stiff raised hand. Jenna knew about her mother, so her dad must have confided everything.

What about silver bullets and metal cages?

Withholding a scream of frustration, Skylar forced herself to speak. "Since we're on the path of truth, I believe I deserve to know more of my own." It took a few tries to get that complete sentence out.

"You do deserve that. But your father made me promise..."

"Promise what?"

"To keep some things from you unless those things became absolutely necessary."

"You don't think that time is now? I've just found out I'm something other than 100 percent human and that my mother wasn't human, either. Neither is my lover or the woman speaking to me. How does that rate as a requirement for needing enlightenment?"

"Your father wasn't sure about you," Jenna said. "He didn't know if you'd ever need to understand."

"He kept my mother locked up."

"For her safety, as well as the safety of others."

"How did he explain that to the rest of the staff? Keeping a werewolf in a padded cell had to have its own challenges. So, which came to my mother first, the wolf or the madness? Or are they one and the same?"

Her voice broke as she went on, recalling things long repressed. "I remember darts. They shot her with darts when they couldn't get close, when she wouldn't let them in. They were careful not to hit me, but there were lots of darts when they finally took me away."

"That would have been medication to calm her down."

"It was barbaric. Would you condone that, Dr. James? If you kept a werewolf in a cell, would you treat it like that? Control it that way?"

Jenna didn't answer that one.

"So, what? Times change? Why aren't you locked away? Why didn't my father go after you?"

"I'm not like your mother, Skylar."

"How do you know? She was beautiful like you. She was lucid at times. What made her so different from you or Gavin?"

She could see the discomfort her question caused in the woman across from her who probably wasn't much older than Trish. But the questions seemed fair under the circumstances. She had a right to know what to expect.

There were secrets, and then there were secrets, Skylar guessed. Maybe her mother had been stark raving mad on top of being Were and Fairview was the right place to handle that. Yet how was she going to find out without being privy to her own family history?

"Different," Skylar pressed. "Explain that. If not bitten, like Gavin or a genetic werewolf like you, if that's what you mean, what does that leave?"

"A creature that's so much more dangerous," Jenna said, her voice low and gentle. "One that has to be carefully monitored for everyone's good."

Skylar sank farther down on the seat. Damn it, they were talking about her mother as though she'd been possessed by some kind of demented demon.

"So she passed the wolf to me?" Skylar whispered, eyes closing, the last of her energy all used up.

"I think that must be the case."

"And it just happened to show up in me now?" Her staccato voice was as shaky as the rest of her and showing the strain. "Can you even begin to explain that?"

"None of us can," Jenna replied. "Very few of us have experience with anything like this."

Skylar opened her eyes to focus on the woman beside her. She had to know everything, wanted to know…and at the same time didn't want to hear any more. But they had already come this far.

Her voice cracked. "Wouldn't it be easier for me to walk out that door and take it like a Donovan? Face my fate head-on and let my body get on with whatever it's going to do? Prove that all this speculation is true?"

"No," Jenna said adamantly. It was a stern warning, a no-nonsense reply backed by the threat of a werewolf's strength and power. And it made Skylar realize that Jenna James had to be here for a reason that surpassed merely being concerned for a colleague's daughter.

Possibly Jenna was here to monitor her, gauge her, study

her since the original Donovan lunatic was lost long ago at Fairview.

And all that was missing from this sordid picture was a tranquilizer dart and a white lab coat.

Chapter 27

Gavin went cold. Numb. Staring at a presence that bridged the gap between heaven and hell by sucking the air and life right out of both. And out of him.

He had a sensation of falling, of the darkness weighing him down, so that thoughts of movement in any direction were impossible. There was no place for other emotions. Fear became an overarching cloud.

He dragged at the air in order to breathe, aware of the need to clear his head. This beast truly wasn't like him at all. If he was its accidental offspring, something had gone terribly wrong with the process.

The thing, creature, monster, abomination, stopped several paces away in a repetition of their meeting earlier in the night, and again the hesitancy seemed strange. Through his stupor, Gavin realized he had to shake off his shock to properly assess this gigantic foe. But all he did was stare.

Again he noted how fur covered its body, with no resemblance to anything human. The dark fur rippled like water over a massive muscle structure each time the creature drew in a breath.

And anything that breathed could conceivably have its air supply cut off, Gavin thought, hoping for an opportunity to test the theory.

But the outline that seemed wolfish at first look went far past that in scope, outclassing Gavin by at least fifty pounds. Maybe out of self-defense or an act of self-preservation, he hadn't allowed himself to remember details of the complete picture. Yet here those details were, larger than life and twice as nasty.

Watch the mouth and the claws, he warned himself as deep-set eyes stared back at him from red-rimmed sockets. Gavin was surprised to sense a terrifying intelligence gleaming from those eyes, which were a light color. Blue? Green? The creature's eyes were the only evidence of an identifiable humanity in the monster, and for a few seconds they tripped Gavin up.

This wasn't merely a super powerful animal, as he'd first thought. It was a walking, thinking machine—which Gavin figured made it ten times as deadly. And it appeared to be assessing him, too.

The claws were extended and at least six inches long, though the beast's big hands, more reminiscent of paws than Gavin's hands, remained lowered. Its impressive muscle wasn't bunched, which would have suggested it was ready to take Gavin on.

Why are you looking at me? What are you waiting for? What the hell are you?

Gavin's pulse hammered at his insides. He didn't attack or do anything but try to stomach the fear and anxiousness of waiting this out.

The beast across from him sniffed the air and growled

menacingly with sounds that raised chills on the back of
Gavin's neck. The pain in his chest intensified. His scars
continued to burn.

He growled back. *You can't get past me, beast. You'll
never get to her.*

He sensed the beast's impatience. Its hunger beat at the
air.

Only death will end this. Yours or mine.

Did it laugh at his threat, as if indeed it heard and understood the challenge? Was it anticipating the ease with
which it might savor a kill?

The terrible humanlike eyes tracked to the right, looking
past Gavin to the gap in the trees that bordered the path.
Alerted to the direction of the beast's new focus, Gavin
inched sideways to block off the view.

Not going to happen. He growled. *Not tonight. Not ever.
Not if I can help it.*

He didn't want to die, and yet he had always been cogni-
zant of the sacrifice he might be asked to make in the line
of duty. Still, not making it through the next few minutes
wasn't an option he was willing to accept.

The monster roared softly and tossed its wolfish head.
Once again it raised its muzzle to sniff the air. Then it
stepped closer to Gavin, and though it was only one step,
and still a distance from him, it sniffed again as if smelling something on Gavin that it might not have anticipated.

The vastness of the silence around them was chilling.
Gavin readied for the fight, raising his claws, demonstrat-
ing his willingness to defend that path to the cabin at all
cost. He had to force himself to anticipate the beast's first
incriminating move. Bile stuck in his throat as he waited.

The giant cocked its head and continued to stare. The
second sound it made rolled through Gavin, pulling from
him another silent protest.

She's mine. Forever. You did this.

The beast's next roar, louder, more feral, caused a chain reaction. The forest came alive with movement, as if a hurricane had dropped from above, controlled by the creature across from him.

Gavin dropped to his haunches and roared his disgust. His chest heaved. He fought for breath and shook off the searing pain cutting through him from being near his maker. Drawing back his lips, he bared teeth that were so much less impressive than the demon's.

The beast snapped at leaves hurling by as if it were a game. Then, without warning, it sprang. The transition from complete stillness to a moving wall of solid muscle took less time than it took Gavin to blink. The creature was on him before Gavin knew what had hit him, its great jaws open and mere inches from his face.

On the ground, on his back, Gavin felt the heat of its breath, felt its heavy bulk bearing down on him before regaining his wits. By then it should have been too late for him to inflict any real damage on the thing on top of him.

He struck out anyway, his claws parting the thick fur to connect with the monster's ribs. The damn thing didn't even react to the blow. Nor did it finish him off, though Gavin's face was a bite away. Instead, it looked him in the eyes as if seeking something. As its light eyes probed his, a razor-sharp claw touched Gavin's cheek and scratched its way toward his mouth, drawing blood, though the beast seemed to have no sense of that or take notice.

I will kill you, Gavin thought. *Somehow.*

He brought up one knee, rammed it into the beast's thigh as hard as he could, and again went at it with his claws. The giant, seemingly oblivious to pain, tilted its head and let out a roar that rattled Gavin's bones.

And then the beast heaved itself backward, lunged to its feet, and made for the path leading to…

The cabin.

Skylar sat forward, looking to the door and noting peripherally that Jenna looked there also.

"Closer," Skylar said. "Whatever is out there is getting closer."

Jenna's gaze snapped to her. "Do you know what it is?"

"I was hoping you did."

"I'm afraid I might." Jenna didn't elaborate.

Skylar tried again to rally and stand. Stumbling sideways, she reached for the rocks surrounding the fireplace to steady herself. There was no reason to be sick. Werewolves required moonlight to transform, and moonlight couldn't reach her here. As long as she stayed inside, she was safe.

Right?

That had to be correct, since Jenna didn't want her to go outside, and the blinds were closed. Jenna seemed adamant about remaining indoors.

"What does it want?" Skylar asked.

"I'm not sure." Jenna looked pensive.

"Could it be revenge on whoever resides in this cabin?"

Jenna turned to her. "Why do you think so?"

"I've seen the cage and the room that contains it. I'm wondering if my father's interest in werewolves might have veered off course, and the one he trapped in that cage got away."

Jenna seemed to stop breathing. Skylar read a lot in that sudden silence, mainly that Jenna didn't know anything about a cage in a room tucked away behind Tom Jeevers's house.

"You told me he wanted to protect wolves, not harm them," Skylar said. "So maybe you can explain how a cage hidden here in Colorado might accomplish that. Tell me you realize that locking up a werewolf didn't work so well when it was my mother."

When Jenna's thoughtful gaze met hers, Skylar saw pain in her expression. "There are things you don't know about that," Jenna said.

"But you do?"

"David confided in me about your mother once he discovered what I am. He wanted information about us and was worried. He had to confide in someone in case—"

"In case he tried the same scenario again and the task killed him?" Skylar used both hands to keep herself upright, sick over having her instincts proved correct. Her father must have captured a Were, and that creature somehow eventually tore the cage apart to make its escape. Maybe her dad went after it, and the creature found him first.

Her mind raced over this conversation with Jenna, sweeping back, moving sideways, leaping ahead to recall what information the doctor had provided either knowingly or unknowingly. One thing stood out. It was Jenna's answer to Skylar's question about how her mother differed from both Jenna and Gavin, and what that revealed.

A creature that's so much more dangerous, Jenna had told her. *One that has to be carefully monitored for everyone's good.*

Before realizing she'd moved, Skylar found herself across the room and next to Jenna, able to stand without support. While this sudden burst of strength surprised her and raised all the little hairs on the back of her neck, Jenna showed no concern at all, only the discomfort of being the one to break all this bad news.

"Why was my mother considered to be so dangerous?" Skylar asked. "What made her unlike you and Gavin?"

Under the weight of the question, Jenna began to display the first hint of what made her seem a kind of were-wolf royalty, if pure bloodlines covered that sort of thing among man-wolf combinations.

Her face became even more angular and set, giving the impression of its having been carved from a slab of marble. Her auburn hair deepened in color and richness, as though the full extent of its color and shine had been purposefully repressed to resemble a normal human's red-gold mane. Jenna stared back at Skylar with eyes flashing gold fire.

Or maybe Skylar just hadn't noticed those things until now.

The effect was stunning and a little scary, and made Skylar take an unconscious step back.

"I've been searching for the answer to that question," Jenna replied. "I spent the past few years trying to understand why your father did what he did to your mother, keeping her at Fairview. When I discovered the truth, or what my pack believes must be the truth, his actions became clearer and made me catch the next plane here."

Pack. Dr. James was the member of a pack of wolves that were so much more than four-legged animals, and light-years from being human. Not one thing completely, or the other. Altogether different.

Skylar tripped past those thoughts, locking on to what Jenna just said.

"You discovered the truth? And that truth is?"

"Your mother might not have been a true werewolf at all, Skylar."

"What? You just…"

Jenna raised a hand to silence the protest. "I believe… *We* believe your mother might have been a Fenris."

Skylar wanted to shout for the absurdity to stop. Put an end to the ridiculous accusations and all the strange terms that had come her way since arriving in Colorado, threatening to make the world a brand-new place.

But in the really creepy way people were drawn to anomalies and tragedies, unable to help themselves, she repeated the term Jenna used, wondering if Jenna might be making stuff up.

"Fenris?"

"Will you sit down?" Jenna said.

"No. Talk, please."

Jenna said "All right," as if not totally sure about that or where this information might lead. She ran a hand over her forehead as she went on, pressing back her wisp of bangs. "You were thinking your mother was locked up because people thought she was some kind of demented demon."

"I didn't say that out loud," Skylar protested.

"You thought it."

"Are you telling me you can read my thoughts?"

"When the moon is full, all Weres, when lacking voices, can speak through our thoughts."

This news spread like whips of fire through Skylar's mind, enlightening, frightening, changing things. New ideas formed rapidly and she had to follow where they led, because if Jenna was right and Gavin could hear her thoughts, he'd hear her calling to him now.

It meant that the night before, at the motel when she wished for his return, he'd have been aware of those thoughts, too. Nor would he have had to guess what kind of reception he'd receive when he got there.

Knowing of her hunger, he brought food. He came prepared to engage in the kind of wild, abandoned sex she craved while in his arms. And he obliged her desire to have him stay with her until daylight. All when there was no way he could have heard those wishes.

But wait just a damn minute, she wanted to shout.

"How could Gavin have heard me before the discovery tonight that I might be Were?"

"If you were human, he couldn't have," Jenna said.

"Is it possible he felt the wolf inside me without realizing it? Could he have read me without understanding why?"

"That's entirely possible."

Too fast. Too much information is coming in at once.

"Go on." Skylar whispered the prompt, waving a hand, feeling sick again but standing firm. "What the hell is a Fenris?"

Jenna's eyes were soft and empathetic when Skylar looked there. "A Fenris is an animal demon."

What? Her body's shaking tipped Skylar into an open-legged stance.

"Do you want to hear this, Skylar? It gets worse."

"Yes. Damn it, go on."

"If I'm right about this, your mother was an entity not seen before on earth, or not for generations, anyway. A Fenris comes out of Were legend and is an entity that can appear to be human and also appear in the form of a giant hybrid wolf."

Skylar considered sitting down before she fell, feeling as if she'd been struck by a particularly potent bolt of lightning. Her skin iced over with shock. Her voice pitched an octave higher.

"What do you mean by it *can* appear to be human? A human-wolf combination is what you all are, isn't it?" She failed to include herself in the remark.

"Yes. But we're just that, wolf and human. The Fenris of legend is not human at all, but the offspring of a wolf god."

The shock accompanying this revelation was an almost tangible thing and so dark it covered Skylar with another layer of chills.

Secrets, unknown identities, and the pain and transformations of the body and soul were concepts pushing her beyond her ability to cope. There were too many revelations. The world had gone haywire, taking her down with it, forcing her to either sink or swim.

She laughed with a slightly hysterical tone and then quickly sobered with her attention riveted to Jenna. "You're saying my father married a demon and that union produced four daughters. That my father knowingly carried on with such a creature—not just a werewolf, but something altogether worse—in a way that might now affect his own children. You do realize how ridiculous it sounds? How sick?"

Jenna's reply came swiftly, and as if she'd thought about this before tonight. "He couldn't have known until it was too late. A Fenris must be able to mask what it is for long periods convincingly, until it gets what it wants."

"Which is what? What could a demon want?"

"Offspring."

Skylar's knees threatened to give way, and held her up with only the utmost willpower as she uttered the protest rising from within her. "That's insane!"

Jenna realized this, Skylar knew. She couldn't miss the effect her information was having. Skylar felt Jenna's strong will reaching out to her like an invisible hand helping to shore her up, as if Weres could not only share thoughts, but energy.

"Why not just a werewolf?" Skylar said. "How did you get to Fenris?"

"Gavin's description of the beast fit with the bits of information I found in your father's archives at Fairview. A werewolf would have been easier to deal with when the full moon wasn't overhead. Even a mad one."

"But a demon wouldn't?"

Jenna didn't answer that.

"They had four daughters," Skylar said.

"Two," Jenna corrected.

"Seriously. You think I can't count?"

"Lark and Robyn were adopted," Jenna stated clearly, in a way that defied further argument. "Probably either to further the whole family image or to keep normal kids close to those who might not be quite so normal."

Skylar stared open-mouthed at her father's partner. "How would you possibly know any of that?"

"I checked birth records, just like you could if you dug deep enough."

"Why would you check?"

"Because the children of a Fenris could possess powers unlike those the Were community is used to and would need to be watched."

"In cages and padded cells?" Skylar shouted.

Skylar heard little after that because the ringing in her ears was getting louder by the second. When the alarm bells grew shrill, she clamped both hands to her head and muttered in a voice that sounded nothing like hers, "I'm part demon. That's the charge? My mother was a demon who seduced my father into a liaison that lasted a few years before her incarceration in a mental ward?"

She sucked in enough air to go on. "Well, hell. Screw the body's rewiring process. As the daughter of a demon and the granddaughter of a god, I might not need help with my transformation, after all."

She'd said that in full panic mode, sure there was no way anyone sane could actually believe this nonsense. Wolf gods? Demons able to take any shape they wanted to and birth children? Her two younger sisters had been adopted by her father?

Standing there, listening to this babble, made her feel less like a demon's child and more like an idiot.

Jenna's hand connected with hers, the Were's long, thin fingers warm and senselessly calming.

"Skylar, it's okay," Jenna soothed in a voice as mesmerizing as Gavin's, but in a different way. The earnest compassion in Jenna's eyes gave Skylar the strength to speak.

"Why didn't he let her go? If Dad knew what she was, and that being locked up drove her insane, why couldn't that demon be freed?"

"I'm sure your father discovered his mistake late in the game. Maybe he didn't realize things fully, even then. But he took action to prevent it from happening again, to anyone else."

"He married her. He had fallen for her disguise. That's one hell of a mistake. So, after he put her away, why did he allow me to see her at Fairview? What would that prove? You must see that the discrepancies read more like science fiction."

"I don't think he could have known anything about what he was dealing with for quite a while, Skylar. Madness covers a wide range of symptoms and behavior, as you well know from your studies."

Skylar waited for Jenna to go on.

"Your visit must have calmed her. She'd gotten what she wanted in you and Trish. However, she wasn't allowed to see you. Until you went there, she had probably given up. David's paperwork on your mother stopped after you left the hospital. There's no mention of your mother after that, which suggests to me that the discovery about your mother's true identity either came with your visit or soon after."

Skylar fine-tuned her focus on Jenna's face, looking for a hint of the wolf Jenna carried inside her, finding only the gold flash in her eyes.

"You're sticking to this fanciful explanation?" she asked.

"Because in all honesty, your theories make me worry about you."

Calmly, Jenna said, "I'm here to help in any way I can, Skylar. David was my partner, but some mistakes are so terribly personal, not even professional friendships can bridge them."

Skylar's spine snapped straight with loathing for the whole idea of demons and wolves. She said insolently, "So, do you have something in mind, now that you're here? Have you brought along a dart or two in case you're right about all this and about me, in case my behavior gets out of hand?"

When Jenna winced at the accusation, Skylar was sorry for the remark. Whether or not these were lies and fantasies, Jenna had done her best to answer some of Skylar's questions.

"I came here to be with you," Jenna explained. "In case you were alone and unsure of what might happen to you here. I thought you might need the company of someone who understands the process and could remain a rock in the bizarre, changing world you as yet know nothing about. I wasn't lying about wanting to help. I didn't know about your lover. And I swear to you now that I would have searched for a way to help your mother if I had been there at the time, no matter what she was."

Skylar's reply sounded very small and faint. "You would have helped a demon as dangerous as you think she could have been?"

If there was a way to do so that wouldn't harm others.

"I believe you," Skylar said. "I believe you're sincere about wanting to help."

How did she know that, though? Was she now reading Jenna's emotions as well as her thoughts? Because doing so meant, proved…

You see? Jenna asked without moving her lips.

And Skylar did see. She was forced to comprehend that Jenna hadn't been lying or making things up. The Were beside her truly believed Skylar's mother might have been a wolf demon in disguise and that somehow this place in Colorado might spark Skylar's first transformation.

"So she died," Skylar said slowly. "My mother died soon after I left Fairview."

"And another one may have shown up here, against all odds," Jenna said.

Pounded by the significance of that and unable to stomach any more bad news, Skylar turned for the door and the moonlight beyond it, hoping to either escape this madness or jump right in with both feet. Being *just* a werewolf was bad enough. Now there was a chance she'd become something worse.

Not much of a choice. Not much of a future.

But either way, good or bad, she had to be sure.

Chapter 28

Gavin ran.

His senses were icy with fear and anger at his inability to stop the beast. The thing moved too damn fast.

There were no sounds of footsteps in front of him on the path, though the scent of malice trailed in the great beast's wake along with the foul odor of wet fur.

Branches tugged at him as he moved. Tree limbs hit him in the face. But he would not slow down. His heart lay in the clearing below, and his lover was in no shape to tackle this kind of nightmare.

He wanted desperately to fight. He would have given anything to avoid what might happen if that fanged thing reached the cabin. He refused to picture it. Fear continued to flow through him, chilling his internal heat, mocking his own tremendous strength.

Darting through the forest, he roared his frustration and swallowed blood from the line the beast had drawn on his face with its claw. He'd gotten away lightly this time. The fact that he could stand, run, breathe, was mystifying.

Why? he asked over and over. *Why did you let me go?*

The area remained quiet, but in that silence his heart thundered. Gavin tossed his shaggy head as if he'd deny everything that had happened to him up to this point. Everything except Skylar. He'd never wish to take that back.

God. Somebody.

He needed to get to her in time.

Brace yourself for what's coming, little wolf.

Reaching deep inside, finding one more spark of energy formerly trapped by fright, Gavin kicked up his speed. He ran like the wind, his boots eating up the trail.

When the clearing came into view, his heart soared. But he also felt the complications about to happen down there as if being psychic came with the territory.

Skylar. I'm coming. Damn it, hang on!

Skylar didn't stop to wonder how she sensed her second visitor of the night. An acute awareness of this took her over the minute her feet left the porch.

Before she drew her next breath, moonlight found her and she stumbled to her knees, nerves immediately firing like crazy. The feeling was like being lassoed with barbed wire, the iron thorns piercing skin and muscle all the way to the bone.

Crying out, head lowered, she groped unsuccessfully for a steadying breath. Instead, white-hot flames shot across her skin, entered her open mouth, slid down her throat. Those flames got bigger each time she made a sound.

A new vibration of power filled the night, as if moonbeams were lethal. Each bone in her body began to ache, pound and pulse. She needed to get back inside the cabin. This was a mistake. This was madness.

She couldn't get up.

She wasn't alone out here, her senses told her. The scent of the figure standing beside her was one she now recognized. Wolf scent, similar to Gavin's.

"Hush now. It will hear you." Jenna's thigh, covered by soft faded jeans, was a comfort of sorts against Skylar's quaking left shoulder.

By *it*, did Jenna mean the moon?

Skylar coughed, and blood came up. So did something else. The sound Jenna wanted her to suppress emerged as a growl of twisted torment, a throaty rendition of Gavin's earlier wolfish protests. He'd been in pain, she now understood. His shifting damaged him in some way, and she shared that pain.

Searing stabs of it slammed into her with a force so hard, she stopped breathing. Nasty, electrical, nearly heart-stopping, this new form of agony rushed in to take her down.

This was happening. Jenna hadn't lied. Gavin hadn't lied. Given that the story, or as much of it as anyone could comprehend, was true, there had to be a way of fighting back. She would have to be better than the hurting, fragile weakling she appeared to be. Especially if it wasn't just any old werewolf virus ruling her DNA. She might be part demon. *Something far more dangerous...*

Though the full meaning of that freaky status eluded her, Skylar figured that, as the offspring of a wolf god, the chances of the Blackout killing her were slim and odds for survival better than average. The rewiring of her body surely presented nothing than an obstacle to be mastered. Or so she hoped.

Moonlight flowed over her, and whatever lay nestled inside her paid attention to that. In an attempt to get out, the thing in her gut pummeled her insides until she doubled over with both hands on the ground.

She stared with horror as her fingers sprouted claws, one by one, each of them springing to life faster than the previous one, with pain that was twice as excruciating. Her breath came in agitated fits, her air supply insufficient for any creature, including those tainted with wolf or demon blood.

There was a popping sound near the base of her skull, quickly followed by another. Skylar hissed with each new torment. Between quakes, her spinal column moved as vertebrae began to lengthen and spread apart.

"Can...do...this."

"Yes," Jenna encouraged, though her voice sounded strained. "You can."

Skylar glanced up to find Jenna's attention on the trees and her body rigid with anxiety. Aware of the tension in the air, Skylar pushed her way to her feet, using her hands to claw her way up through the moonlight. Barely upright, she stood, unable to straighten beneath the weight of her body's insufferable demand to change from its human shape into something else.

She managed to lift her head. And there it was, just out of sight—the thing she'd almost seen on the mountain before Gavin had blocked it from view. The thing Gavin had tried so hard to protect her from. This was the bad guy.

Her arm felt heavy when she raised it, though that arm looked much the same as usual. An unnatural sliding sensation in her hip sockets left her feeling sicker, yet she breathed better when upright.

Her wrist came away red when she swiped at her mouth. Blood, from biting her tongue. But the fact that she was standing seemed to be a miracle, and Jenna's concentrated alertness forced her to get a grip.

A new shadow flowed across the path between the trees, getting larger as it neared. Lightning fast, that shadow, merely a blur, reached the edge of the driveway and hurried on to vault the fence.

Jenna didn't stir from her guarded pose. Skylar bit back a scream as that shadow barreled into her. With only a growl of introduction, the shadow became a beast whose thick body pushed her back and up the steps. So scared her ears rang, Skylar fought hard to remain conscious.

She shouted. No sound came out. Her throat seized, squeezing off a howl. Her hands, hanging at her sides, were pinned by the moving mass of muscle, rendering her beginner's claws useless in the face of such a quick attack.

She was through the door and against the wall inside the cabin, trying not to faint, alarmed by the captivity and wondering why Jenna hadn't made one single move in her defense.

It was then Skylar recognized the scent and feel of the beast holding her against the warm stone wall and realized why Jenna hadn't responded. The werewolf beside her wasn't the cause of the trouble ripping through the moonlight. This was Gavin, here with her.

Gavin, the werewolf.

He was huge, angry. His muscles moved like liquid over his tall frame as he growled softly with his face close to hers. She looked right into his blue eyes and found Gavin there.

After making sure she could stand on her own, he said silently, *I guess there are no more secrets.* He brushed her face with his in a tender, loving gesture before rushing back outside.

She was coming unglued. Sanity no longer ruled here, Skylar thought, scraping the wall with a swipe of her claws.

The world was in serious trouble…because, with no distinct boundaries in place to protect reality, nightmares were taking over.

Gavin joined the female Were standing as silent as a sentinel in the cabin's front yard, gazing at the trees. She'd obviously sensed trouble brewing without his having to tell her what he'd seen out there. It took him a minute to remember she could read his thoughts.

Not normal, he sent to her. *Not sure what it is or where it came from.*

It followed you? The she-wolf, still in human form, didn't speak out loud.

Other way around. It headed this way and I followed.

Can you describe what you saw to me?

Gavin shook his head, unwilling to explain. *Met it before.* He raised his claws. *Gave me these.*

The she-wolf acknowledged that by briefly closing her eyes. When she reopened them, she turned to face him. *Aggressive?* she asked.

Monstrous. Yet it could have hurt me again tonight, twice, and didn't. Why?

The she-wolf named Jenna appeared to contemplate that. She threw a glance over her shoulder at the cabin. Disliking the implication of that look, Gavin shuddered.

Maybe it won't hurt us, he suggested, worried. *Because we're what we are, the thing must realize it's the bane of our existence, but also a relative.*

So, what does that leave to spark its interest here? the she-wolf asked. *Or who?*

Gavin knew damn well who that left. He'd known for some time. The creature had acted strangely tonight when Skylar was on the mountain, its aggressive behavior seemingly at half strength. That beast must have recognized

Skylar's scent on Gavin's skin when it sniffed at him quiz-
zically, taken a liking to that scent.

Fresh blood, Gavin thought. *But there goes my theory
of Weres being off-limits to Weres, since Skylar isn't...*

Human, the she-wolf finished for him.

He waved his claws at the cabin. *Will she ever forgive
me for that? For making her a monster, like me?*

You are not to blame, I promise.

Gavin took that remark in with another skip in his pulse.
The she-wolf shook her pretty head as if to ward off arguments and confirm this as fact.

Nevertheless, he couldn't be sure, couldn't see how Skylar's wolf would make an appearance without him putting
it there. The guilt over that would kill him eventually if
the abomination on this mountain didn't get to him first.

It will fight us for reasons we don't understand, he sent
to the other Were, who again gazed thoughtfully at the
cabin. He added, *So I hope to hell you're stronger than you
look. With two of us in the way, we might have a ghost of a
chance of preventing that thing from getting what it wants.*

The next look she gave him was appraising.

I didn't even see it coming, he confessed. *And we both
know Skylar won't stay inside for long.*

Taking a step toward the fence, the she-wolf said solemnly, *I know what this is.*

She didn't say what that was, though, and this she-wolf's
thoughts weren't so easy to read. Some kind of barrier stood
guard over her Otherness, allowing her to project the image
of being human, even when in the moonlight and stressed.

Where did this woman come from? Why should he trust
her?

Why the hell wasn't she shifting right now?

As I see it, I'm all you've got, was her response.

And she was right. What other option did he have for protecting Skylar from a monster's sudden interest?

He was about to tell the she-wolf that, but didn't get it out. At the fence, her body stilled. With a flick of her head to toss back her hair, she raised her face to the moonlight. Chin lifted, lips parted, she unbuttoned her bronze-colored blouse, slipped her arms free of the silk sleeves, and dropped the shirt. The damn thing fluttered to the ground in slow-motion.

She wore nothing underneath. Naked from the waist up, and with her taut back to Gavin, she kept her focus on the heavens as she reached for the waistband of her pants.

Chapter 29

Skylar stumbled to the open doorway. Panting from the strain of downplaying the pain racking her body, she leaned hard against the door frame with her gaze riveted to a fantastical sight she wasn't entirely sure could be real.

Jenna stood by the fence, completely naked. Her hair was loose now, and radiant in the moonlight. No underwear or tan lines marred the sleek, wiry, silhouette. Her arms were raised, her head thrown back as if she embraced the moonlight and actually welcomed its shape-shifting treachery.

Seconds passed, barely enough time to register that sight, before the sound came of flesh sliding over flesh. The unmistakably sickening pop of bones breaking followed, and then all of Jenna's body parts fluidly made the leap from human to werewolf in unison. In seconds, Jenna simply flowed into her other form, growling just once to externalize the discomfort.

Skylar held what breath she managed to take in. Viewing Jenna's transformation caused a responding reaction in her own body, which had been fighting hard indoors to retain its human origins.

Tugged forward as if by a magnet, her feet soundlessly hit the porch floorboards. Although she didn't get far, both werewolves in the yard turned to look at her.

It was astounding to see them both wolfed up in their alternate shapes. But something loomed in the periphery beyond them—the same dark, dense presence she'd met on the mountain. In her memory she saw its outline, felt its weight.

This required immediate attention, though her focus veered back to the yard where in a truly frightening new rendition of a nightmare, wolf Jenna dropped to her haunches, opened her mouth and howled.

The sound that echoed in the clearing was twice as loud inside Skylar's head. Somehow she recognized this as a multileveled call that was equally an invitation and a warning. Loud, frightening, that howl seemed more terrible than anything Skylar had ever heard.

Her own mouth opened to let out a cry of protest, though the cry didn't happen. Instead, she repeated the sound Jenna made, and her human vocal cords churned out a rolling, growling sound that joined the echo of the other one in the crystal-clear, pure mountain air.

Unconsciously, she moved down the steps and into the yard where moonlight—her enemy, antagonist, torturer—slapped her in the face with a sharp, silvery sting painful enough to make her head fly back, and then immediately, savagely, flowed over a stretch of her bare throat.

A set of hands tore at her shoulders, their claws digging grooves in her flesh. Except this time Skylar wanted no protection, no coddling or signs of personal weakness making her insides heave. She wrenched herself away from Gavin's grip. Standing tall, fending him off with a shake of her head, Skylar waited for whatever would happen next.

The overwhelming pain of several minutes ago didn't make a comeback, yet her claws were there when she looked. She began to heat up inside, her temperature soaring to a combustible degree.

Squirming in clothes that felt way too tight and restrictive, she had a sudden burning desire to be free of all the things binding her to her human outline. She wanted to let go and get this over with. Yet her legs remained her legs, their shape familiar and encased in denim. The brush of her hair against the back of her neck produced the usual tickle.

What the hell? Did a werewolf have to strip to achieve a full-body transformation?

Skylar.

Gavin's anxiety piled on to her own.

"No. Gavin, please. I have to find out what this is like, and what I am."

Bad timing, Skylar. We're not alone.

She gave the trees a sideways glance. "Let it come."

This beast isn't like us. It's more dangerous.

She threw a wary glance to Jenna, now a streamlined rust-colored werewolf with a serious edge, and said, "As dangerous as my mother?"

Jenna's wolfish eyes tracked Skylar in a predatory manner, but no medicated dart gun or syringe glistened in her hand. Gavin was in the dark here about the details. He didn't know what Jenna had revealed about her mother.

He bumped her shoulder to get her attention. *It's bad. Trust me on this.*

Again, Skylar looked to the she-wolf crouching by the fence. "What is it?" she asked Jenna, pretty damn calmly for the craziness of the situation they faced and the panting, staccato voice she'd spoken with.

They were werewolves, for God's sake. Not just people. Three werewolves stood in this yard. Well, two and a half at the moment since only her claws proved her affiliation with the clan.

The world had just gone to hell. That thought was seconded by a great howl that answered hers from the shadows beneath the trees.

Gavin's automatic response to the sound crashing through the night was to challenge it with a gruff growl tinged with its own hint of darkness.

Behind him, Skylar uttered a gasp of startled surprise. Near the fence, Jenna, the she-wolf, straightened with her head tilted to one side.

The air moved, though the wind had died. Silence gripped the night.

You said you know about it. He directed this thought to the she-wolf, as well as the idea that he was almost as dangerous as anything else that might turn up in the next few minutes. *Is Skylar right? This beast wants revenge for something only it knows about?*

Receiving no reply, he cursed the gaps in his knowledge.

"What does it want now?" Skylar asked in a voice way too steady for a human about to confront the monster they all knew was coming.

Us, he answered, not sure Skylar could hear him through thought.

You, Jenna corrected with a glance to Skylar. *You asked for the truth, Skylar, so let's be clear about this one thing. I think it's come for you.*

Gavin heard Skylar's teeth snap shut and looked to his beautiful young lover. Even now, his unbridled obsession for Skylar made him want to take her to the ground where he could ease the physical cravings for her that were setting him on fire.

His body hummed with a desire for her made ten times worse by the wolf in him easily recognizing its mate in her. Though she only wielded a set of claws so far and exhibited no other outward signs of an upcoming shift, he sensed the wolf beating at her core, realized that wolf wanted to be free.

Damn it, didn't they all?

He knew he could tug that wolf of hers into being if he chose. Pull it from her with a whisper. Coax it out with a hand on her face. But with the fetid breath of a monster so close by, he knew better than to touch her in any way that might bring more harm.

Skylar stood in the moonlight without swaying. Her face remained ashen, though it glistened with a coat of silver light originating from high above their heads. Her hands were frozen in a raised position, showing off ten lethal claws.

Her gaze moved to him, connecting with his gaze and producing waves of adrenaline that kicked his heart into overdrive. She was thinking she'd be ready for this, yet she had so much to learn.

Here, the she-wolf, suddenly announced. *Look.*

Reluctantly, regretfully, Gavin tore his attention from Skylar, his gut knotting. Following the she-wolf's focus, he found the eyes in the dark that were observing everything in the yard. Those eyes shone with a reddish glow across the short distance between the cabin and the path up the mountain.

He'd seen those eyes up close, firsthand, and thanked the heavens they weren't getting any closer. Boldly, Gavin strode to the gate, where Jenna joined him. Separately, they paced the fence line, their muscles tense and their senses on full alert.

It was Skylar who made the next sound that broke the awkward, loaded silence. She called out to the awful gleam of those eyes, "If you killed him, and he's gone, what more do you need?"

Her voice, full of the fear they all felt, carried. As if it were an invitation too tempting to ignore, the monster Gavin had hunted, chased and thought of with hatred every damn day since the first time he'd encountered it, stepped forward, though not quite clear of the trees.

Its pressurizing effect on the atmosphere reached them in the yard like a bad wind blowing through. Skylar groaned out a whispered "Oh."

The she-wolf, a few paces to Gavin's left, hopped over the fence. Though she didn't go to meet the devil, Gavin considered how brave this Jenna was to close the distance to those trees by even a few measly feet. Although he would have joined her, Skylar's labored breathing, coming in audible starts and stops behind him, kept him from leaving her.

There was no peace to be had with those beastly eyes glaring back at them from the dark. No sense of comfort in his close proximity to the cabin. If he swept Skylar inside again, Jenna might make a stand on her own.

Then again, if they all made it inside, the beast that very likely broken free of the silver cage in the shed would easily tear through a closed wooden door.

I can't picture it, he said. *No human could have captured and trapped this thing. It's too damn powerful.*

Jenna didn't argue or allow her attention to drift. Her concentration possessed an energy all its own.

Skylar made another sound that raised the hair on his arms and made him turn to partially face her. The sound was a word. *Smell.*

With no idea how she could be withholding her shift since beams of moonlight bounced off her in silver sparks—the same moonlight that pelted him and left him voiceless—Gavin thought, *Don't breathe in that bastard's foul stench.*

Her response was quick and unusual. "It's injured."

He was aware of the she-wolf's attention turning their way.

What do you mean? Gavin asked. *Explain.*

"It's been hurt," Skylar said. "Blood and old infections are the cause of the smell."

Gavin wanted to shout "Good!" And he hoped those injuries might eventually claim the damn thing.

Hell. Jenna cursed vehemently several more times, continuously looking from Skylar to whatever watched them from the shadows. *I was right. This thing has come for her and won't wait much longer. Gavin, get Skylar inside. Now.*

Gavin knew better than to argue.

Chapter 30

So, that was it, Skylar thought, allowing Gavin to lead her inside. The directness of Jenna's command brooked no argument from either of them after that final statement.

This thing has come for her.

Mind racing, Skylar looked up from her position at the base of the fireplace, which afforded her a clear view of the door. Gavin stood with his back to it, his body finally retracting, shuddering, compressing back to the man she recognized with an effort that left his dark hair in his eyes and his scarred chest slick with sweat.

She wanted to throw up. She wanted to throw her arms around Gavin but didn't dare. They both had been completely exposed tonight, their secrets shattered, and the shock of those things formed a barrier not easily breached right then.

"Neither of you are anything like what waits in the dark," she said.

Gavin's voice was deep. "Wouldn't your friend know more about that?"

"I'd never met Jenna. Only heard about her."

"No, we're not like that demon," he agreed. "I couldn't intentionally hurt anyone."

"But it can," Skylar said. "That thing can do harm?"

Gavin nodded.

"You know that because you've seen it before. You've met it before tonight," Skylar pressed, needing information in the same desperate way some alcoholics needed a drink. "And before last night, when we were out there."

"I wasn't born like this," Gavin said, standing there, apart from her, trembling.

With sudden comprehension, Skylar made the jump to follow his train of thought. Jenna told her Gavin had been bitten.

"How did it happen?" she asked. "What did that creature do to you? Was it the same one, and can you be sure?"

She could see that Gavin had long avoided the words he spoke now, and see, too, how painful they were for him.

"I was hunting down the cause of a string of animal deaths and reported disappearances," he began, pausing for a breath. "Not only in the wild, but domesticated stock and pets. I tracked drag marks one evening up the hill, following this same path. I was sure the culprit was a mountain lion."

"The path in front of this cabin?" she asked.

"Yes."

"Instead of a mountain lion, you found that thing?"

"Yes."

"You called that creature a man-hater. It left these scars?" She pointed to his chest with a finger ending in a sharply curved claw. Scared to find the claw still there, Skylar dropped her hand and looked away, trembling the same way Gavin did, her body fighting the fever of Otherness.

"I don't know how I survived," he confessed. "For a long time, I wasn't sure I had."

"I'm sorry." Though sincere, her whispered sentiment came nowhere close to covering the horror of what happened to him.

"You've nothing to be sorry for. This had nothing to do with you," he said.

"You might be wrong about that, if it has in fact come looking for me."

Her lover slid a hand over the wall beside him before inching away from the door. "Do you believe that?"

"I'm starting to believe it."

"These—" Gavin pointed to his bare chest where the parallel scars were no longer white and nearly invisible, but a livid, fiery red "—happened two years ago. Long before you came here. How could that thing be waiting for you?"

Although Skylar ached to touch his chest and trace the scars with fingers not sporting the markers of a mythical creature, her claws were a stubborn reminder of how far things had moved past any semblance of being normal.

"My father has been coming here for years. What's happening now must have something to do with that," she said.

"How, though? Who can tell us what's really going on?"

"I can," Jenna said from the doorway, already gracefully slipping back to her human form and unconcerned about ending up naked in company. "But right now we have to get out of here as quickly as possible."

Of course the creature stalking them would have other ideas that probably didn't include allowing them a smooth getaway. Skylar knew that with her own kind of insight as she glanced between slats in the blinds, listening for the groan of the fence being breached. Without seeing anything out there, she felt the nearness of the creature in the same way she'd sensed its closeness earlier, chills and all.

"Too late," she said. "It won't take long for that thing to reach the yard." She looked to Jenna. "Can it hear us?"

"I'm guessing it can." Jenna searched the yard over Skylar's shoulder after catching the blanket Gavin had given her to cover herself up with.

When Skylar backed away from the window, Gavin was there beside her in that quiet way he had of returning to her when least expected and most needed. She found comfort in his body heat and melted into him. His scent was a familiar slice of the heaven she'd been able to sample before this horrid turn of events, and that scent was now an integral part of her.

Gavin, the man-wolf, wrapped his arms around her protectively. "We just need a little help," he whispered with his mouth in her hair. "And some answers."

Skylar looked to the chair, where the gun no longer rested on the seat. She had lost it on the mountain and nearly forgotten about that. "Help in the form of silver bullets?"

Gavin followed her gaze.

"You could have ordered some of those bullets," she said to him. "Why didn't you arm yourself for your next meeting with the thing out there? What kept you from taking this creature down when you could have?"

Gavin said, "That's just it. I didn't have the chance. Although I've been searching for it, the creature only appeared again a few nights ago after I became aware that you were in this cabin."

He tightened his hold on Skylar and went on. "I've got a special blade reserved for that beast in my back pocket. Firing a gun would have alerted people to the disturbance and brought more rangers in. The potential of the beast harming other rangers seemed too great a risk to take."

He paused again before going on. "I hadn't really ever seen it, and had no accurate idea what kind of enemy roamed out there. The night it found me is a blur. I hit my head when I fell, and couldn't even picture that sucker until..."

When Jenna interrupted, Skylar got the impression Jenna wanted to save Gavin from reliving his ordeal. Jenna said, "So, it knows Skylar's here. That's what we're dealing with now, though we're not really sure why it might be looking for her."

"Revenge for what my father did?" Skylar suggested. "Revenge that didn't end with his death?"

"We have to stop it any way we can," Gavin said, glancing to Jenna. "You know what this is, you said, and you agree that it shows some interest in Skylar. How did you figure that out?"

His tone was authoritative and firm. To Skylar's surprise, Jenna willingly answered those questions.

Still gazing out the window, her dad's partner said, "I think Skylar's father didn't just stumble upon this creature here in the mountains. What I've come to believe is that David might have brought it here."

Chapter 31

Gavin's protest over Jenna's declaration was cut off by the memory of finding the cage in a building that Skylar's father had rented.

"What?" Skylar said in confusion, stinging his right thigh with a scrape of her claw.

He covered her hand with one of his.

Jenna, focusing on the yard, spoke over her shoulder. "It's the only answer that makes sense."

"Make sense to whom?" Gavin countered.

"Your description fits," Jenna said.

"What are you talking about?" he demanded, sensing Skylar's ongoing distress rising to intolerable levels.

Jenna fell silent for several seconds. Then she said to Skylar, as she turned from the window, "I think this beast might be related to your mother."

All the fight went out of the woman in Gavin's arms. No one in the room laughed at the absurdity of that statement.

"You called it a monster," Jenna said to him. "Do you call yourself one? Or me? Or Skylar? Did you label this beast a monster because of what it did to you?" Her eyes met his. "No? Then some part of you realizes this creature is different in very notable ways. I'm wondering what those differences are and if we're actually dealing with something new."

Skylar felt his body stiffen further. Her claws disappeared. "You're thinking my father found another one?" she said faintly, as if the idea was too insane to speak aloud.

"Another what?" Gavin asked, but his question was ignored. The intensity of the energy between the two females in the room grew substantially when Jenna's gaze returned to Skylar.

"It's possible that he did bring one here," Jenna said. "Hell, anything is possible."

"You told me she came out of legend, something not seen in generations, if ever. If that was true, what would be the odds of finding another one like her?"

Picking up on pieces of this conversation, Gavin absorbed the vague details swimming in the minds of both of the females—thoughts of monsters, white rooms and hospitals. Was Jenna suggesting there were monsters at Fairview?

"Maybe this one came for her, and finding her gone, found your father instead," Jenna suggested seriously.

"Then he managed to capture it?" Skylar sounded unsure.

Jenna nodded. "He might have brought it here to hide the creature away."

Skylar didn't seem to have anything further to say about that, but he sure as hell did.

"I think you need to backtrack for those of us not in on the story," he said. "What are we facing here? What are you hinting that thing is—the beast that changed my life with its teeth and claws?"

"Demon." Skylar again spoke faintly, muttering that word as if trying to believe it.

The back of Gavin's neck twitched, not only from hearing that term, but from the shock of more pieces of the puzzle falling into place. The answer Skylar had just given was darkly fantastic, yet if it were true, it explained a lot.

Can it be true?

He turned Skylar around to look into her face, seeing immediately that she believed this might be so. Her eyes were huge, her pupils dilated with fear to a deep, flat black, while the skin surrounding them was so very white.

He wanted to kiss her. He wanted to remove her to someplace safe, where they would never have to confront these kinds of issues again. Until the next full moon.

"Your father came across one of these creatures before?" he asked.

"So the tale goes." She flicked her gaze to Jenna, which let him know that Jenna had been the bearer of that news.

"Something happened to that other one?" he pressed.

"She died. Full of needle marks at Fairview, in a padded room," Skylar explained.

Which didn't really explain much at all. Not to his satisfaction anyway. So he started over.

"You said *she*."

"What the hell do we know about demons?" Jenna said when Skylar's quivering mouth stayed closed. "Except that one of them was able to reproduce."

Horror at this announcement struck a solid blow to his chest as if it were a living fist. Gavin saw how Jenna eyed Skylar and, in return, how Skylar's wolf was about to explode within her as a way of coping with things the human woman couldn't.

His tone was harsh. "A demon held at Fairview produced children, or whatever the hell its equivalent of children would be?"

The room went quiet around this question. Gavin's next one couldn't have been stopped or kept to himself, because that just wasn't possible.

"Where are those offspring now? Could that beast be one of them?"

This would tie in nicely with the whole revenge theory being batted around, he reasoned. Maybe this creature sought to exact its own form of punishment on those responsible for keeping its parent in captivity. Possibly Skylar's father brought that offspring here to hide it or…what?

Who the hell knew what Skylar's father had done in that shed?

"Good reasoning," Jenna said, following his thoughts. "Sound, even. Except for one thing."

Skylar whirled to face Jenna.

But with a tremendous crashing sound, the front door splintered into pieces, scattering wood, hardware, and hinges everywhere.

And the night rushed in.

Chapter 32

All three of them moved at the same time, launching through the bedroom door and using the farthest window to make an exit. Skylar didn't even notice the sharp shards of broken glass from the window she followed Jenna through. Fear made her oblivious to her surroundings and blissfully numb.

They raced for the Jeep, parked on the dirt driveway, but moonlight was in the way. Sprinting through that light was like slogging through ankle-deep mud.

Somehow, miraculously, none of them shifted before jumping inside the car. Maybe the fierceness of their concentration lent a hand, or their incredible speed. Too afraid to look at what might be following, Skylar focused straight ahead, only slightly relieved when she, Jenna and Gavin slammed the doors, as if that would keep a demon out.

Luckily, the keys were in the ignition and all it needed was a turn. Heartbeats filled the tight space when the engine sputtered to life. Gavin stepped on the gas and the

Jeep flew forward. With both hands on the wheel, Gavin expertly maneuvered the car in a U-turn, intending to head for the road.

Skylar dreaded speculation that the demon Jenna spoke of wasn't going to let them off so easily after announcing its presence. In her heart, and in her twisted gut, she sensed its intentions, and was too scared to speak.

Flashbacks of memory came—dark shadows passing behind the car the night she drove, seen only out of the corner of her eye and in the rearview mirror. Wolves on the loose, Gavin had said. Nothing about demons seeking revenge. No mention of demons at all.

Inside her, tucked deep, nestled the new fear that her father might indeed have brought one here, as Jenna suggested. The thought became all the more terrible because of what that demon had done to Gavin.

Its behavior would make her dad, in the long run, responsible for the creation of one werewolf, and possibly more that they didn't know about.

Gavin spoke. "I don't know where to go. If that thing follows, we can't lead it to town."

Skylar wished they could go to town. People, in a big group, might be able to tackle a beast. There'd be a chance. Gavin was right, though, and determined as always to protect the community from physical and mental harm. Innocent people not only had to be protected from a raging monster, but the idea of that monster's existence.

Gavin was at that very moment pondering how to keep her safe, and Skylar loved him for that, and for so much more. Someday she'd tell him so. If they survived the night, he'd need to understand how she felt in spite of their short time together.

"I do know," he said, without looking at her. "God, Skylar, I feel the same way."

Jenna interrupted. "Hey, we're not dead yet. Can we make a plan?"

"I'm all ears." Gavin's voice was gruff with emotion. He kept glancing Skylar's way with his hungry blue eyes.

"Now that we've got our breath back, we probably need to realize that I was wrong about running. Going back there might be the only option," Jenna said.

Gavin continued to drive. "I don't think that would be healthy."

"Shall we go in circles, then? All night if we have to? After that, what? For all we know, a demon can be a demon whenever it wants to, with or without a full moon," Jenna argued.

"Whereas I can't be a werewolf without that damn moon," Gavin said. "That's your point, right? A human can't hurt this creature, so we're at a huge disadvantage after tonight?"

He added seconds later, "Jenna, are you able to shift without the moon's shiny silver impetus? Somehow I sense that you can."

"Yes," she replied honestly. "I can and have. It's tough, and it's nothing any Were in their right mind would want to attempt too often. That said, too much adrenaline, too much emotion, can bring on an urge to shift for those born to it."

Skylar heard Gavin's next question in his thoughts before he uttered it aloud.

He said, thoughtfully, "Back there, you said my thinking was sound, except for one thing. Since your advice is to go backward, how about if we start there?"

No explanation came from Jenna.

Gavin thumped the wheel with his palms. "What's so terrible that I can't hear it? Worse than the existence of werewolves, demons that track humans and the fact that

none of this is myth? Christ, I'm not sure anything could
be worse."

Why are you blocking me from this? he was thinking.

"It's me," Skylar said, and those two little words made
a big impact on the chill ruffling through the car. "I'm that
one thing Jenna was talking about. I may hold the key to
some of this mess."

Gavin swerved to the right, onto the dirt. The tires
kicked up sprays of mountain debris as he put on the brakes
without seeming to give a damn about anything other than
what she'd said.

The car stopped so fast, they all flew forward. Gavin
turned to her, waiting for her to explain her statement. Skylar saw no place to hide from the confession he wanted,
since he could read her thoughts if he tried. However, if
the answer drove him away, she wasn't sure what she'd do.
A future without Gavin in it presented a bleak picture... If
there was to be any future for her at all.

She and Gavin were connected, with a bond that had
snapped into place with the first shared look. She would see
him standing at the cabin's gate, and the way he'd looked at
her in that moment, for the rest of her life. The two feet of
distance between them in this car were two feet too many.
She'd have traded anything to be in his arms.

"I..." Her voice faltered.

Her lover deserved to hear the truth about the dilemma
she faced. He deserved to know what Jenna told her, and
that she really couldn't rest until that theory was proved
true or false. Gavin had to understand how scared she was
to tell him any of this, though that's exactly what she must
do. Right now.

"You can tell me," he said. "You can trust me, Skylar."

"Okay." She gathered her courage. "Apparently, I could
be the child of the demon once housed at Fairview. One of

its two children. So unless the beast out there is my big sister, who was in Miami the last time we talked on the phone, the creature on this mountain can't have sprung from my mother's womb, as far as I know. That's something."

Stunned speechless, frozen, Gavin's beautiful eyes were on her. He didn't drop his gaze to search her for signs that this could be true, the way she might have if the tables were reversed—something demonish in her outline that he might have missed. A red gleam in her eyes?

After the shock of her answer began to wear off, his blue gaze softened and he said, "I see."

Just that. *I see.*

They sat opposite each other, trying to make sense of this information when there was no sense to be had. No one cared to offer up a suggestion about how to prove or disprove her statement, or how proving it mattered. An underlying added stress for Skylar was the fact that if the monster followed them, they were easy prey at the moment, parked by the side of the road. Sitting ducks.

But the beast didn't show itself, and that, too, was yet another oddity in a long list.

Gavin eventually turned the wheel and got the Jeep back on the road leading away from the cabin, where under the canopy of trees, moonlight dulled to a dim and distant glow. Out of all the other things he could have chosen to say, he chose this one. "So, you have a sister."

Skylar closed her eyes briefly, thankful to be able to deal with this remark. "Three of them," she said, despite what Jenna had told her about two of them being adopted.

"I don't have any siblings. I haven't seen my parents since…well, you know."

She got that, all right, and said in a rush, "I want to know everything about you before *this*. How you grew up, where you grew up and why you became a ranger. What kind of food you like. What sort of bed you sleep in. Your favorite color. Will I get to hear about those things, or is it too late?"

"I promise you will know all of those things," Gavin said.

Her battered soul required the normalcy of small talk and familiar themes. Her revved-up body craved the werewolf beside her with a nearly out of control passion.

Animal instincts were at work, she supposed, like the ones telling her to run and to howl at the moon. Would Gavin and Jenna let her go if she opened the door? Allow her to find her fate? She didn't think so, and didn't have to read that in their thoughts since it was plainly written on their faces.

Gavin's emotions ran in fiery streaks along her nerve endings. He wanted all those same things and to know her background, too. At that moment they were wounded, desperate souls in search of a good grounding. They were two hungry souls in need of the promise of a good, long future.

It was stupid to imagine the beast wasn't following, though, or watching without showing itself. Did only she feel its breath? Hear its call? Sense it waiting? Was revenge the reason it was after her?

Who'd hurt it, if not her father, in that silver cell?

Did a Fenris reason, think, plan its revenge with intelligence?

Could her mother have been just like it?

God...can any of this be real?

She said, "Stop. Stop the car."

Startled, Gavin again slowed.

"Jenna's right. We need to go back."

"That's nuts," Gavin objected.

"I can't run away. It will never end if I run tonight."

Jenna spoke up. "It's our best bet. Maybe we can capture the demon."

"Capture it?" Gavin repeated. "No. No way. Then what? Keep it locked up? Do the very thing it might be rebelling against?"

"I didn't mean that," Jenna said. "I'd never do that. I meant if we could capture it, we could ask what it wants. Maybe it understands more than we think."

"What if it doesn't?" Gavin asked.

"Do you want it to do more damage? No matter what we like or dislike, would you wish a meeting with that demon on any unsuspecting hiker or summer resident?" Jenna didn't hesitate to tell it like it was. "This is what we do. What my pack and others like us do to keep the peace and keep ourselves safe."

"What do you do?" Skylar asked.

"Whatever it takes to ensure the future and keep the secrets of our species safe," Jenna replied. "As harsh as that may seem to you right now, it's important. Trust me on that."

Skylar got that, no problem. The sticking point continued to be wondering how a demon like this one could have fooled her father and produced children. Her. And Trish. Then again, maybe her mother wasn't like this one at all. Maybe she was something else entirely.

"Go back," she repeated, tired of the speculation and in dire need of closure. "Please, Gavin. Either take me back to the cabin or let me out right here."

He shook his head as he began a wide turn. "We do this together or not at all."

He looked in the rearview mirror, at Jenna.

"It's not much of a plan, though," he muttered. "So we have about three minutes to make one."

Skylar said, "I just want to see this thing up close and tell it how sorry I am if in fact my family hurt it."

"Then what?" Gavin's frustration showed in his tone. "You're best friends?"

"No." Skylar was deadly serious. "That beast and I acknowledge that we're family."

"You're kidding, right?" Gavin eyed her instead of the road.

"Hate to break it to you, Gavin, but I think she's being sincere," Jenna said.

Chapter 33

No demon waited for them on the road, in the driveway or the yard. Instead of relief, Gavin experienced a flush of new adrenaline that made his muscles dance as he faced the cabin. He had wanted to find this demon for a long time, and when he finally had the chance there were two women by his side with beastly tales of their own to contribute.

Well, not women exactly, though at the moment they were reasonable enough facsimiles.

Every nerve in his body was edgy and on full alert. After switching off the engine, something he didn't really want to do, the night became eerily quiet. Moonlight reflected off the hood of the car and shone through the windshield without reaching his thighs. He noticed Skylar pressing herself against the seat as if that light contained incinerating properties and, in fact, it kind of did.

"It's still here," Skylar said, studying the cabin through the windshield. "Close."

Though he couldn't really determine the truth of that in

any tangible way and felt very little beyond the pull of the moonlight waiting for him, Gavin went along with Skylar's assessment.

His breath came in shallow puffs too inadequately timed to keep pace with his racing heartbeats. Instinct told him to get out of the car and find the sucker hiding from them for the moment, but he was too worried about Skylar to open the door.

Jenna made the first move. Tossing off the blanket she'd draped around herself, she stepped out of the car, and with a soft sighing sound again flowed incredibly smoothly into her werewolf form.

Something in the way she did that tugged Gavin into following her lead. Never easy for him, his bone-breaking shift doubled him over. His body convulsed, still fighting the change rather than fully accepting it, but this shift came faster. He rallied in less than a minute.

Jenna growled. Rolling his muscled shoulders, Gavin growled back. From different sides of the car, they focused their attention on the cabin, though neither of them made a move in that direction.

Skylar finally got out of the car and looked at him over the hood. Her eyes met his greedily. Then, without showing so much as a twitch toward a shift in form, she took off toward the cabin on her long human legs.

He went after her with the auburn she-wolf on his heels. Up the steps, across the porch, Gavin chanted, *Slow down, Skylar!*

Her heat was high and her anxiety level through the roof. She'd feel she had more at stake here in facing the beast than they did, when that was far from the truth.

Through the splintered front door, into the living room, they ran. No sign of the monster remained there except for the scattered remnants of that front door, though Skylar paused in a frozen stance, looking over her shoulder at the bedroom.

No demon jumped out at them in the bedroom when they entered it. Gavin supposed that any creature once kept in a cage probably wouldn't like to linger within four square walls.

Skylar spun around to stare at the window they'd broken and used as an exit. Raising her pale face, she sniffed the air—a strangely spooky action for someone in human skin. Then she lunged for the window and dragged herself over the sill. He followed her with Jenna on his heels, not sure what was going on, other than his guess that Skylar was using some kind of special radar to zero in on her prey.

He almost laughed at that thought, fairly close to his limit on patience. The night had been crazy from the get-go, and he felt pumped-up. His thoughts turned to the gun with its silver bullets, which he couldn't have picked up with his wolfish hands anyway, if Skylar hadn't dropped it somewhere on that mountain. He wished things weren't moving so fast and that he could transition back and forth as easily as Jenna. His stamina was already suffering.

Maybe with time he'd become more adept at exchanging one shape for the other.

If he survived.

Outside the cabin, Gavin began to scent the trail the demon had left. By then Skylar was heading for the path leading up the mountain. Other than planting himself in front of her, he doubted anything would stop her from confronting her destiny, and he couldn't fault that wish. In her place, he would have wanted the same thing. He'd need to find the truth.

As he moved after Skylar, he watched her for signs of the moon forcing her to change shape, wondering how she had so far avoided the silvery call that twisted through him.

Higher and higher they climbed: one semi-human demon and her two furred-up companions on a mission that surely would lead to someone's death. He'd be damned if it would be Skylar's.

Gavin's thoughts raced, producing clear images with each breath of moon-filled air. In his mind, he saw the beast, massive, dangerous as hell. But could it be a real demon? Was there any way Skylar's blood could possibly be tainted by a relationship to such a thing?

Then again, if Skylar did have demon blood in her, they were in the same boat. If the beast they were after actually turned out to be a demon, its curse had also fallen on Gavin. That beast's blood had mingled with his, and that's what forced him to change. In that respect, he and Skylar were blood compatible. So again, the question became one of why Skylar wasn't morphing now.

Halfway up the hillside, she stopped, breathing hard, trembling big-time. Gavin closed in, pressing his body to hers possessively. *What do you see?*

She wasn't able to speak, and didn't try. Her eyes held a wild cast and were again black with fear. By her side, Jenna growled an encouraging rumble and continued to survey the area, also having noted the heavy weight of the burdened atmosphere. Jenna's thoughts were clear. She was wishing her pack were here to help.

Skylar surprised them both when she called out "I'm here," as though she perceived something he didn't.

It quickly became obvious she had.

The beast he'd been searching for, the monster that had made his life a living hell, appeared ahead of them on the path as if Skylar had simply conjured it out of thin air.

Or called it to dinner.

The giant beat with life, its body visibly vibrating in the dappled light. This was no bit of overworked imagination, Gavin's gut told him. The fact that he'd met this abomination a few times already didn't dull the effect of this sighting. The thing ahead of them on the path was too big and too otherworldly. Everything about it screamed for him to run.

In that loaded silence, no one moved. The demon didn't advance. Unlike their prior meetings, it failed to circle its prey or even acknowledge Gavin's presence.

It was too busy staring at Skylar.

Her thoughts had stopped reaching Gavin some time ago, replaced by a buzz of static in his ears. Panic gripped him. Jenna stood as though she'd been turned to stone, her unwavering attention on the demon.

"I know what you are," Skylar said to the creature. "And why you're here."

She was fighting to get the words out, squeezing them through her constricted throat.

"You've met my father, I believe. I'm Skylar Donovan, and they tell me I'm the child of one of you."

The red-rimmed eyes across from them were unblinking and remained fully trained on Skylar. Gavin's internal heat flared against the threat, the fires stoked by his nearness to the creature that had made him what he was. But the beast's restraint truly plagued him. Perhaps some demons picked and chose their victims, and then took all the time they needed to attend to that singular objective.

Did this one understand human speech?

When would it pounce?

"I didn't know about you," Skylar went on. "No one I knew did. I'm not sure if my dad hurt you or if someone else might have, but I've come here to tell you how sorry I am for any hand my family might had in seeing you harmed."

She waved to include him and Jenna. "I don't think I'm

like them." Her hand moved toward the moon. "So maybe what they say about me being like you is true. Do you see a connection?"

The beast slid forward, stopped, sniffed with its big head lifted, and then lowered its face until it was level with Skylar's from a distance of five feet.

"Maybe," she said, pushing the limits of Gavin's tolerance for dangerous standoffs, "you knew my mother. Her name was Greta."

Gavin had called this thing a beast and an abomination, but he saw now those things didn't begin to describe what faced them. It had to be a demon that cocked its long-snouted head, straightened to its full and substantial height, and roared with a bellowing blast of anger that sent Gavin and Jenna stumbling sideways. Gavin pulled Skylar with him, his claws embedded in the back of her jeans.

"Do you understand me?" Skylar asked, righting herself, struggling out of Gavin's grasp to face the creature. "Have you come here to hurt me?"

Another great howl went up, filling the area with a harrowing echo. Thing was…that sound hadn't come from the monster across from them.

Thrown off-balance by the sheer surprise of the sound, both Gavin and Jenna whirled toward this new threat without considering the consequences of turning their backs on a demon.

Chapter 34

Skylar was knocked off her feet and flung to the side, but somehow, with the grace of a cat, managed to land on her feet.

The night filled with the sound of deep, menacing growls and snapping teeth as a great weight descended from behind her, bending her forward and cutting off her air supply.

Face in the dirt, heart pounding at a disastrous rate, she saw shadows darting around her, heard Gavin's burst of exhaled breath and Jenna's protesting yip. An iron-like odor of blood saturated the ground. The lights went out. No. She had merely closed her eyes. The moonlight hadn't gone anywhere.

Coarse, wiry fur smelling of damp, dirty places, brushed across the back of her neck, just above her collar. She shivered and cried out as a scrape of bony claws pierced her shoulder, cutting right through the cloth of her shirt.

A cry went up that wasn't hers, and was immediately answered by another. Dark paws passed in front of her eyes, inches away, scrabbling for traction, attracted to the blood seeping from her wound.

To her right, Jenna was up and moving, encouraging her to do the same. Hunched over, fighting off an onslaught of swiftly moving bodies, Skylar curled into a ball and rolled away from the nightmare in front of her, only to be confronted with yet another nightmare once she got to her knees.

Gavin, fierce in his werewolf form, pulled animals off her and tossed them aside. Jenna jumped in front of Skylar, growling, doing her share of damage, but not before Skylar saw what those animals fighting Gavin and Jenna were. Wolves. Real ones. No human in them.

They kept coming. Gray blurs with their teeth bared. Some of them called out when Gavin fought through them. Others yowled as if they were not only starved but mad with a rage that knew no bounds. The sight of two werewolves didn't deter them because the smell of blood promised a delicacy too good to pass up.

And maybe they just didn't like what they saw.

Wild animals...

Skylar had time for just that one thought before she was grabbed from behind. Two massive arms closed around her, lifting her off her knees and out of the dirt. The scene in front of her began to fade as she was dragged backward, away from the fight.

She kicked out without connecting with her aggressor. The grip on her waist was tight and growing tighter, a discomfort that made it impossible to cry out.

This is it, she thought. *The beast has found its prey.*

Kicking out again with both legs, squirming as much as she could, Skylar refused to give up. *Not an option.*

She found room to breathe and made a charge. "You…

killed…my…father." Those whispered words set the stage for what she was sure was about to happen to her. "He is all I knew. All we had."

More chaos. Dark blurs. Two dark forms rushed at her, one of them lunging for the beast that had her secured. A flash of red that came with the name Jenna jumped on top of the demon, bearing down with her sharp canine fangs. A darker figure with a seductive scent she knew all too well attacked the arms holding her captive with his own wall of moving muscle.

"Gavin!"

The beast loosened its grip and roared its displeasure. Though tough as nails and fighting for a hold, Jenna flew off, discarded with one good shudder. Another fling of its arms dislodged Gavin and let Skylar fall.

Gavin stumbled back and dropped to a crouch, ready to spring again. But, before he got off the ground, the beast was on top of him, growling, knocking Gavin back with a superior speed and strength that suggested to Skylar that this was no fight at all and that the beast that could have snapped them all in half if it chose to.

Yet for some reason, it didn't seem to want to inflict that kind of damage. The monstrosity just sat there, pinning Gavin, roaring over and over as if shouting curses in an alien language.

Why?

Why would such a dangerous creature hold back?

Skylar advanced on the beast, and the beast sprang back so fast, she had to turn her head to find it. Gavin, caught unaware and too riled up to read her body language, leaped in front of her.

One good shove from the beast and Gavin, in all his werewolf glory, backpedaled five or six feet. Another pivot and shove, and Jenna was there next to him, growling with fire in her eyes.

Neither werewolf had time for a replay, though. With a shiver and a long reach, Skylar was again in the creature's grip and being carted away before the werewolves had time to blink.

What the hell was that? Gavin demanded, running for all he was worth after the beast that had taken Skylar.

Fenris.

Jenna was nearly as out of breath as he was, but still faster. He had to kick things up a notch to keep up with her. *If it hurts her, I'll...*

Maybe it won't.

Then what does it want?

I don't know.

Can you find where they've gone, Jenna? We can't be too late. Just please get me there.

Moonlight streaming through pine branches fueled their run. Firing werewolf synapses enabled them to cover ground at an astonishing speed, though Gavin feared it wasn't good enough. The demon stayed well ahead of them, climbing higher and higher up the mountain. Eventually, it would reach the rocks.

Hell. Then what?

His brain turned off the rest of his questions. All his effort was necessary for him to reach Skylar before the demon reached that peak. One slip from up there and there'd be no coming back.

Wait, Skylar. Wait for me.

Did she hear him?

One more bend in the path and the rocks became visible. Crystal veins in the granite made them sparkle in moonlight, which would have been pretty at any other time.

They had reached tree line, too high up on the mountain for much to grow.

Gavin saw them immediately. The great hulking creature had Skylar in its grip as it barreled upward, oblivious to the steep drop on its left.

It moved higher, to where the air became thinner, and breathing, for a runner, whether a werewolf or not, was no easy task.

Then it disappeared.

Gavin roared, sucked in what air he could and ran on, hearing Jenna panting behind him. The rocks came into view, and above them, several outcroppings. They had to have run for miles. The elevation was extreme.

Around one more bend, he skidded to a stop, and sensed Jenna doing the same. His heart couldn't have beat any faster. His blood was nearing the boiling point. But he was frozen in place.

Skylar stood on a large rock ledge, with her back to a boulder. Her arms were at her sides, bracing her stance. Her fair hair whipped in the wind, partially covering her ashen face.

The demon, less than a foot away from her, was trapping her there, pacing back and forth and facing her with its great mouth open.

Something inside Gavin went ballistic. Anger turned his vision white, then black, then red. With a running jump, he leaped from rock to rock, growling, furious, no longer caring about anything except reaching Skylar and somehow finding the strength necessary to kick some Fenris ass.

His body responded to the request for strength with a fresh flush of power. He heard a sound like the crack of lightning, and his legs just took him there.

Landing on the rock several paces from the Fenris, he

held up a hand of warning. The demon, its dark fur moving in waves in the wind, turned its big head.

This one is not for you, Gavin said, raking a claw over the scars on his chest. *You've done your share of harm here, and it's time you left.*

The Fenris glared back.

She's not like you. Not really. Look at her. Would you take her away, stop one more breath? She's done nothing to you. Skylar is innocent of anyone else's crimes. Let her go.

Still no response came from the monstrous werewolf that everyone supposed was a demon. In fact, he thought that this thing looked and smelled as if it might have been to hell and back.

Standing firm, Gavin spoke again. *If sacrifice is what you need, then take me in her place. Thanks to you, I'm halfway gone already.*

The Fenris's eyes blinked and then refocused on Gavin. They were light eyes. Red-rimmed, but light in color. Gray? An intelligent gleam backlit them, making those eyes seem way too human. This was a trick. Had to be.

The demon moved, appearing next to Gavin before Gavin's next breath. No werewolf could possibly move that fast. Jenna and Skylar had been right. Just when you thought the world couldn't toss up anything worse, it coughed up worse by the bucketful.

Gavin.

This was Jenna, taking advantage of his current thoughtful state.

Gavin. Please back away. Slowly. No fast moves or threats.

He shook his head. *This ends here.*

Maybe not the way you think it will, Jenna said. *Listen to me. Trust me. Back away now.*

Not happening.

He watched Skylar, using the rock to brace herself, and said to her, *No, my lover. My love. I won't let it hurt you.*

Still visibly quaking, Skylar pushed off from the stone. When the creature's head turned toward her, she looked into that face, into those eyes. Then Skylar swayed and put a hand to her forehead. Gavin heard her say "No," and "Can't be."

Gavin. Jenna called him again. The adamancy in her voice prickled.

His attention was riveted on Skylar. His gaze covered every detail of the body he already knew so well, sure he must be missing something. Though Skylar's fear buzzed like electricity in the air, her face no longer reflected that same level of fright. Her features seemed to have softened into a look he'd witnessed while staring down at her in bed, with his naked body pressed to hers.

What the hell is going on? he demanded.

It knows her, Jenna said. *Recognizes her.*

Gavin's growl of protest stuck in his throat. *Skylar?*

Skylar ignored him, intent on remaining upright as she searched the Fenris's face. Gavin heard her say to the beast, "He kept you in a cage. I can't imagine what that must have been like. God. Was it because you're so dangerous and willing to hurt others?"

Was the damn thing talking to her in return? Gavin didn't hear anything else. But Skylar was too close to that demon…and to the edge of the ledge she stood on.

His anxiety made him inch forward. Skylar didn't notice. *Keep it busy,* he sent to her, not stopping to consider if the beast could hear him.

Her focus didn't waver. Looking at the Fenris, she said, "He didn't do that to hurt you. I knew him to be kind, so hurting you couldn't have been his intention. He must have brought you here to protect you. Maybe he kept you caged in order to protect others. And to protect us."

Gavin saw her knees begin to weaken. He watched Skylar sag back against the stone, and he stepped forward, intending to reach her. It was Jenna, still furred up and incredibly strong, who held him back.

When Skylar closed her eyes, he wanted to shout, but no sound emerged. Her chest expanded as she sucked in a breath, made a sound like a stifled sob and pushed herself back up, bringing herself closer to the demon. She was face-to-face with the abomination, and Gavin couldn't stand one minute more.

But then Skylar spoke to her captor, in a voice teeming with barely contained emotion.

"Oh, God. Is it you?" she said.

Chapter 35

Is it you?

Skylar's heart seemed to clench inside her chest as the question she asked echoed in and around the rocks. She wasn't sure this was happening.

This wasn't a joke. No mistake. She had to speak but couldn't find a pattern of words to confront the images racing through her mind of white coats, white rooms, a mattress on the floor and food that had to be eaten with bare hands from disposable paper trays.

How could she have missed the signs now lining up?

Why hadn't she recognized this presence, even from afar?

Finding her breath, she spoke slowly, precisely, trying desperately to control her emotions.

"He told us you died."

Noise from the periphery didn't matter to her. Her lover was there, waiting, fighting his need to help when Jenna kept him from doing so. Gavin was trying desperately to understand what was going on. Her father's partner, a good woman and a fierce she-wolf, also waited. But there was no way to explain this, no way to really comprehend that it wasn't just a Fenris she faced here.

This was her mother.

She felt like sitting down. Falling down. The discovery was overwhelming. She felt herself sinking.

"What do I need to do?" she asked the demon that had long ago taken human form. And though this creature might have deceived her father, she had also shielded six-year-old Skylar from medicated darts.

This same being had wanted to be with her child as badly as that child wanted her mother. It was all there in the demon's eyes. Recognition. Familiarity. Frustration. Confusion. Untapped emotion.

"I'm here," Skylar said. "You know me."

The demon tossed her head and looked to where Gavin and Jenna stood.

"You made him," Skylar confirmed. "You made Gavin a werewolf. Is that what it's like? You sometimes lose control and become the thing you fight against? That's the behavior that made Dad keep you away from others?"

The demon's attention, drawn by Skylar's speech, came back to her.

"Did you hurt Dad?"

The demon backed up, taking several small steps at a time, its eyes still on Skylar.

"Stay," Skylar said with a pleading tone. "Please. I'll find a way to take care of you."

She stumbled forward with both hands outstretched, her new claws obvious in the moonlight. The Fenris stood very still for a few heartbeats, as if waiting for Skylar's touch, but it didn't allow the contact.

"He brought you here, didn't he? He kept you here so that no one would find out about you. So that I wouldn't find you again," Skylar said.

She resisted another step, both drawn to and repulsed by the creature in front of her. The creature whose blood ran in her veins.

The Fenris's eyes blinked slowly. Its mouth moved as if it wanted to speak.

"I'm sorry," Skylar said. "I'm sorry for everything, and that if you had a plan for your future here, among humans, it couldn't have worked very well."

The Fenris lifted one massive paw, turned it over invitingly but then retracted the gesture. She sliced her chest open with a four-inch-long claw, and let a drop of blood drip from her fist.

"If you changed once, can you change again?" Skylar asked, understanding what the creature meant by the display of blood. Maybe they weren't one, or exactly alike, but that blood belonged to them both.

The Fenris knew who Skylar Donovan was.

"Can you be her? The mother I saw? I know about the moonlight, and what it does."

The beast in front of her suddenly flickered, as though it had never been solid in the first place. An outline appeared. It was a waifish, slender woman with dark hair and a gaunt face that stood in the Fenris's place for seconds only, but long enough to make Skylar's eyes fill with tears.

They were tears of loss, confusion, fear of the past and of the future. Tears of longing for the mother she never really knew and now might lose, though that mother wasn't human.

"Please," she whispered, taking another step, the tears falling unchecked down her cheeks.

But the image of the woman quickly disappeared, replaced by the massive body of the Fenris, a frightening creature that so few people knew anything about.

The Fenris made a keening sound, deep in her throat, that made Skylar snap upright.

"No," she said. "Please don't."

With one more toss of her head, one more blink of her light eyes and an accompanying howl of pain, the creature turned. And with a great leap into the air, the Fenris soared from the rock into the valley beneath, not to any escape route this time, but to her death.

Gavin was there in a flash, afraid to touch Skylar though he wanted to, ached to. Skylar was teetering on the brink of the rock the Fenris had leaped from. He said nothing because what was there to say?

Skylar had called that demon *mother*.

That couldn't be right, but Skylar was still in danger.

I'm here, he said, over and over, softly, tenderly, afraid to find cover and change back to his human shape. Afraid to move away from Skylar.

It was a long time before she looked his way: an interminable, unendurable number of minutes. When her eyes registered his presence, there was so much pain in them, he choked back a response.

Speaking was difficult for her, but she said in a voice that cracked, "Sorry."

Gavin fisted his hands to keep from grabbing her as she went on. Another foot backward, and she would fall.

"That's what I carry in me," she said. "At least in part."

The tears glistening in her eyes broke his goddamn werewolf heart.

Hell, so do I, he said, daring just one small step forward. *Maybe that was fate, too, for those who believe in that kind*

*of thing. Maybe I'll be the best person to understand you.
I'm willing to try.*

He tracked every tear that ran down her cheeks.

"She didn't do it on purpose," she explained. "She didn't
intend to hurt you. She'd been caged, and she got loose.
She didn't want to go back there."

There was a further hitch in her voice. "What will happen to me if I inherit that tendency for danger?"

*You won't. You're half human, and it turns out that
half is a good one. You've been strong enough to keep the
changes at bay.*

"She could have killed me with one swipe of her claws,
Gavin. She wasn't dead. All those years, she was alive and
living like this. And now she's gone."

I know. Skylar, I know.

"The myths are wrong. She wasn't a monster. She died
for me. She gave her life to save me from having her in
my life. I saw that in her. She didn't kill my father. He did
his best to keep her safe from others and from herself. She
knew that. He must have slipped, fallen."

She turned to face the drop to the valley. "When I look
back, I see the things my father did to protect us. We knew
how to use guns. He introduced me to Danny, a cop, possibly assuming that kind of relationship might offer me a
greater defense in case I needed it. He distanced himself
from us so that we wouldn't come here, where he...where
he tried to take care of her."

It's over, Gavin said softly.

Skylar's eyes met his. "Really, it's only the beginning."

We'll face whatever comes our way.

"Our way?" she repeated.

*Can you finish your school work here? Close to here?
Would you regret leaving Miami? I'd like you to stay here
with me. I need you to stay.*

"Will you two get a room?" Jenna said, appearing beside them in her human form wearing little more than a very sober expression. "You're making me crave my guy, and it's a long flight home. And yes, my Matt is like us. That's important and saves a lot of trouble and heartache."

Jenna's tone was light in an attempt to ease the blow Skylar had received. They all realized this and silently thanked her for it, though he felt Skylar's pain as if it were his own and knew she wouldn't truly get over this for a long, long time, if ever. Such was the way of darkness once it had gotten a foothold.

And he shared her feelings because they had imprinted, bonded, connected, as two halves of a pair.

A lot of questions still needed answers. Questions like how her mother's human-like form could have lasted long enough for her to be married and have children. And when Skylar's father had found out what his wife really was. How he'd taken that shock.

Questions about how a Fenris got here in the first place and met David Donovan, and whether that meeting was chance, or somehow preordained.

How had this Fenris recognized her daughter?

What the hell was a Fenris, really?

How would that kind of blood affect Skylar?

None of those answers would be coming now, not without a lot of research. Maybe they were the same questions Skylar's father had needed answered for the sake of his own peace and sanity. Still, it had to be clear to Skylar that her father had loved her. He had loved his daughters enough to leave them in order to keep them safe. And to protect them from the truth.

Gavin needed a voice, so he could tell Skylar these things. A real voice. The longing to hold Skylar beat at him mercilessly.

We have all the time in the world to search for what answers we can find, he said. *This is the place for you. Here. With me.*

Skylar's heart began to slow, syncing its beats to his heart. He guessed the shock of all this might never wear off.

You might have faced a demon, Skylar, but I'm not going to let you face the future alone.

Her life had taken a strange turn, as his had. He understood about this. He knew.

There are no more secrets. You don't have to be afraid.

"I'm going below to search the valley," Jenna said. "Just to be sure. To ease my mind." She glanced over the ledge. "I'll meet you at the cabin, where I hope there'll be a stiff drink waiting. These Colorado nights are too damn cold."

Gavin closed the distance to Skylar, reached out to her and held tightly to his half human, half something else lover.

She allowed him to carry her, probably because she was shaky and emotionally depleted. But both of them knew she didn't really need this kind of treatment, so it made having her in his arms feel even more special.

Back under the cover of the trees, Gavin set her down. He willed himself back to a form more conducive to sharing with her the depths of his love for her. And whether he was human or werewolf, most of those things bordered on being X-rated.

They both needed to vent some emotional steam.

Pressing her to the tree with his partially bare body, he realized that talking wasn't necessary after all. Having Skylar all to himself, body, mind and soul, was. Selfishly, unabashedly, he craved her full attention.

He wanted her to know how much he cared, and that he would always be there for her. With her.

His mouth hovered over hers, seeking the perfect place

to land, waiting to see if she could even respond. His hands covered hers, linking their fingers in a lover's knot. *Will you go for this, my love? Do I have the right to demand anything right now? So soon?*

His hips ground against hers suggestively, in an unconscious gesture. He'd thought he might lose her. God, if he had…

He couldn't stall his longing to possess her. Nothing that had happened tonight had dulled that desire.

He anxiously waited for her to make a move with his heart dancing inside his chest. Finally, Skylar's lips parted. Her mouth met his with a breath that was blissfully hot and slightly salty from the tears she'd shed.

He accepted that kiss, relished it with relief and a raging hunger. When that wasn't enough to assuage his beastly cravings, his hand moved to her zipper, her hand moved to his, and the jeans came down.

Long legs—the first thing he'd noticed about Skylar—wrapped around him, bringing her damp, fiery heat too damn near to his aching erection. She wanted this as much as he did. She needed this, too.

"Foreplay," he muttered. His fevered lips devoured hers as his hands lifted to settle her into place. "I swore to you that we'd have some."

"First thing you have to know about demons," she whispered back, sliding down over him and pausing to utter a throaty curse as he helped her along, "is that we don't understand that word."

Skylar was willing herself to move on, for now, and using him to do it. Gavin was all for that.

With tears still shining in her eyes and her body needing an outlet for pent-up emotion, Gavin stroked her, each movement reaching her core, where her wolf, or whatever the hell had taken up residence there, accepted him willingly.

Hearing Skylar's throaty cry was like a release. He felt the internal quakes that rocked her, and he moved inside her blistering heat like the madman he was, wanting all of her and vowing to take care of the little wolf demon in his arms for as long as that infernal imprinting thing lasted... plus a hundred years.

And then, when she cried out, he joined her in one long, satisfied exhaled breath. Filled with the hope and promise of finding peace for the first time in a very long while and a bright new future with the woman in his arms, Gavin closed his eyes and whispered Skylar's name.

* * * * *